ENCOURAGING TRUST

"Your teeth are still clacking like horses' hooves." Drake's voice whispered along her neck as he rubbed Victoria's quivering shoulders. "I assure you it is in your best interest to stay warm."

The mere touch of his fingers sent a smoldering shiver through her veins. "I am feeling much better," she said softly. "Thank you."

He took hold of her shoulders, and her breath came to a screeching halt. He seemed to recognize her reaction to him, and his lips curved upward into an unconscious smile. "You must trust me on this. Can you do that?"

"Trust you?" she repeated in a suffocating whisper. To put her family's future totally in this man's hands? She shook her head. "No, I can't do that."

He lifted her chin with the tip of his fingers. "Yes, you can," he said in a silky voice and lowered his head, capturing her lips with his.

To Marry a Marquess

Teresa McCarthy

A SIGNET BOOK

SIGNET
Published by New American Library, a division of
Penguin Group (USA), Inc., 375 Hudson Street,
New York, New York 10014, U.S.A.
Penguin Books Ltd, 80 Strand,
London WC2R 0RL, England
Penguin Books Australia Ltd, 250 Camberwell Road,
Camberwell, Victoria 3124, Australia
Penguin Books Canada Ltd, 10 Alcorn Avenue,
Toronto, Ontario, Canada M4V 3B2
Penguin Books (NZ), cnr Rosedale and Airborne Roads,
Albany, Auckland 1310, New Zealand

Penguin Books Ltd, Registered Offices:
80 Strand, London WC2R 0RL, England

First published by Signet, an imprint of New American Library,
a division of Penguin Group (USA) Inc.

First Printing, August 2004
10 9 8 7 6 5 4 3 2 1

To Mom and Dad

Chapter One

*L*ady Victoria, daughter to the late Earl of Wendover,
sank into the leather chair beside the rosewood writing
desk, gripping her aunt's accounting ledger in her hands.

No, this couldn't be true.

An uneasy chill spread down her back as she flipped
through the marked pages of credits and debits. The expen-
ditures of the past year were all itemized. Invoices and bills
were totaled. Family jewels and silver had been sold. The
quaint cottage in Yorkshire had been mortgaged. Taxes were
due in two months.

Debts and more debts. The columns showed continuous
losses. It was all there for her to read.

"Oh, Aunt Phoebe." Victoria slouched forward, tucked a
strand of mahogany hair behind her ear, and closed her eyes
in anguish.

Leaning her elbow on the desk, she brought a shaky hand
to her brow, breathing in the scent of lavender that still lingered in the air. It was Phoebe's scent. Her aunt must have
left the library only minutes ago.

Victoria swallowed past the lump in her throat and
opened her eyes, turning back to today's date. The numbers
in the right-hand column of the page were smudged with
fresh tears.

Sickened, Victoria shifted a blank gaze toward the library
window. A moaning wind blew hard about Hanover Square,
sending dust and grime swirling in the air, mimicking the tumultuous emotions clouding her mind. The trees outside the
Chester townhouse resisted against the mighty force of na-

ture, but they eventually bowed, not able to combat the storm hovering in the distance.

Wiping a hand across her eyes, Victoria turned her attention back to the ledger. The storm would come. It was inevitable. Her wonderful aunt would be all but penniless in a few months. Victoria's chest tightened in dread at the thought of Phoebe in debtor's prison.

No, her heart answered with a stab of pain. Not Phoebe. Not the lady who had been her guardian angel, taking her in at the age of twelve, as if she were her very own child, after Victoria's parents had died.

Victoria's lips trembled and her nose started to sting. She had never planned on peeking at her aunt's books, but curiosity had taken hold of her like a demon in the night. One minute she was fiddling inside the crammed drawer, searching for an ink well and an extra quill for William, her aunt's six-year-old son, and the next minute she was staring at the accounting ledger that had literally fallen into her lap. Impulsively, she had opened the book without ever thinking that she would be invading her aunt's private domain.

It had been wrong of her to look in the book, but she was glad she had done it. Aunt Phoebe, her father's sister, was all that was good. Beautiful, poised, and without a hateful bone in her body, Phoebe moved about London, conveying such an easy grace that once she had actually caught the Prince Regent's eye at a masquerade ball. After that episode, Victoria vividly remembered Uncle Henry refusing to be present at anything the Regent was attending, unless it was ordered by royal decree. And if Henry did not attend, Phoebe refused to go either.

No, Henry Chester had loved Aunt Phoebe with an all-consuming passion, and she had loved him back. When Henry died, Phoebe had been heartbroken, but she moved on, trying to make a good life for Victoria, William, and Sarah, Phoebe's niece on Henry's side. Sarah had been orphaned as well, but her parents died when she was but two. Unlike Victoria, Sarah, now eighteen, had never remembered her parents.

Though Victoria remembered her uncle fondly, it didn't change the fact that Henry had never been good with money.

He drank a little too much at the gaming tables, losing enormous sums, and ventured into madcap plans of becoming rich, only to lose much of his fortune in a scheme gone awry. He meant well, but he wasn't good at keeping or making money.

Mentally tallying the columns, Victoria realized Uncle Henry had been punting on the River Tick when he died two years ago, and it seemed poor Phoebe had been selling off everything to her name just to keep afloat.

Oh, Uncle Henry. Not you, too.

Victoria had learned that trusting a man with one's future always bordered on trouble, and that is why she meant to choose her own road in life. Her father had failed her by dying and leaving her with nothing, and even dear Uncle Henry had failed Phoebe, Sarah, William, and her by his irresponsible behavior.

No, trust of the male gender was not something that came easy to Victoria. She tried to suppress the anger that curled inside her at the men whom she loved and had abused that trust. In truth, she felt like a stretched piece of rubber, ready to fly in endless directions if she let one more male decide her fate.

"Vicki, where is the ink? I have been waiting a very long time. Almost a hundred hours!"

Victoria jumped at the sound of William's voice. She turned her gaze toward the doors where the boy hurried into the room. His play sword, a long wooden replica, swung at his side while yellow curls bounced playfully about his face.

She fought the ache in her throat and snapped the ledger closed, trying to control the trembling within her. What would happen to Sarah and little William if funds did not arrive in time to pay the debts? What would become of Phoebe? What would become of them all?

"Botheration! Vicki, are you listening to me? I've been waiting in my chambers for . . . forever! You were going to show me how to draw a pirate ship. 'Member?"

Victoria smiled. "Of course, I remember, silly. I was looking for extra ink." She reached toward the back of the jammed drawer and pulled out the ink and quill, easing the accounting ledger back into place. "There, all set."

William peeked over the edge of the desk. "Are you hiding treasures in there, me princess?"

Victoria threw a hand to her breast. "Oh, no, Captain. I would never hide treasures from you."

William jumped on top of a nearby wing chair and sliced his sword through the air. "Never fear. I will fight all the pirates on the high seas and save you! Your treasures are safe with me!"

Victoria chuckled and rendered the boy her deepest curtsy. "I am in your debt, sir. What do you ask of me?"

William took a flying leap onto the Aubusson rug, then puffed out his chest like a preening peacock. "You must show me how to draw a pirate ship!"

"I will, Captain. You have my solemn word."

The sword swooshed through the air. "Very well. Let us begin at once, me princess. And don't worry about the pirates. I will protect you with my life! Let us be off before the villains find us."

When William's small hand slipped across her palm in such a trusting grip, Victoria's heart turned, and she knew without a doubt that she would protect this boy with her life.

"I think a pirate with a skull on his flag is a good idea, don't you think, Vicki? We could put that in the drawing, huh?"

"Anything you like, me captain."

"I will have the bestest ship in the whole wide world when I am grown. Did you know that?" William looked up expectantly, his innocent gaze fixed on her face.

Victoria smiled at the twinkling blues eyes glancing up at her. "Of course. The bestest ship for the bestest captain, me captain."

The boy laughed.

Victoria's heart squeezed. She would never let this boy go hungry. Never! She owed her family all the security they had given her when she had come to them a fearful and penniless twelve-year-old. Her parents had left her nothing, but it had mattered not to Phoebe or Uncle Henry.

Victoria had been with Phoebe for more than nine wonderful years, and she would never change a minute of it.

"Do you think we could have another ship, Vicki? One with a good captain?"

"We must have two ships, or we would not have a fight between good and evil."

"But good always wins, right, Vicki?"

"Yes, William," she paused, "good always wins in the end."

At that moment Victoria promised herself that Aunt Phoebe, Sarah, and William would always have a decent home. They would never be hungry or want for anything. Never. As long as she had breath within her, Victoria would do what she had to do in order to see that her family was kept safe and secure.

"Confound it!" Jonathan Gorick Kingston, the Marquess of Drakefield, hurled the *Times* to the floor, his black brows slamming together in disgust. Drake, as his friends knew him, gave his butler another blasting glance of disbelief.

Stanby, the bearer of the ghastly news, bowed his bald head in agony, stuffing one of his hands, which were double the size of the average man's, against his breast. "I have it from a most reliable source, my lord."

Drake paced the drawing room of his London townhouse, his Hessian boots digging into the Aubusson rug with every angry step. A lock of jet-black hair fell from his queue as he wiped a tense hand across his face, pinching his right forefinger and thumb to the bridge of his nose.

"I cannot believe it. Nightham would have said something to me."

"My lord, if you don't mind me saying so, sometimes a man in love does stupid things."

Drake's jaw clenched. *A man who thinks he is in love, that is.* "But the man is not in love, Stanby. I tell you, I would have known. Nightham may have a secretive streak, but this does not signify at all!"

Dropping his hand to his side, Drake flipped open the gold pocket watch dangling from the chain attached to the ribbon of his waistband. He had received the French-made timepiece from his loving mother, God rest, and it had never left his person except at night when he placed it beside his bed in its gilded bronze watch stand. The beloved piece kept him punctual and orderly everyday of his life.

Orderly? He slapped his free hand against the nearby wing chair. His friend's entire situation was inconceivable.

With another curse, Drake snapped the pocket watch closed. Order was the key to life. Order and predictability. And now Nightham had done the exact opposite. Blast the man!

"Devil take it, Stanby. I need a drink."

"My lord." Stanby gave his employer a curt nod, handing him the ready glass of brandy. "Heard it from Crotchet, Lord Fairbury's cook, who heard it from the groom, who heard it from Lord Nightham's groom, who is no longer his groom by the way, who heard it from—"

"Yes, yes." Drake downed the amber liquid in one long swallow, raising a stiff hand in the air. "Plain, old-fashion gossip line to be precise. Always a reliable source."

"Quite right, my lord."

Drake frowned as he turned toward the hearth. "There's no plausible reason for Nightham to marry by special license, and especially to a penniless female. He saw what happened to me."

Stanby stood by, his expression worried. "I do have his direction, my lord. Only a few hours ride, I believe."

Drake turned, thrusting a stiff hand through his blue-black hair. "Indeed? Then have the grays brought about immediately. Seems I won't be going to my grandmother's after all. I'll talk some sense into that idiot, even though it pains me to do so. But talking to the man won't do any good if Nightham is already married."

"Very good, my lord." Taking one last worried look at his master, Stanby departed from the room.

Drake clanked his brandy glass on top of the rosewood table behind him, refilling his drink. The beating of the nearby mantel clock mimicked the ticking of his brain where chaos and confusion had swiftly replaced all thoughts of regulation and order.

Marriage to a pauper?

He slowly sipped his second glass, gripping the mantel with his free hand. Nightham's decision was like a knife to his heart. Old wounds began to open again, bleeding him of the defensive armor he had built up over the years. He was determined not to let the same thing happen to his friend that had happened to himself. The union of a penniless woman and a wealthy earl like Nightham would only bring trouble.

But the loss of one's coin would be the least of Nightham's worries. Drake instantly recalled the pangs of humiliation he suffered only a few years ago. A conniving, treacherous woman marrying for money could change a man's life forever.

When Honoria died, Drake vowed never to marry a poor woman again. It might kill him next time or squeeze every drop of blood out of his heart, and to him, that was certain death. At a score and seven, he was too young to die.

"Papa!"

Drake lifted his head, pushing his emotions to the back of his mind as his four-year-old daughter burst through the doors of the drawing room. "Come here, Margueretta."

"Papa!" The girl flew into his arms like a well-aimed cannon-ball. "You thaid that later you would give me a hor-thy ride."

The high-pitched voice carried a soft lisp that turned Drake's heart. He loved this child more than life itself.

Dressed in a pink and white striped robe that flowed about her small form like an angel's, she gave him a kiss on the cheek. Her skin was as white as alabaster, and smelled of fresh rose petals from her bath. Silky, ebony hair spilled down her back in a cascade of rolling waves. Two chocolate brown eyes looked up at him expectantly. "Are you going to be my horthy, Papa? Are you?"

"A horsy?" Drake's smile widened as he swung his daughter into the air. "I suppose I can squeeze in a horsy ride for my favorite girl, especially since you will be returning to Grandmama's house today."

His grandmother, the Dowager Duchess of Glenshire, relished her time with Margueretta as much as Drake did.

Drake gave his daughter a ride on his back and let out enough neighs to make the fiercest of stallions take a step back.

Margueretta laughed, rolling on the floor beside him. "Grandmama promithed me a cuthtard pie!"

"A custard pie?" Drake stopped abruptly, raising his black brows in mocked outrage. "She is giving you my favorite pie?"

Margueretta's laugh became a hysterical giggle, her warm hands clapping against his face. "Oh, Papa, you are tho thilly."

The shadows across Drake's heart momentarily disappeared.

"My lord?"

Drake stood and pulled Margueretta onto his hip, turning his gaze toward Nanna, Margueretta's nursemaid, who peeked into the room, a smile on her face. He nodded, giving the older lady his permission to take his daughter.

"Here now, Lady Margueretta," the lady continued, "we will travel to see Her Grace today. You need to be dressed, child. You don't want to keep your father waiting."

Drake frowned as he let his child slip to the floor. "My plans have changed. I won't be able to go with you right away."

Margueretta's dark gaze met his with a pleading look. "But I want you to come with me, Papa. Pleeeeeathe."

Drake's stomach knotted with guilt. He brushed a hand through her silky waves. "Wish I could, poppet. But I need to help a friend. I'll meet up with you at Percy Hall later. You must listen to Nanna and hurry so as not to disappoint Grandmama."

"Oh," his daughter said, looking down at her pink toes. "Your friend needth you very bad then?"

The word friend sounded more like *fwend* from Margueretta's lips, and Drake bit back a smile. He knelt down in front of his daughter and tilted her face to meet his. "Very bad, indeed. But the next time I see you, I shall bring you a special gift. What say you to that?"

The smile she sent him pierced straight through his heart. "A thpecial gift?" she asked, her eyes wide with excitement.

He grinned. "Very special."

"Margueretta," Nanna called softly.

Margueretta flew into her father's arms and gave him one last hug. "I'll be waiting, Papa."

Drake swallowed hard as black, wavy tresses disappeared up the stairs. Though his late wife had scourged his heart, he had always kept a hidden place for his daughter, a corner of his heart set aside only for her. For Margueretta's sake, he vowed to marry a woman who would not have money matters on her mind.

If luck were with him, in his marriage of convenience, he would have an heir as well. To marry for love was for fools. But respect was a different thing altogether. His new wife would not come to the marriage a pauper, and with money of no consequence, there would be no question of her loyalty.

Drake dropped his gaze to the crumpled *Times* resting beside his boots. Confound it. He would stop that marriage between Nightham and that pauper. He would go as far as to offer a good amount of coin to the woman if she would agree never to see Nightham again. He would make her a generous offer, or he would make her life miserable. But time was of the essence here.

Biting back a curse, Drake flipped open his pocket watch, snapped it closed, and swallowed the raging emotions clogging his throat. Maybe he could still reach Nightham in time.

Lady Victoria descended Lord Nightham's carriage, not able to dismiss the dull ache of foreboding that crept along her spine. The sky was overcast, and a cool breeze swept through the village. Spirals of mahogany hair whipped against her face, and she shakily pushed them away.

The entire escapade had been a secret from the very start. Not even her family knew what she was doing. But there was no time to feel sorry for herself. Nothing would change the fact that she was about to enter into a marriage of convenience.

She managed a tremulous smile as Charles Millington, the second Earl of Nightham, took her gloved hand in a possessive grip and led her toward the Boxing Boar Inn at the edge of village. "No need to worry, Victoria. This marriage will suit us both."

Lord Nightham was a handsome man with a hard-muscled frame, golden blond hair, and devilish blue eyes that seemed to hold a host of secrets. If she didn't know better, she would have thought he had known all about her dire circumstances before she had told him the truth.

Though he had acted the very epitome of the gentleman since she had met him at the Dowager Duchess of Glenshire's ball last month, she still felt uneasy about her decision. She knew he held the particulars about her family in strictest confidence, and she should have been happy that he had chosen her for a wife.

But the fact was, she did not love the man.

However, it had to be done, for her family's sake, and done quickly, so her family would not interfere. They would never approve of her marrying Nightham for the sole purpose of providing for them a secure future.

But Nightham wanted to be married without the pomp and circumstance of a large wedding, and that suited her just fine. He explained that his mother was a delicate woman and would not be able to bear the stress of the invitations and parties. Victoria understood perfectly, feeling somewhat relieved. A swift, private wedding seemed the logical step for both of them.

She had been barely out in Society since Uncle Henry's death, and Nightham had been an answer to her prayers. Yes, indeed. A swift marriage of convenience would give her beloved family security. In return, Nightham would have a wife and mother for his future heir.

At first, Victoria had thought they were to be married in a church, but as soon as they arrived in the village, the earl calmly explained the church pews were being varnished, and the ceremony was to take place by special license at a nearby inn.

As her booted feet crunched over the gravel pathway toward their destination, she lifted her head and caught sight of Mrs. Hinckleberry, the hired escort from London, scurrying ahead of them, her plump feet stumbling precariously toward the tap. Alarm sent Victoria's heart racing. It was obvious that would be the last they would see of her. She had been paid for her journey and was to immediately return to Town in a hack after taking some refreshments.

Realizing she was alone with the earl, Victoria wondered for the hundredth time why he had chosen her among all the beautiful ladies of the *ton*. She had no dowry, nothing but herself. But he needed her for a wife, and she needed him for the money. At this point, that was enough. She could not afford to linger on her decision.

A few minutes later, in a secluded dining room inside the inn, she braced herself against a nearby chair. Swallowing hard, she took in the cracked yellow walls and the mildewy odor leaking in from the drainage ditch outside. Sweat beaded along her forehead, and she blinked to keep herself from fainting. Recovering from a bad cold and worrying over her plans, she had barely slept a wink the past few days.

As for her gown, a plain blue muslin, it was nothing a bride would want to remember for this momentous occasion. But Lord Nightham had told her there would be plenty of time to shop in London for gowns after they were married.

When the vicar, a slight man with rounded shoulders, suddenly appeared with the witnesses, a plump servant lady and an older man with barely any teeth, Lord Nightham pulled out the special license.

Victoria didn't like the mischievous smile on the vicar's face, but she ignored it. She focused her attention on her fiancé. He was dressed in a cream-colored waistcoat and navy jacket. Tall and handsome, he was every schoolgirl's dream. But he did not love her.

The vicar cleared his throat, glancing at Victoria, then back to Lord Nightham. "You are a lucky devil, my lord."

"A devil maybe," Lord Nightham said, smiling, "yet I find myself in a rather favorable position at the moment."

Nightham gave Victoria a wink, appraising her with a possessive caress that sent a chill along her spine. Had she somehow misjudged him? No, certainly not. He was merely a man who was about to be wed, a man about to claim his husbandly rights. But could she trust him? Her fingers gripped her gown. Could she trust any man with her life ever again?

Minutes later, the sentences, the vows, the one-word answers, all seemed to tumble forth like a horrible dream, seeping past Victoria's senses in a giant blur. When Lord Nightham placed his ruby ring on her finger, it was all she could do not to run away. Sweat had soaked through her chemise onto her gown, dampening her chest.

As the earl's—no, her husband's—lips claimed hers, panic finally began to penetrate the shield she had put up for so many days. Blood rushed from her head as he whispered her name.

She had made a mistake. A terrible mistake. The words rang over and over in her mind until her knees wobbled, and she felt a strange roaring in her ears.

"Lord Nightham," she said softly. "I—"

But before she could finish, her knees finally gave way and the room went black.

"The lady is ill," Nightham said with a frown, catching Victoria in his arms. "Dash it all! Go fetch a doctor."

The vicar's eyes went wide. "There's no doctor here, my lord. He was taking his breakfast early this morning at the inn when he was called to a birthing in the neighboring village. Ain't been back since."

Nightham scowled. "You there." He looked to the servant. "Is there no one who can help us?"

The servant frowned. "There be a woman down the road, m'lord. Begging your pardon, but she ain't be catering to the likes of you. Won't step outside her cottage. Daughter ran off with a military man and ain't seen hide no hair of her since."

"If you ask me," the older man, serving as witness, interrupted, raising a bushy white brow as he stared at Victoria, "lady swooned like one of those fancy birds in Town. That's all gov'nor."

A muscle ticked in Nightham's cheek. Uttering an oath, he shifted Victoria in his arms, angling his head toward the plump servant, telling her to follow him as he brought Victoria up the stairs of the inn and into one of the bedchambers. He pushed some coins into the woman's hands and frowned at Victoria's pallor.

"It's more than just a swoon. The lady has not looked well the entire ride. Stay with her and give me directions to that woman down the road. I won't be long."

After receiving directions, Nightham hurried down the stairs the way he came, only to find the vicar and the old man long gone. He spent a few agitated minutes looking for them while a niggling suspicion began to gnaw at his brain.

He had no marriage certificate and no vicar. He needed that piece of paper. Dash it all. It was his future.

The sound of clamoring feet snapped his gaze toward the stairs. The servant who was to stay with Victoria had bolted through the private dining room and out the back of the inn. An ugly thought suddenly occurred to him. Mayhap the vicar was not a man of the cloth at all, but a swindler pocketing his money. Nightham knew he was not the smartest of men, but by Jove, he thought he knew a vicar when he saw one.

Clenching his fists against his sides, he hastened outside to go after the woman. "You there! Stop, I say!" But the earl never saw the man coming up behind him. Pain seared Nightham's back, sending him falling against the inn with a thud.

"Take that, your lordship. It won't be a wedding night for you, but a funeral march."

Chapter Two

*I*t took only a few seconds for Victoria to realize that she
was in a strange bed with only her shift for clothes. She
vaguely remembered being carried up some stairs and given
something for her nerves. Laudanum? A round-faced
woman had offered her a drink and then fled from the room.
She had been the same woman who had served as one of the
witnesses.

Victoria lifted a hand to her brow. Her head felt fuzzy
from the medicine, yet the past few hours flashed through
her mind with a distinct clarity. Dear heaven, what had she
done?

She slowly turned her head, spying a small engraving on
the nightstand beside her. Narrowing her eyes, she read the
words etched on the porcelain pitcher. *Boxing Boar Inn.*

She glanced beyond the nightstand, noticing her gown
thrown over the top of the changing screen, and her throat
tightened with dread. Had Lord Nightham removed her
clothing, or had it been the servant woman?

Panicking, she fumbled beneath the covers and felt the
ruby ring circling her finger. Where was Lord Nightham?
Would he return? Of course, what a ninny she was.
Nightham would surely come to her, demanding his husbandly rights now. She cringed at the very thought of him
touching her. Though his few kisses were not unpleasant,
she had no love for the man, at least not like the love Aunt
Phoebe had for Uncle Henry.

Her bottom lip trembled as she tilted her head toward the
small window at her side. A pair of white curtains floated in

the afternoon breeze, letting the soft rays of the sun spill onto her bed. How many hours had passed since the wedding ceremony?

"You are awake, madam?"

Victoria gasped and felt the blood drain from her face as she shifted her gaze to the corner of the room. She fought back the urge to scream at the sight of the man stepping toward her. His shoulders filled the room with such arrogance, her throat ran dry. Slick tan breeches molded to long muscled legs and narrowed hips, accentuating his powerful strength. Glossy hair, black as midnight, fell behind his back in a queue, leaving a small lock hanging loosely about his left temple.

Why, he . . . he looked like a pirate!

"Who are you?" she finally asked in a haughty tone after she gathered her wits, or at least a modicum of sanity.

He seemed to ignore her question, and as if he were having tea with Prinny, the man flipped open a gold watch, scowled, snapped it closed, and returned it to his pocket.

His black-silver gaze pinned her to the bed. "I believe the real question is, where is Nightham?"

Victoria's eyes flashed with anger. "You insufferable lout! I demand you leave here at once!"

The intruder gave a slight bow. "Forgive me, madam, I had no thought that I would be attending a ball with a princess or I would have worn my most expensive silk and velvet."

Humiliated, Victoria jerked the covers to her chin. Where was Nightham? And what was this man doing here with the door latched closed? "Leave here at once. This is positively insufferable."

"Insufferable?" The man glared at her as if she were a pesky fly in his ale. "Why, *my lady*, if indeed that is what you are, this is not insufferable. This is intolerable."

Victoria gasped, feeling violated and stripped of more than her dignity. Did he not know that she was married to the earl?

"I need to see Nightham." His voice boomed above her thoughts, making her bite back a hasty retort. "Where is he?"

His face moved so close to hers that she could see her reflection in what seemed to be a canvas of steel gray, the foreboding color of an approaching storm that she had no wish to encounter.

"Where—is—Lord—Nightham?" he repeated.

Her blood froze in her veins when the thought suddenly occurred to her that this was one of the men Lord Nightham had warned her about. Although Charles had mentioned that he had placed a few vowels here and there, he assured her that he would pay them off as soon as he returned to London. However, he had distinctly informed her that some men, even some unseemly lords, would claim that he owed them absurd amounts of money, when he did not. But because of Nightham's title and wealth, the leeches of the world would continue to plague him.

Well, this insufferable rogue was not about to obtain a single guinea from Lord Nightham or her. He may be undeniably handsome, but his arrogance crushed any hope of a conciliatory conversation. She lifted her brow in disdain. "I have not the faintest idea where he is."

The man shot her a disbelieving glare.

She forced her lips to plunge into a cool, stiff smile. Oh, she saw the flash of sarcasm in that piercing gaze. His steel gray eyes said everything that words did not. She was a tramp, a jade, a hoyden. He had no idea she was Lady Nightham. But it was his snort of disgust that sent her anger climbing.

"Do you deny your own status in life?" he asked with a hint of sarcasm.

She sat up. Did he know about her family's monetary situation? Impossible. He wanted Lord Nightham's coin and she would set him straight on that account. "Now see here, sir, you have no right to come barging into my chambers demanding answers that do not concern you. I must insist that you leave."

"*This* very well concerns me," he snapped.

She watched as he pulled out that infernal pocket watch again and checked the time. Daft as King George, he was. She would not hand over a single coin to this blathering nitwit.

"You will not obtain anything from me," she said sharply. "If you do not take your person from this room, I'll . . . well, I'll scream."

To her surprise, he threw back his head and laughed. "Be my guest, madam." He stepped back and sent her a mocking bow. "Scream and we shall see who comes running. Who will look foolish then? What would your dear Nightham say?"

Her breath caught at the insolence of the man.

Yes, what would Lord Nightham say when he returned and saw her with this . . . this pirate? The scandal would be unbearable for her and her family. The rushed marriage was one thing, a compromising position with this man was quite another. Perhaps this man was not as stupid as she thought. Undoubtedly his looks had women swooning at his feet. Moreover, there was an air of command about him that even Victoria could not dismiss.

"About the coin . . . I believe you will see the light once you have heard my offer."

Goodness, did he believe she would swindle her own husband? He was mad. "I think not."

He threw his hands on his hips, looking more the pirate than ever. "Confound it, you will or I'll force you from here myself."

Force her? She stiffened her spine. By heavens, she would not give him anything. No small wonder why Nightham had warned her. She was about to open her mouth when she jumped at the knock on the chamber door.

With a muffled curse, the man stomped across the room and threw open the door. "What is it?"

A quivering urchin was slumped against the threshold, breathing heavily. "The gent's dying," the boy said as he slipped past the pirate, handing Victoria a red-stained hand-kerchief, pointing toward the back of the inn. "Told me to give it to you. You have that reddish-brown hair all right. You're the one."

Victoria stared at the bloody handkerchief, her heart hammering in her chest. The cloth had the Nightham crest embroidered on the corner. "W-what happened?"

Without warning, the man beside her grabbed the piece

of cloth in her hands and studied it with a dangerous scowl marring his perfect features.

Victoria stared back in shocked silence.

The boy retreated, his wide gaze switching between the pirate and her. "Gent's been out there a good while. But I ain't knowing who did it. I ain't. And ain't told nobody either."

The hair prickled at the back of Victoria's neck. This boy seemed to be telling the truth. An icy chill of doom swept through her, and it was all she could do not to scream and run out the door to Nightham.

"I believe you," she said calmly as she slowly swung her feet over the side of the bed, trying to keep the boy from bolting. "I won't harm you. Just take me to him."

"Stay here."

Victoria froze at the command. She looked back at her intruder. A pair of dark gray eyes shot her a firm warning. She lifted her chin. As if she would listen to him. "I most certainly am not staying here. Nightham needs me."

One black brow rose in challenge. "I will return with the information, but you will stay here." It was not only a command, it was a threat.

Victoria's gaze fell on his taut expression, and she pressed her lips together in frustration. A second later the intruder left with the boy.

At the sound of the door slamming behind them, guilt sliced through her like a white-hot sword. If she had only objected to this quick wedding, Nightham would not be hurt.

After waiting like some dumb, anxious animal, for who knows how long, she finally threw back the sheets from the bed and decided to inspect the scene herself. She would dress and follow them. Nightham needed her.

What had she been thinking staying in the room under that man's orders? She had stayed in the room far too long already. Who did he think he was?

Panic like she had never known gathered in her breast as she hurried across the room. Her hands shook as she grabbed her gown, telling herself that Nightham would be fine. It was probably just a little scratch. However, deep down inside, she didn't believe it at all. Something told her that she would never see Nightham alive again.

Kneeling down in the alley behind the inn, Drake closed his eyes as he held Nightham's hand. Pain swept through him at the sight of his dying friend. There was nothing to be done. He had pressed a cloth against the wound to stop the bleeding, but the knife had cut too deep, and the doctor was nowhere to be found.

"Drake." Nightham's voice was so weak that Drake barely heard him.

Drake opened his eyes and angled his head toward his friend. "Save your breath, old boy."

"No hope . . . m-must take care of her."

Drake grimaced, knowing Nightham was speaking of the woman. "She wants to marry for money. Can you not see that?" The words burst forth without thought, and he regretted it instantly.

"No . . . failed her . . . m-must compensate." Nightham's face was white and his lips were turning blue. "P-promise me, Drake. T-take care of her."

Drake's stomach clenched. A death bed promise. How could he refuse? "You are ever vexing me, friend. Did you love her so?"

"Remember . . . the pig?" Nightham's pale blue eyes held a twinkle of mischief as he ignored the question.

Drake's smile widened. "Ah, the time you let it in the master's living quarters and blamed it on me? You were always a sneaky devil."

"Never . . . d-dull moment . . . eh?"

Drake swallowed hard. He and Nightham had grown up together. As boys it was Nightham who had painted Lord Roxey's pew with brown paint an hour before church service because the baron had taken him to task the day before. It had been Nightham who had showered the ladies' punch bowl with whiskey at the Winter Ball because the hostess had shaken a finger at him. Drake shook his head at the bittersweet memories. In each incident, Drake had been blamed, but Nightham's devilish humor seemed to make up for his vice. But it was that devious streak that had always placed Nightham apart from the others. There had always been a bit of selfishness in his ploys, but they always seemed so harmless, it mattered not to Drake.

Drake pushed the blond hair out of Nightham's eyes. "No, never a dull moment, not with a scoundrel like you."

"Scoundrel." Nightham frowned, locking his hopeful gaze on Drake. "P-promise me."

Drake nodded, wishing he could promise his friend anything but this. "You have my word. I'll take care of her."

"Always the hero." With a smile on his face, Nightham sighed and drew his last breath.

After making the appropriate arrangements, Drake, filled with grief, returned to the woman's bedchambers and halted at the sight of her willowy form retreating from the room. She had changed back into a simple blue gown and looked enchanting. Mahogany hair flowed about her head in long, shiny curls, and her face was that of an angel.

"You're leaving?" he asked, blocking her retreat, inhaling the scent of fresh roses.

"The boy said he's dead." She lifted her chin, her gaze meeting his. Tears filled a pair of soft aquamarine eyes, and for a fleeting moment, Drake felt an odd ache to hold her, comfort her. His chest tightened painfully as he thought about Nightham.

Had his friend loved this woman then?

"I need to go to him," she said, her voice shaking.

"We need to talk," he said more harshly than he intended. "You were to stay here until I returned."

She did not challenge his command, but retreated inside the room and sank back onto the bed. "But you don't understand. I must see him."

Drake closed the door and whipped a hand through his hair, recalling the promise he made to his friend. He took another glance at the woman sitting on the bed, her back straight, her chin up, her hands clutching the reticule on her lap. Not the usual flighty female of Nightham's acquaintance. Perhaps his friend had loved her?

Yet, this woman had a spine, and if Drake was not mistaken, she had a certain intelligence as well. His stomach pulled at the thought. Beautiful and intelligent? A rather intriguing combination. He glanced above her head, not able to push away the attraction he had for her.

He drew in a suffocating breath. Honoria had been both beautiful and poor, letting him believe that she loved him, and he, the fool that he was, had showed his love by marrying her. Nine months after the wedding, their first and only child, Margueretta, was born, the only gift of value in the entire union.

Honoria had used his money to her selfish heart's desire and ignored their baby. She led such an irresponsible life, carrying on with so many men that he lost count. And then it happened, in the country, while on an excursion with one of her many admirers, her carriage was swept off a cliff, and she was killed.

Drake clenched his jaw and stole another glance at Nightham's woman. "You're correct. Nightham's dead. The magistrate is downstairs inspecting the crime scene. It seems it was the work of a footpad. No need to venture down there. The body's already been moved."

"B-but I must go." She stood. "You don't seem to understand."

He took a step toward her. Yet he felt an instant need to protect this woman. She did not need to see Nightham's bloody body. "Let me rephrase it so you do understand," he said. "You cannot go down there. I will not allow it."

Victoria stared into a pair of hard, gray eyes. Anger stirred in her veins. Her head felt full of cotton, and she could barely think, but she understood a command when she heard one.

"*You* will not allow it?"

He raised his hand, his lips thinning. "Nightham does not need another scandal associated with his murder. He is dead, and nothing you will do can bring him back to life."

Scandal. Murder. Victoria opened her mouth and closed it. A scandal could ruin her family. A rushed wedding was one thing, the suspicious death of an earl was quite another.

"It seems as though you are out of luck, *my lady*. Nightham is dead and you will have to return to the place from which you came. You will never be a countess or anything else."

Victoria felt the color seep from her cheeks. After a long pause, she found her voice. "You won't obtain a single guinea from me."

"A guinea?" His eyes narrowed dangerously, and she felt a fluttering in her stomach. "It is I who would have given you more than that."

He did not want her coin? Victoria's mind swam with reasons why he would pay her. Could she have mistaken his identity? Was he some acquaintance of the earl, or possibly a distant relative, since Nightham was an only child? Confusion overtook her as she watched the play of emotions on his face. Anger, grief, pain. Who was he? "You would have given me money?" she asked.

"If Nightham had lived, I would have paid you to leave him."

Victoria's heart felt numb. She opened her mouth to speak, but with the authority of a king, he stepped closer, pressing his hand in the air to stop her.

"Have no fear, Lord Nightham's dying wish was that you were to be properly taken care of, even though you were not his wife." He paused. "Or were you, Lady Victoria? Were you his wife?"

Victoria flinched at the sound of her name on his lips. She assumed he retrieved it from one of the servants. But what about the ceremony? Did he know what had transpired? No, he was asking her that very question. And what about the witnesses and the vicar? Had they disappeared? What about the marriage papers? Had she signed anything at all?

She suddenly remembered her wedding ring and carefully covered it with her right hand. She swallowed hard and made her way slowly to the window.

"Come now. Are you already a countess? The church is but a small distance down the street. I need only to take a walk down there to seek my answer."

She could feel his eyes glued to her person. With a slight tug, she pulled off the ruby ring and set it on the sill behind the curtain and turned. She had needed to marry Nightham for his money, but the earl had known that. She refused to divulge to this insufferable oaf what had transpired between Nightham and her. And who would believe her if she told the truth? People might think she had something to do with her husband's death.

"I was never his wife." The words came out in a slight stutter, but he did not seem to notice her nervousness.

Though it was a white lie, she told herself it was somewhat true. She had never been Nightham's wife, in the real sense of the word, so to speak. And she still did not have the marriage certificate. She wondered if she had been a wife at all.

The man seemed to breathe a sigh of relief at her denial. "Very well then. I will follow through with Nightham's wish. I will see to it that you are sent two hundred pounds a year, and in return you will say nothing of your little visit here."

Her eyebrows shot up in outrage. "What do you know about Nightham's wishes?"

For the first time she saw a semblance of a smile on that pirate. A smile that said he was vastly satisfied with his offer of help. This man was offering her money to keep the day a secret—a secret that he had no knowledge of. How dare he!

She would not embrace a single crumb from this wretched man, even if she were starving. "Two hundred pounds, you say?"

His eyes flashed with contempt. "Very well. Four hundred pounds a year. Lord Nightham would have wanted it that way. We were good friends."

Friends? Victoria curled her hands behind her back. Lord Nightham was dead, and this alleged friend was acting as if the earl's death were nothing at all.

"My, you are generous. Four hundred pounds a year now?"

He clenched his jaw.

She gritted her teeth. "Why not? It's quite a sufficient sum." *Sufficient enough to shove up your haughty nose.*

She batted her eyes, sinking back against the sill, bringing her arms across her breasts, and hiding the stinging tears that threatened to spill. She would not give this man the satisfaction of knowing how much she hurt inside. If she had stayed home, Nightham would still be alive.

"What about Lord Nightham?" she asked, her voice deceptively calm.

As if avoiding her gaze, the man tilted his head to the side, his black hair gleaming against the setting sun. His profile was strong, almost classically handsome. But she realized now he wasn't quite perfect. His nose was a bit too long, and when he turned toward her, she could not help but catch the sorrow that flitted across his face.

So, the pirate had a heart after all. She had no wish to feel sympathy for this man, but she did. However, trusting him was an entirely different matter.

"His body will be sent home to his mother." He glanced away from her again. "I'll send his carriage along as well."

Victoria cringed at the mention of Nightham's mother. The poor dear would be in a state of shock. Somehow, she would have to make things right with the woman. But how to do that without causing a scandal mystified her.

"I have already paid the magistrate to keep the specifics of the death as quiet as possible. Even he admits that the thief could be anywhere by now." His accusing gaze swung her way. "You must realize that eventually Nightham's death will be news. The papers will say that he was stabbed by a footpad, and that is all. You were never here."

She pressed her lips together in annoyance. What a lobcock!

"The earl's ruby ring was missing," he continued with a frown. "Nightham never took it off. It would be a prize for any thief. Yet it was strange, when I searched Nightham's pockets, I found his money still left on his person."

"His ring?" She never thought about the object as evidence against her, until now.

Arching a scrutinizing brow, the man strode toward her and touched her forearm. "Not to worry. You can trust me."

She looked away, keenly aware of his warm flesh upon hers. But she could not trust him. She would not trust him.

"You will be quite safe returning to London. I'll take care of the matters entirely."

The tenderness in his voice shocked her. Why was he

concerned about her now? Safety was precisely what she was worried about. If he ever discovered that she had Nightham's ruby ring, she might not make it back to Town at all. A thief killed Nightham, but that thief did not take his ring. She did. The man may believe she planned the killing.

Yet she could not ignore the questions whirling in her mind. Was she married to a dead man? Or was the marriage ever legal in the first place? And if so, was the marriage certificate still on Nightham's body? No, the man would have found it. Still, what about her signature?

Suddenly, it was all too much for her, and she made her way toward the bed to sit down.

The man's keen gaze followed her. "Are you ill?"

"No," she responded sharply. Of course, she was ill. She was sick to her stomach! Perhaps she ought to tell this man that she had already married the earl. No, she could not. He would believe the worst. Oh, what to do! Here she was worried about herself when poor Nightham was dead. She was absolutely wretched.

The man cleared his throat, his voice softening as he spoke. "I'll send for a maid. We need to start back to London without delay."

Victoria shook her head, her hands twisting on her lap. "No maid. I have very little. I can gather my things and meet you in a bit." She paused. "I just need some time."

Like a general giving orders, he conveyed to her when to meet him downstairs in the private dining room, then he quickly departed.

After the door closed, Victoria fell onto the pillow with a sob. Oh, heaven help her, what had she done? Nightham was never coming back, and it was all her fault. Her marriage might not even be legal, and if it were, the scandal would be suicide. What would her family do now? She had made a mess out of everything.

After a minute of indulging in grief and self-pity, she sat up, pulled back her shoulders and mentally scolded herself. Nightham was dead, and she was alone. However, it was Nightham's mother who would be the one to truly suffer her son's death. But Phoebe, William, and Sarah must come first.

Guilt pricked at Victoria's conscience. One day, when things were better, she would venture to Nightham Manor and explain the entire situation to the countess. She owed the lady the truth, no matter what the ninnyhammer downstairs had said to her. And she certainly would not be going anywhere with him!

She hurriedly rose from the bed and locked the door. Her gaze snapped to the window where a robin sat chirping in a tall elm tree situated within an arm's length of the inn.

She immediately made her decision. She had always been good at climbing trees. She just hoped her legs could handle the drop.

Drake sat in the taproom, snapping his pocket watch shut for the third time. The shock of his friend's murder overwhelmed him, but it was the disturbing death scene that formed a hollow ache in his soul. There was nothing to be done but to fulfill Nightham's request to take care of the female.

Frowning, Drake shifted his gaze to the stairwell. He had been waiting thirty minutes already. Where in blue blazes was that woman? After what he had been through today, he had no use for more chaos, but he was inclined to believe that Nightham's acquaintance was going to do her best to drive him mad.

He stretched his legs toward the hearth and grimaced as a pair of aquamarine eyes flashed in his mind. He knew his behavior was abominable, but he had no help for it. She was a pauper and deserved a few contemptuous glances for her deceitful plan. However, he was reasonably sure she had nothing to do with the hideous death of his friend.

He blinked. Or had she? The question simmered in his mind as he swirled the glass of brandy in his hand. He would never fall prey to a beautiful face again. He had no need to be involved with another Honoria. But the tumultuous feelings he had for Nightham's lady were beginning to worry him.

His gaze narrowed on the orange flames dancing before him. Surely his friend could not have married her. But then again, she was registered at the inn under Nightham's name.

Yet the upstairs maid had assured him that Lord Nightham had placed Lady Victoria—that was the name the maid had given him—in the room soon after she had departed from the carriage. Nightham had left her with another female servant, having never stepped foot in the chambers again.

Drake whipped his fingers through his hair. It could not have been grief he had seen in those turquoise eyes. She could not have loved Nightham, not a penniless chit.

Still, there was no reason for Lady Nightham to know of her son's scandalous escapade or of the woman upstairs. If he had his way, no one would learn about Lady Victoria, ever. He owed Nightham at least that much.

Drake's gaze moved to the door of the tap as a tall, fair-haired gentleman in a many-layered black cloak nodded him a greeting and took a seat at the far corner table.

Drake did not know the man, but from one gentleman to another, he nodded back, drumming his fingers on the table. He would have waited in the private dining room, but he wanted to listen to the locals as they slowly congregated in the tap. The conversation centered on the murder. It was inevitable.

"A lord, he was."

"Knifed in the back."

"Fight over a woman, I think."

"Blood everywhere."

Drake winced, but he had yet to hear Nightham's name. He had to get the woman out of the inn swiftly. He had paid the servants not to talk, but one never knew.

He looked at the stairwell again, knowing from this angle that he would see her enter the private room with no one the wiser. He knew there was another door to the kitchen from the private dining room, and he had already decided to take his leave from there.

How long was it going to take her? If this were her way of trying to procure him to her chambers, she would be sorely mistaken. He started for the stairs, his Hessian boots clacking against the pine planks as he climbed the steps. He raised a hand to her door, and rapped hard against the wood.

Silence.

The smell of rotting wood seeped through the floor-

boards beneath him. He glanced down the hall. Two dusty
sconces lit the corridor. It was a deplorable inn, a place his
friend should never have come.

He rapped on the door louder, scowling as he remembered the key lying on the table inside the room. "Madam, it
is time we left."

He stiffened when the answer was nothing but the rumble of voices from the tap. Had the lady run out the back?
No, he would have seen her descending the stairs.

He stared at a knot of wood on the door and frowned. The
notion of him not fulfilling the promise to his friend made
him clench his hands in rage. He knocked again with no response, biting back a curse at the very idea of the woman
slipping through his fingers.

"Lady Victoria?" Nothing.

A shiver clipped down his spine, making his blood run
cold. Something was wrong. And, dash it all, he felt something for that woman he had no right to feel. He must be
mad.

Nightham had died in his arms, and that very same day,
Drake was yearning for a woman he could not have.

Ramming his shoulder against the door, he broke past the
lock. His gaze immediately shifted to the curtains blowing
steadily across the window. "Lady Victoria?"

Her name fell easily from his lips as he hastened across
the room, breathing in the lingering scent of roses. Looking
past the window, he noticed a huge tree that brushed up
against the inn. He stared in shock, his jaw tightening. She
had scooted down the tree and jumped!

He slammed his fist against the sill and cursed.

Beyond the ground, shadows blended into the night,
making detection impossible. A murderer was on the loose,
and the confounded female had left his protection.

First Nightham and now this! Though he had no notion
of the woman's full name, Drake made a solemn vow to find
her.

Devil take it! It was a matter of honor now.

Chapter Three

Victoria held a teacup to her lips and stared blankly out the window of her aunt's townhouse. A drizzling rain beat against the cobblestone streets, adding to the miserable feeling churning inside her. It had been two weeks since Nightham's death, and yet it seemed like yesterday.

Her family was to return home today. They would not have known of her absence since they had been staying in the country near the Duke of Glenshire's Estate for the past two weeks. Victoria had asked to be excused from the journey because of a slight cold, and though Phoebe had planned on canceling their outing in the country, Victoria had insisted that the lady do nothing of the sort.

After much cajoling, Phoebe reluctantly agreed to travel without her niece, but only on the promise that if Victoria became worse, she would send a letter by special messenger immediately. Mrs. Dorling, their housekeeper, was the sole person who knew about Victoria's absence. Although the elder woman did not like the idea of Victoria's flimsy excuse to visit a sick friend, she told Victoria she would say nothing to Lady Phoebe, since the poor lady had enough to worry about.

Sighing, Victoria placed her drink on the rosewood sideboard and fished inside her pocket for the ruby ring. She would never sell it, and she dared not show it to anybody. She could never claim to be a countess. People might believe she killed Nightham. Her family would never survive the scandal. And who knew if she had been legally married to the earl in the first place?

Nightham's death had been reported in the papers, but the news had been scant at best. The pirate must have paid a good sum for the story to be hushed.

Sheer panic rippled through her veins at the thought of that man. It was a miracle she had escaped him. After she had descended the tree, she made a mad dash to the stables and discovered a driver heading back to London with his master's coach. A few blinks of her lashes, and she had a lift back to Town.

She would have been a good wife to Nightham, she told herself. Her family had needed money. What else could she have done? There was no man to provide for Aunt Phoebe. Little William needed proper schooling. And Sarah deserved a proper dowry. But now, all seemed lost.

Where were the papers to prove her marriage, if there was a marriage in the first place? And should she seek answers from a solicitor and risk the chance of being thrown into Newgate for Nightham's murder? Or was it best to stay quiet?

Her head had been spinning with questions since Nightham's death. But at the moment, keeping quiet seemed the best alternative until she decided what to do. Tears burned the back of her eyes as she thought about the earl. She could not outwardly mourn him because everyone would know of her predicament and accuse her of murder. She had only made things worse by her impulsive actions.

Her stomach churned as she thought about her family's situation. It had been two months earlier when she had come across her aunt's ledger. She had met Nightham at a ball days later. Aunt Phoebe rarely accepted invitations to balls because they reminded her too much of Uncle Henry. Phoebe kept to the fringe of Society, living in a small world of close-knit friends and cozy soirees, but it seemed that the ball had been one of her exceptions.

"Hellooooo! Anyone here?"

Victoria quickly pushed her ring back into her pocket and wiped the tears from her eyes as William's voice reverberated throughout the house. Her family was home.

She smiled when she caught sight of the boy taking a fly-

ing leap in the hall and landing on his bottom with a pro-
nounced thud.

"Whew! That was fun, Mama. Can I do it again? Can I?"
The boy jumped up, ready to partake in another jump, when
Aunt Phoebe held him back.

Victoria laughed, watching her little cousin wiggle like a
worm on a hook, trying to disengage himself from the strong
arm that held him.

"Enough, William," Phoebe exclaimed vehemently. "I
declare, you smell like a dead fish. Take off those wet things
this minute. You have tracked mud everywhere. Look at
those stairs, young man."

Aunt Phoebe looked stern, but beneath that taut expression was a heart as soft as cotton, and Victoria loved her desperately.

"William, I'm warning you," Phoebe replied. "Not another step or you will spend the rest of today and tomorrow
in your room. Do you understand, young man?"

"Yes, Mother." His bottom lip formed into a large shovel
while his blue eyes twinkled with mischief. Before Phoebe
had a chance to grab him again, he jumped out of her arms
and bounded into the drawing room.

"Vicki," he cried. "Did you miss me?"

Victoria grinned as her cousin's muddy shoes thumped
across the rug. Unruly golden locks peeked out from a dark
blue cap. She pulled him into her arms, swinging him
around full circle, then set him down.

"Well, William." Her wary gaze took in the boy's devilish smile. "What gift have you brought back for me this
time?"

William, known for carrying around tiny creatures of one
sort or the other, especially after a trip from the country,
thumped his chest with his fist and peered up at her with two
of the most innocent blue eyes in the world. *"Moi?"*

Victoria raised a finely arched brow. At six, the boy was
smarter than most ten-year-olds. "Yes, you."

"Oh, Victoria, you missed a marvelous time."

Phoebe walked into the room, pulling off her gloves and
straightening her lavender traveling outfit, giving William a
stern eye at the mud he had dragged in.

Victoria managed a smile.

At forty years old, her Aunt Phoebe was still a beautiful woman. Her blond hair, swept high on her head, posed not a streak of gray. Her bubbly personality only added to the beauty of her slender form and her wonderful heart. Though the lady swooned a little too often, the males that swarmed around her seemed to enjoy that feminine eccentricity.

"I should have insisted that you come along with us, my dear." Phoebe gave Victoria a squeezing hug and stepped back, her eyes narrowing in concern. "The minute I left, I knew I ought not have left you alone with that cold."

"But I'm quite fine, as you can very well see," Victoria said, hiding her pain.

"Pshaw! Nothing can become something if one does not take care of oneself. I was just telling Sarah that we should have insisted that you come along. You talked me into it, you know. And you do not look fine. What are those dark circles under your eyes?"

Victoria smiled. "You are a worrier, Aunt Phoebe. I am in the best of health. But I do admit, I missed you all terribly."

"Depend upon it, my girl. I will never leave you alone again. I know you are very capable, and I am certain Mrs. Dorling cared for you like a mother, but I did worry, you know."

Victoria took her aunt's hand in hers. "Mrs. Dorling served me chicken soup and hot tea for three days straight. I recovered faster than William could hop across that rug."

William giggled. "Want to see me do it again?"

Phoebe eyed the child with a disapproving glare. "No thank you, William. We have seen enough of your hopping for an entire year." She turned back to Victoria and gave her a wink. "Nevertheless, we did so many things in the country. Why, we even dined with His Grace, the Duke of Glenshire."

"Indeed, we had such a grand time."

Eighteen-year-old Sarah, her brown curls bouncing about her heart-shaped face, smiled as she passed through the doors and enveloped Victoria in a loving embrace. "We missed you terribly, and I won't hear of you staying home the next time we venture into the country, even if you do have the sniffles."

"Next time, I promise to go with you." *If I am not in Newgate*, Victoria thought with dread.

Sarah gave an amusing nod toward her aunt. "I daresay, we will be traveling there soon, if Aunt Phoebe can help it."

Victoria lifted an inquisitive brow. "Ah, do I see a handsome man throwing his amorous advances in your direction?" She touched her finger to her aunt's shoulder.

"Now, girls." Phoebe's cheeks grew red. "The situation is nothing like that."

"Like what?" William protested, pulling on his cousin's violet skirt. "Who is throwing arms and ants at Mama?"

Phoebe's eyes widened. The girls giggled.

"Amorous advances, silly." Sarah patted his curly blond head and scooted him off toward their housekeeper and part-time nanny, Mrs. Dorling. "And it would be best if you had no more information than that."

The plump lady smiled as she stood by the open doors waiting for William. The boy squirmed in Mrs. Dorling's arms when he caught the wink his mother gave the housekeeper.

"Let-me-go, I say! Botheration! I do not want a horrid bath!"

Mrs. Dorling grabbed his flying arms. "'Tis not a bath, William. You are to be a pirate in your own wee boat. A captain must be clean as a whistle when he meets up with his crew."

William looked up, eyes wide. "Why the blazes did you not say that in the first place?"

Phoebe glowered at her son. "William, your language, please. Go upstairs and a tray will be sent to you before you go to bed."

William frowned, then looked back at his housekeeper. "Very well. Take me to your ship, my lady." He skipped passed the drawing room doors, but before his head disappeared from view, he managed to lean back and throw in the last word. "And you silly girls think I don't know what amors advances are, do you?"

Mrs. Dorling tugged, but William would not hear of it

until he finished what he wanted to say. "Botheration! You think me an idiot? That means old Georgie's going to marry Mama!"

Victoria jerked her head toward Aunt Phoebe, who in turn rolled her eyes and sank onto the green sofa behind her. Sarah threw her hand to her mouth in surprise.

"Georgie?" Victoria choked out, taking a seat in the wing chair opposite her aunt. She pursed her lips, struggling to hide the smile that tugged at the corners of her mouth.

"Georgie?" Sarah squeaked as she took a seat beside Phoebe. "I had not realized it had progressed that far. The Duke perhaps, but Georgie?" She lifted her light brows in question.

"I have no notion how that boy of mine knows everything that happens almost before I do."

Victoria was caught off guard by her aunt's flustered expression. Along with Sarah, she waited for Phoebe to explain the situation.

Phoebe's face paled and she clasped her hands together in frustration. "You see, George . . . I mean His Grace, the Duke of Glenshire, is quite smitten with me. And yes, he did ask me to marry him. William must have heard me speaking with the duke at the Dower House where we were visiting the past few weeks. Percy Hall, you know. But I did not call him Georgie!"

"Did I miss something on the trip?" Sarah asked. "Or did you just pronounce that His Grace asked you to marry him?"

Phoebe's cheeks turned pink. "Yes, he did." She then turned to Victoria, as if it were every day a woman was asked to marry a duke. "Dearest, you were introduced to His Grace at the ball given by his mother about two months ago in Grosvenor Square. His sons were not in attendance, and you never met the Dowager Duchess because she fell ill. Of course, there was that one blond gentleman, I never knew his name, but he paid particular attention to you, did he not?"

Victoria gave her aunt a noncommittal smile. Oh, yes, she remembered that night all too well. She had met Lord Nightham at that ball, but she had never put two and two together, until now. It had been such a large extravaganza, everyone in London seemed to have attended. Had the duke known Nightham well? The earl's death had already been reported in the papers, but would there be a scandal? And what about the pirate?

She stared at Phoebe, her mind surveying her options. Perhaps this duke was the answer to her prayers, as long as that pirate, whoever he was, had not divulged information about Victoria being in the village when Nightham had died. But if anyone discovered her secret, it would be very probable that the duke would never marry Phoebe.

Victoria knew she would not be able to trust the duke with her secrets, even if he loved Phoebe. And it wasn't fair to tell Phoebe either. Perhaps after the duke married her aunt, then Victoria could reveal her past, but not before. But hiding her past would be all but impossible if that pirate showed his face.

"His Grace and I have known each other since we were children." Phoebe stood and walked toward the hearth. "It seems that time has rekindled an old flame."

"And he wants to marry you, Aunt Phoebe?" Victoria asked, raising a brow toward Sarah.

"I have yet to make up my mind," Phoebe said. "It's only been a couple of years since Henry died."

Tears sprang to the older lady's eyes, and Victoria ached with an inner pain for the woman that had loved her like a mother. Though Uncle Henry had gambled away the family's money, he had loved them all.

"What type of man is this duke?" Victoria asked.

Phoebe cleared her throat and smiled. "Oh, quite handsome, and the duke's mother is a dear."

"I do seem to recall a bit about him," Victoria said, smiling. He was tall and handsome and something else, but she could not quite put her finger on it. "I assume he is wealthy, but I have to ask. One never knows these days. Dukes can be voracious gamblers. Does he have the means to support you and the children?"

"Children?" Sarah rose from her seat in indignation, her brows furrowed above her glaring eyes. "Good heavens. I am no longer a child, Victoria. I am eighteen, only three years younger than you."

"Forgive me." A soft smile touched Victoria's lips as she continued her interrogation. "But this is of the utmost importance, Aunt Phoebe. I need to be certain that the man could care for you properly. Is he truly kind? Will he watch over you like a husband should?" *Can you trust him?*

"Indeed," Sarah said with a determined look, taking her seat. "Will he be a good husband?"

"Girls!" Phoebe's hand shot up in outrage. "Though I love you both dearly, I believe that I am old enough to make my own decision. *I* will be the one to determine if the man is worthy to be called *my husband*. I have no wish to hear another word on this subject." She stared at the two girls, waiting for a reply.

They both nodded in grim embarrassment at their questions. With another warning glare, Phoebe strode across the Aubusson rug, her skirts rustling past the door.

"We will be returning to the country next month. Elizabeth, I mean, Her Grace, the Dowager Duchess, has invited us. There will be a formal invitation coming soon."

Phoebe glanced over her shoulder. "I will see you both at supper, and we will say no more about—"

She was interrupted by a shrill shriek exploding from upstairs. Victoria and Sarah shot from their seats.

Phoebe shook her head in dismay. "Nothing to worry about. William seems to be at it again. Depend upon it, he has brought some creature home for Mrs. Dorling. I truly thought I had checked every pocket on that boy, but goodness knows how many hiding places he has for those vexing little creatures."

She shook her head once again and climbed the stairs, heading in the opposite direction of the screams.

Half-giggling, half-grimacing, Victoria and Sarah scurried up the stairs toward William's chambers. As soon as they opened the door, a wave of rose scented bath water slapped them in the face.

"Watch out there ye landlubbers," the boy yelled.

William stood naked, except for the towel wrapped around his torso, which was slipping down his white little belly. One hand held the towel, the other pointed toward the ceiling. One pink foot was stationed on the floor, the other was planted on top of the exhausted Mrs. Dorling who was bent over on hands and knees.

Yowling, William took a flying leap toward the bed. "There is treasure about, and I be the only pirate who will find it."

Sarah took a firm step forward. "William Joseph, come here immediately."

"Fear not, princess." His voice thundered across the room. "Your father, the king, has not come to save you. You best go below before my crew becomes restless."

Victoria stalked across the wet floor. "For goodness sakes, William. You are quite impossible." She shot him a quick smile, which instantly made him retreat back a step.

"Leave me alone, princess. I am your captain."

Victoria grabbed hold of his arm. "But now you have become our prisoner, little pirate."

Sarah came up beside them. "You will do as we say or you will walk the plank."

Victoria chuckled when Mrs. Dorling threw her the boy's nightshirt and cap.

William groaned. "This is not part of the game, Vicki." The shirt flew over his head, followed by a smacking kiss on the cheek by Victoria. "Yuck! I'm a pirate! Girls and land-lubbers do not help pirates dress and they don't kiss them!"

"Game or not little brother," Sarah added, buttoning his shirt and giving him another loud kiss. "It's time you go to bed and stop playing pirate. And next time, the boat goes outside."

"Next time?" Mrs. Dorling's voice rang out, her expression weary. "Believe me, there will be no next time."

At the dining table later that evening, Victoria noticed that the ornate silver candelabrum that usually sat in the center of the rosewood sideboard was missing. Her stomach coiled in dread as she glanced about the room, noting that a few other pieces were gone as well. More missing silver. How much time did they have left before they were put on the streets?

"William needs a man," Sarah said in exasperation as she opened her white linen napkin and waited for Phoebe to join them. "But I declare, not any man will do. He needs a man who would make a good father. Every time I turn around that rapscallion is in some type of trouble. In the country, it was all Aunt and I could do to keep him civil. I shudder to think about visiting there again with him."

Victoria recognized the concern in her cousin's eyes and felt the same herself. "What about this duke? You must have more information than his looks. Will he cast William out of the house to some school up north, far away from Phoebe?"

"Oh, no. He is nothing like that. His Grace is fifty years old, and his wife died years ago. He has three sons. I met Anthony who's sixteen, and now away at school. I suspect the older two are just as handsome. Then there is the Dowager Duchess, the grandmother. Quite a nice lady, but you know, Victoria, I felt as though she could see straight through me, noting every one of my flaws, inside and out."

Victoria blinked. Hopefully, her cousin was wrong.

"But there is also the duke's granddaughter."

"Granddaughter? Truly? How old is she?"

"I will tell you how old, young lady." Phoebe stepped through the doors and took her seat at the head of the table. "The girl is four, and the child of the duke's eldest. The mother was killed in a tragic accident, leaving a grieving husband behind. Her carriage slipped off a cliff."

The oxtail soup was served, and after a moment, Phoebe looked up. "They say he hardly smiles anymore."

"Who?" Sarah asked. "The duke?"

Phoebe shook her head. "No, his eldest son. Talk has it he resembles something of a pirate."

Victoria choked, grabbing a glass of red wine to wash down her food. Pirate, indeed. She took another gulp of wine, recalling the only two pirates she had ever known, the mischievous one upstairs and the menacing one back at that inn.

She flashed a tremulous grin in her aunt's direction. "A p-pirate? How utterly ridiculous." But as she spoke, she knew ridiculous was too tame a word. It was horrid.

Phoebe frowned at Victoria's reaction. "I had no cause to upset you. How careless of me to mention the mother's accident."

Victoria's parents had died in a carriage accident, but that was not what upset her. She regained her composure and waved her hand in the air. "No. The soup. Went down the wrong way."

Victoria caught Sarah's curious gaze. Her cousin would have to wait for answers because when the footman pulled the top off the platter of chicken, a green blob jumped into the air and struck the table with a thump. The footman leapt back in surprise and dumped the entire dish on top of Phoebe's head, tray and all.

Phoebe shot straight out of her chair and screamed.

The footman stammered an apology. "So very s-s-sorry, my lady. 'Tis only me working today, and well, I ain't been checking all the platters since . . ."

He wanted to say since the mischievous William returned home, Victoria thought with a smile, but the poor man's face turned three shades of red as he fought for a plausible explanation, helplessly dabbing at Phoebe's ruined gown.

Victoria and Sarah sat covering their mouths with their hands, watching a huge frog hop down the lace tablecloth, teeter on the edge, then jump to the floor with a ferocious croak.

Phoebe pushed the footman out of her way while she wiped a chicken leg off her gown. "WILLIAM!"

A flash of white zoomed by the doors of the dining room.

Victoria exchanged amused glances with Sarah. Phoebe pounded up the stairs, her voice echoing off the walls.

"William! Do not think for one single minute that I did not see you down here, young man!"

When Victoria slipped into bed that night, her mind whirled with thoughts of that pirate. He could not be the son of a duke. It was just not possible. She plumped her pillows into a soft mound, slamming her fists into the sides.

She recalled the night she met Lord Nightham at the ball given by the dowager duchess. Could there have been a closer connection between Nightham and the duke? If so, then it seemed plausible that Nightham knew the duke's son—the pirate.

Her stomach churned with uneasiness as she pushed her

feet further toward the foot of the bed. What if her pirate was indeed the duke's son?

She flinched when something brushed across her feet. At the sound of a squeak, her eyes snapped open in horror. In the light of the moon, a white mouse scurried from beneath her covers, racing across the floor. She jumped from her bed and onto her vanity chair just as the hideous beast scampered back in her direction.

"William!"

Her door instantly swung open, and a small shadow hovered in the hallway.

"What be all the shouting about, landlubber?" William's bare feet hit the floor in a string of happy thuds. "Oh," he said innocently, followed by a mischievous chuckle as he glanced up at her. "I see you have met me second in command, Cap'n Whitie."

The boy hurried over to scoop the mouse into his hands. Then he turned to leave, but not before he sent her a devilish smile and a six-year-old's piece of advice. "Ye should know, pirates do not like being slobbered on," referring to her kiss in his bedchambers. "I should like it above all things if you do your kissing with your prince."

Prince, indeed!

Victoria watched in awe as the door closed behind him. Grimacing, she crawled off her chair and carefully tiptoed to her bed, palming the covers, feeling every crinkle and curve for anything that could be lurking about. She felt things that were not even there.

Climbing back into bed, she cringed, not certain which pirate was worse, the big one or the little one. Nonetheless, what she did know about pirates vexed her to no end. They were odious creatures, every last one of them.

That same evening, in the library of Percy Hall, the country home of his grandmother, the Dowager Duchess of Glenshire, Drake took a seat in the bottle-green wing chair beside the hearth. Surrounding him, rich wood wainscoting met with thick crimson carpets, giving the room a warmth much like the duchess herself.

Drake thought of his grandmother fondly as he lifted a

crystal decanter off the mahogany end table and splashed some Madeira into his glass. She was a woman of indiscriminant taste and unconventional means. He could not thank her enough for showering Margueretta with love and giving his little girl a home, a place where Drake felt at home as well.

A kind, gentle woman, the dowager never approved of his gallivanting about Town with the ladies, taking him away from his daughter for weeks at a time, and doing who knows what else. Gambling, fencing, boxing, you name it, he did it. But she had always loved him, the only woman besides his mother and daughter who ever had.

Crossing one well-polished boot over the other, Drake swirled his drink and took a sip, reflecting upon the recent turn of events that had turned his life upside down. He could not forget that mahogany-haired goddess from the inn and wondered if he ever would.

He tilted his head toward the fireplace, blinking against the reddish-orange flames dancing before him, flames that reminded him of both her hair and her temperament. He pulled out his watch, then snapped the timepiece back into his pocket.

A heaviness centered in his chest when he thought about Nightham. The funeral had been brief with a small piece in the paper. Nothing had been said about the woman. Only that the earl had died from a footpad's knife. There had been rumors, but nothing that amounted to anything. And it grated on Drake's nerves to have the bounder responsible for Nightham's death still about.

Drake had paid well to ensure his friend's privacy and to avoid a scandal that would affect Nightham's mother. He also had spent a good deal of time and money discreetly searching for Lady Victoria with no luck. The female seemed to have disappeared off the face of the earth, or at least from London.

He could only guess that Nightham had met her in Town. At a ball perhaps? A soiree? Through mutual friends?

Sighing, he placed his glass down and rubbed the back of his neck. The strain from the search for the woman and the death of his friend had begun to take a toll on him. Despite the fact that the woman had eluded him, he would never give up.

Confound it. He had made a promise. Yet in the back of his mind he knew there was another reason for seeking her out, but he refused to search that part of his heart. Never again.

"Papa! Papa!"

Drake smiled as Margueretta rushed through the doors and into the library.

"Papa, you thaid, you would give me a horthy ride."

"Did I now?" He nuzzled her neck, taking in the sweet scent of rosewater that lingered over her skin. "Last time I saw you, the horsy ride was very short if I remember correctly."

"You had to help a friend."

Drake thought about Nightham and grimaced. "Did you receive the gift I left for you in your bedchambers?"

"Yeth, Papa. Thank you." Her small white hand pulled out a tiny timepiece locket that hung around her neck. "It tickth, Papa. Lithen. Tick. Tick. Tick. I will keep it forever and ever and ever." She threw her hands around his neck in a tight squeeze. "Will you find that thpecial clock, will you, Papa?"

"It's being made in a place very far away, poppet."

"And will thith," she pulled at the locket, "be part of your thpecial thingth too." Her dark gaze looked hopeful.

Drake gently tapped her nose. "Yes, but you will have to guard it very, very closely for me. Can you do that?"

Her eyes lit up with pride. "Oh, I will, Papa. I will. I promith, I will hold it forever and ever."

Drake's heart skipped a beat every time he looked at his child. "How would you like a ride to London on Papa's back?"

Margueretta let out a gleeful gasp and clapped her hands. "Yeth. Yeth. To London, to London, my horthy."

Smiling, Drake pulled off his jacket, tugged at his neck-cloth, and unbuttoned his waistcoat, rolling up his shirt-sleeves. "Ready, my lady?"

Margueretta giggled. "Ready, Lord Horthy."

Drake hunched down on all fours while a laughing

Margueretta jumped onto his back, holding onto his mane of black hair.

"Whoa," she yelled, her little bottom bouncing up and down in the air. "Whoa," she giggled again.

"Almost there." Drake trotted toward the open doors to the hall. "Grab tight, my lady."

"Now what have we here?" a male voice sounded in the hall, sending Drake's four hooves grinding to a halt.

Drake groaned, focusing his eyes on two sets of Hessian boots, reflecting back up at him. His gaze followed tan breeches clinging to two pairs of muscular legs. The devil. His brother James and his friend Foxcroft had come to call.

"Papa'th giving me a ride," Margueretta squealed.

Twenty-two-year-old James laughed as he bent down to give Margueretta a kiss. "Papa's giving you riding lessons for the circus?" He paused to stare at Drake. "And neigh to you horsy."

Drake glared at his brother. No doubt, the two men were here about Nightham, and from the looks on their faces they weren't leaving until they had some answers.

"Can I play horsy, too?" James said, patting Drake's black hair, a shade darker than his own. "See here now. I can be the front of the horse." He quirked a brow toward Drake. "And you dear brother, you can be the other part of the horse. By Jove, what an idea! You . . . you can be yourself!"

The two hovering men hooted with laughter.

"Come here, Gretta," the other man said, whipping the girl off her now thoroughly disgusted horse. Twenty-five-year-old Viscount Foxcroft hoisted her up in the air, catching her in his arms. The sandy-haired man had been friend of both Drake and James since childhood.

"Weeeeee," Margueretta squealed. "Do that again, Foxth."

"Here we go, Cabbage. But watch out for Lord Horsy. He might give us a swift kick in the you know what and send us flying into the wall."

Fox, James, and Margueretta cackled with laughter.

Drake grimaced, slowly rising to greet the men while brushing the dust off his breeches. When he gave them a glare that sent most men scrambling for cover, the laughter stopped abruptly. Although the two men were by no means small, Drake hovered over them by a few extra inches.

"What in the—" Drake looked down at his smiling daughter and bit back a curse "—world are you two doing here?"

"What indeed?" James held a teasing glint in his warm brown eyes, then glanced at Fox. "Daresay, word has it around London there was a horse for sale here and we came to inspect it." He sniffed the air and moved closer to Drake. "By Jove, smells like a barn in here."

Margueretta let out a giggling snort as Fox dropped her to the floor. No sooner had James opened his mouth than both men started poking and prodding Drake from head to toe as though he were a horse for sale.

Fox cleared his throat. "Ah, this one could be sold at Tattersall's at a fair price. Do you not think so, Lord James?"

Margueretta giggled, throwing her hands to her knees as Fox attempted to check the inside of Drake's mouth. "Oh, but I see he's a stubborn one, he is. What say you, Lady Margueretta?"

The little girl nodded and laughed. "Thubborn!"

Drake clamped his mouth tight. He gave them his most contemptuous glower, knowing Margueretta was loving every second of it.

"Oh, Uncle Foxth." Margueretta pulled at the viscount's blue brocade jacket. Her big brown eyes regarded all three of them as if they were very stupid men. "*He* ith not a horth. That ith my papa. You call him . . . Drake."

Drake's name came out as Dwake, and his eyes twinkled as he met the amused gazes of the other two men.

Minutes later, after *Dwake* had galloped his daughter to her waiting nanny, he rejoined the two gentlemen in the library.

Drake reached for the crystal decanter and turned to them. "Not in London chasing the ladies? But the Season has begun, gentlemen. I cannot fathom the reason behind your visit, for you will have only the pleasure of my company tonight."

He raised an inquisitive brow, searching for a sarcastic reply, but there was none.

"You must know about Nightham." James stood, his fists tightening at his sides. "The story is all over London that his body was sent back from that inn. And from what I can deduce from your servants in Town, you took off in a hurry that same day he was found dead. You were there, were you not? Why the devil did you not tell us? The funeral was over before we came back from Brighton!"

Drake leaned against his desk and sipped from his glass. "True. All true. You must have seen the papers."

"True?" Fox shot up from his seat beside the fireplace. "Nightham was our friend, too! You should have sent word to us right away. Dash it all! The man was murdered!"

Sitting on the corner of the desk, Drake tipped the last of the liquid down his throat, wondering what to say.

"Drake?" James demanded. "What happened?"

Drake peered back at the men as a handful of embers snapped in the hearth. He slowly slipped off his desk and retreated into the leather chair behind it, his mind clouding with the memories of that disturbing night. Grief still cut deep into his heart.

"Nightham was knifed. I found him behind the inn."

Grimacing, Fox leaned forward. "Thought it was something like that. Probably saw something he shouldn't have." He paused, frowning. "Rumors are flying at White's that Nightham had a special license on him. What about the woman?"

Drake's brows shot up in surprise. Rumors at White's?

Fox narrowed his gaze on Drake. "By Jove, I knew it all along. Nightham had no brains when it came to females. An inn in a small village. What else would the nodcock be doing? He was always a bit sneaky, you know. Tell us. What of this female? I demand an answer."

"You demand an answer, do you?" Drake's tone was cool as he leaned forward, glaring back at his friend. "Nightham is dead and you demand an answer!"

"Enough." James threw his hands in the air, separating the two. His brown eyes widened in surprise as Drake and Fox sank back in their seats.

Drake frowned, recalling the entire escapade with Nightham and Lady Victoria. He could still smell the rosewater from his daughter's bath lingering on his shirt. The scent made him think of the woman, and that made him think things he had no right to think.

"Nightham did not marry her," he said, avoiding their gaze and biting back a curse. The lady had slipped through his fingers as easily as oil through a crack.

"At least there's one blessing in all of this," Fox said. "Should save his mother some grief. Poor soul. But who is this mysterious woman?"

A muscle twitched in Drake's jaw. "She disappeared. Scared, I think."

"Disappeared?" both men replied.

"Disappeared," Drake said, shifting his gaze toward the dying fire. He had told them too much already, and as much as he hated to confess the rest, it was almost impossible to stop now. He owed that much to Nightham.

Fox leaned back in his chair. "Man always had an eye for the pretty ones. He had a downright gem on his hands, did he?"

"I say," James replied thoughtfully. "The woman didn't just disappear. She gave you the slip, didn't she?"

Drake glared at his brother.

James stared back, a teasing glint in his brown eyes. "Well, who would have known? You wanted the woman for yourself, but she didn't want you. Isn't that so, big brother?"

"Shut up, James. You go too far."

"Do I? Your latest flirts have been beautiful, yet they have all gone after you. But what of this mysterious lady? Did she love Nightham then?"

Drake clenched his teeth. Did she love Nightham? He was wondering the same thing himself. "It was not that way at all. I made a promise to Nightham."

As the night progressed Drake eventually furnished the details to the two gentlemen about Nightham's death and the promise he made. He knew James and Fox would keep the information in confidence. They knew the lady involved was comely in her own right, but that was as far as Drake went on her description, conveniently leaving out the lady's hair color. Fox had a fetish for reddish-brown locks.

When the men stood up to leave, James turned to his brother. "Ah, almost forgot."

"What now?" Thoroughly exhausted, Drake frowned as they made their way to the front door.

"Father's to be in London next week."

"And that is supposed to thrill me?" As if he wanted to know where his father was all the time?

"So . . ." James whisked his hat off the hall table.

"So?" Drake stepped toward the door.

Miles, the butler, handed them their cloaks. Fox side-stepped the brothers, but Drake had distinctly heard the man's muted chuckle.

"So," James threw one foot over the threshold and glanced over his shoulder, "I did come here to find out about Nightham, but I daresay, thought you would like to see who your stepmother is going to be." Without any further explanation, James turned around and pulled the door closed.

Drake whipped the door open. "What the blazes are you talking about?"

James looked up. "The new duchess-to-be. She stayed here at Percy Hall while you were gallivanting about Town. Grandmother knows all about her."

"The devil, you say?"

James threw his head back and laughed. "No, but she is a beautiful, well-bred widow, if my sources are correct."

"And who are your sources?"

"Father, of course."

When James finally took his leave, Drake mounted the oak staircase, retreating to his bedchambers. "A blasted widow!"

"Jonathan."

Drake's gaze slowly moved down the hall. The Dowager Duchess of Glenshire emerged from her bedchambers. She was a small woman dressed in a pristine white robe buttoned to her neck.

Drake met his grandmother's stern glare. At seventy, she could still see through a brick wall, and she was the only person who called him by his first name. Even his father called him Drake.

"Jonathan? Do I smell trouble?"

Gray eyes met gray in a battle of wills.

Drake lifted a knowing brow. "I will leave the situation alone, unless it needs tending. Good night, Grandmother."

"Good night, Jonathan."

Drake stomped into his bedchamber with the lady's infernal gaze attached to his back. First, Nightham's death, and now his father was engaged to someone Drake didn't even know. Probably a pauper, too!

Drake pulled the tie from his hair, recalling a pair of aquamarine eyes. Haunting eyes. Innocent eyes. Downright enchanting eyes that had bewitched him.

With an oath, he pulled out his pocket watch and slipped it into the gilded bronze stand on his night table, setting it in place so the watch now served as a clock. He stared at the stand and felt as if time were running out like the sands of an hourglass. But time or not, he would do something about that promise to Nightham, or he would die trying.

Chapter Four

"*I* have it from Mrs. Dorling that no sooner had we left than you were out visiting a sick friend. Yet it seems strange that you could not venture with us into the country with a cold in your head?" Frowning, Sarah rested the candle on the nightstand next to Victoria's bed.

Victoria let out a shuddering sigh as a drizzling rain tapped against the windowpane of the bedchamber. Sarah's long white nightgown glowed eerily against the candlelight.

"Come now, Victoria, you must tell me what happened. I know all your friends. None are that ill that you would have to be gone from the house for almost twenty-four hours. Even Mother suspects something is wrong. Mrs. Dorling is not about to worry her with your absence, but I am a different story altogether."

From her bed, Victoria took hold of Sarah's hand. "Oh, Sarah. It is so wretched, I don't think I can tell even you."

"Goodness, you know you can trust me."

Victoria bit her lip in dismay and regarded Sarah with a wary gaze. She could trust Sarah with anything, even her life. But she could never trust a man again. The men in her life had failed her all too often.

"Does Aunt Phoebe know I left the townhouse that day?"

"No. Only Mrs. Dorling and me."

Victoria closed her eyes. "It's such a mess. I don't know where to start."

"Start anywhere, dearest. It cannot be that bad."

Victoria shook her head in disgust. "But it was a madcap thing to do. I have made a mess of it all."

"What is it? You must tell me."

"I believe I will go mad if I do not tell someone. It all happened two months ago when I came across Aunt Phoebe's financial reports in the library." Victoria took in a deep breath. "You must believe me that I did not mean to pry, yet what I discovered in those pages made me ill."

Victoria looked into Sarah's innocent face and felt a stab of regret at her impulsive behavior. "Aunt Phoebe has virtually nothing left. Her debts are rising and she is selling off the silver to make her way."

Sarah stared back in horror. "No?"

"Yes, I believe Uncle Henry lost more in those ridiculous ventures of his than Phoebe first thought."

Victoria swallowed hard, swinging her feet around the other side of the bed. "You can see how I felt it my duty to do something as quickly as possible. Phoebe has been so good to me."

Sarah stood, her hands fidgeting. "No, I don't see that at all. You should have at the very least told me."

Victoria followed her cousin's agitated movements and wished she had never spoken. "Well, it just seemed logical that I would be the one to help Phoebe out of this mess."

Sarah spun around. "Good grief, you are not suggesting you stole for us?"

"Certainly not." Victoria avoided her cousin's shocked gaze as she walked toward the window where the wind began to whistle against the pane. "I, um, married an earl instead."

"What?" Sarah fell back on her cousin's bed, her hand covering her mouth. "Did you say you married an *earl*?"

Mutely, Victoria nodded.

"Oh, Victoria."

Victoria swallowed as she turned to face her cousin. "It was idiotic. Stupid. All those things. Believe me, I know. But I did not know what else to do. My father left me with nothing, and I became a burden to Phoebe, a loving burden, but a burden all the same. It only made sense to help her." *I trusted my father and he let me down*, she wanted to say, but didn't.

"You are not a burden," Sarah said defensively.

"Oh, I know Phoebe loves me, but after what I have disclosed, can you not see that Uncle Henry was totally irresponsible, leaving Phoebe in horrendous debt?"

Victoria put up her hands. "And before you defend him, let me say that I loved the man dearly. But Phoebe has had to carry the weight of his reckless behavior since he died. She trusted him with all her heart and what did that lead to? Heartache and possibly debtor's prison.

"Can you not see that I needed to make a decision to help the ones I loved? If that meant marrying a rich earl, then so be it. It was a marriage of convenience, no love between us. Oh, I liked the man, but any mistrust on his part would not sink like a knife into my soul." She bit her lip, recalling Nightham's death.

Sarah wrung her hands on her skirt and rose from the bed. "But is this earl truly your husband?"

"To be perfectly honest, I'm not certain. There was a problem while I was at the inn. Actually two." She thought about the pirate and her hands twisted nervously on her nightgown. "No, much more than two."

"But an inn? And you don't know if you are wed to the man?"

A blush worked its way up Victoria's neck and across her cheeks. "It's not like that at all. The earl had a special license, or at least he told me he did. I was married in a private ceremony at a small inn, and then I fainted. But I never received the marriage certificate. Actually, I never signed anything." She paused. "And we were never . . . together."

"A special license? A private ceremony? You fainted? And you have no marriage certificate?" Sarah plopped onto the bed, her face white with shock. "Well, it sounds so reasonable, Victoria, I find myself speechless."

Victoria looked beyond the drizzle of the night as frustrating tears began to collect in her eyes. A clap of thunder sounded, and she dropped her gaze to the walk. A black cloaked figure paced the street corner beside the lamps below.

A cold shudder ran through her as she turned toward Sarah.

"I know it sounds mad, but it truly did happen. There's more to it . . . things I cannot bear to tell you."

Wiping a hand over her eyes, Victoria glanced back through the window. The figure had disappeared only to be replaced by a sheet of heavy rain. "I was a stupid fool to have put our family in this insufferable position, and I am heartily sorry for it. Aunt Phoebe has an offer from a duke, and now the scandal may ruin us all."

"Oh, Victoria." Sarah rose, pulling her cousin toward the bed to sit. "Had I known of your plan, I never would have let you leave this house."

"I know, and I have made a mess out of everything. But I will think of another plan, depend upon it."

"No more plans. I beg you. But you must tell me more about this earl."

"I met Lord Nightham at that ball when I met the duke."

Sarah stiffened. "Phoebe's duke?"

"Yes."

"That tall, blond man who danced two waltzes with you?"

Victoria nodded. "Since then, Lord Nightham pursued me. He wanted me to marry him, and I finally said yes. He bumped into me a few times at Hyde Park when I was out with either Mrs. Dorling or William. I realize now that he had planned those coincidental meetings to see me, and I still don't know why he chose me, but he did. He tried to be discreet about his intentions, even sending me letters through a servant boy, because he wanted to save his poor mother the worry over his search for a wife. The poor lady has palpitations, he said."

"Mrs. Dorling had mentioned you had a few admirers at the Park, but I never suspected one of them was Lord Nightham."

"He was the only one. He gave me a way to help Phoebe, William, and you, so I took it."

"But you should not have done it, you know."

Victoria felt her chest tighten with guilt. "I know. He was such a good man."

"*Was*? You mean *is*."

"Was."

"What do you mean?"

Victoria cleared her throat. "Just what it sounds like. Past tense. Not present."

Sarah blinked. "Are you telling me Lord Nightham is dead?"

Victoria nodded silently and walked across the floor to her bureau, pulling out the top drawer. "We agreed to marry at this quaint village about a half-day's ride from London. A lady named Mrs. Hinckleberry escorted us. I don't know where she lives, but she was foxed the entire ride and disappeared as soon as we arrived at the inn."

A thunderous boom shook the house. Both women jumped.

"Here it is." Victoria's hand emerged, exposing a small gold ring set off with a brilliant ruby. "This belonged to him."

Sarah picked up the candle and moved closer. "Oh, my." The light hit the gem, setting off a pink glow about the room. She looked up at Victoria. "What happened?"

"After I fainted, I found myself in one of the inn rooms with a strange man hovering over my bed, while unbeknownst to me, Lord Nightham was slashed to death outside the inn."

Sarah gasped. "Slashed? How dreadful."

Victoria's lips pinched. "There's more. The stranger promised Lord Nightham that he would take care of me, monetarily, that is. After a time, I believed the man to be family and then a friend, but I find myself uncertain of either one anymore."

Her gaze lifted to her cousin's stunned face. "You see, at first, the man did not take me for a lady. He thought I was marrying Lord Nightham for his wealth, which I was, of course, but Lord Nightham knew that."

Sarah's gaze softened as she came forward and put her hands gently on Victoria's shoulders. "Did he take liberties with you?"

"No." Victoria shook her head. "But he was a hateful man. I escaped him and returned here with no one the wiser. I could not bear to tell anyone about what happened. No one knew I married the earl except those few at the inn. And now, I am not certain I married him at all. You must have read about Lord Nightham's death in the papers."

Sarah blanched. "There was something said at Percy Hall about a deceased earl, and the duke seemed terribly upset about the man's death, but His Grace seemed to put on a good face when Phoebe was near."

Victoria slipped the ring back in the drawer and sank onto her bed. "Whoever the stranger was who knew Nightham made mention of having the scandal hushed. However, the thought of Lord Nightham's mother burdened with her son's murder haunts me to no end. Someday, I wish to ask her forgiveness."

"You should tell Phoebe," Sarah replied shakily.

Victoria's eyes widened. "No. Please, I don't want her involved. Don't you see, people might think I killed Lord Nightham? Besides, I could never claim to be his widow. I have no certificate to prove the marriage ever happened. I don't even have the vicar's name or the witnesses'. It would be a wretched scandal. If I could only wait until your mother marries the duke, you would all be safe."

Victoria lifted her chin. "Don't look at me that way, Sarah. You know it is the only way. After Aunt Phoebe is married, I can seek the help I need to sort this all out."

"But this is positively dreadful." Sarah's bare feet brushed against the rug beside Victoria's bed. "And who is this man that followed you to the inn?"

"I don't know." Victoria let out a nervous laugh. "And I never want to see that detestable man again. Of course, I think he wished me dead instead of the earl. Why, the man's probably glad he's seen the last of me."

But her heart pounded wildly as two hard gray eyes focused in her memory. Glad? No doubt the man was positively livid!

The man stared across the street at the townhouse, his eyes attached to the soft candlelight flickering in the upstairs window. He studied her silhouette, her slender body and that magnificent mane of hair. The gangly-legged freckled-face girl had turned into quite a beauty. But she had no man to take care of her now. Lord Nightham was dead.

He laughed to himself. The lady had no man but him.

His grin grew broader. She would gladly take him as a husband after her disgracing exhibition at that shabby little inn. He would see to that. It was a stroke of luck that the vicar had been an imposter. Nightham had no brains at all. Nevertheless, the fraudulent minister and the two servants had to disappear. Permanently. Each deed had been done with one quick slice of his knife. It was pathetic how easy the killings had been. But it was Nightham's lingering death that had been the best.

Still grinning, the man turned to leave. He didn't see the carriage until it was too late. The oncoming vehicle splattered mud high into the air, covering the man's shiny black boots all the way to his beaver hat.

"Idiot driver!" The man threw his fist in the air. "I'll kill you! Kill you, do you hear me?" He cursed with a vengeance as he tried to flick the slop off his coat.

But as he did, he missed the blond-haired boy pressing his nose against the townhouse window across the street, making plans of his own.

Chapter Five

*T*wo weeks later Victoria sat in Phoebe's carriage as the vehicle headed back to the townhouse. For Victoria, the party at the duke's residence in Grosvenor Square had been troublesome indeed. She peered down at her gloved hands, hoping the darkness of night would help hide the uneasiness in her face from Phoebe and Sarah.

Though the duke's first son had not made an appearance at the soiree, she shuddered as she thought about the duke's second son, Lord James. His coal black hair, chiseled jaw line, and muscular build were similar to the duke's except for the sprinkle of gray about the older man's temples.

If those men had worn their hair any longer in a deeper shade of black, and if she exchanged slate gray eyes for their brown and added a few inches in height, they would have resembled her hideous pirate from the inn.

Clasping her hands about her reticule, Victoria stared out the window. The lamps, carriages, and buildings passed by in a blur of shadows as Nightham's death haunted her.

"His Grace was most kind tonight, was he not, my dears?" Phoebe asked, her heart in her eyes.

Victoria gave her aunt a genuine smile. "I do hope the duke knows what he's up against. The man may have three boys, but that fact does not stack up against one William."

Sarah's eyes held a teasing glint. "Do you dare think he should be warned of the pirate that lurks in our family?"

Phoebe fidgeted with her gloves. "I daresay, George has seen William at work. Besides, he has plenty of that in his own household, too." Phoebe looked up and gave Victoria a wink. "The oldest son is hideously handsome they say. Though I have not had the pleasure of his acquaintance yet."

Victoria smiled at her aunt, but inwardly grimaced.

Minutes later, Sarah elbowed Victoria in the ribs as they entered the townhouse. "You should have seen the black spider that fell into the duke's soup back at Percy Hall. Mama about had a fit."

Victoria frowned. "What did the duke say?"

"Not a word," Sarah said with a straight face. "But his glaring gaze said more than words ever could. Even William turned quite red in the face."

As Sarah made her way to her chambers, Victoria found herself alone in the hall with her aunt.

"What is it, my dear?" Phoebe frowned, slipping her hand into Victoria's. "Is it about that viscount? I saw Lord Foxcroft kiss you, my dear, and I have it on the best authority that he is every bit of the gentleman, most of the time. You need not worry." Her eyes sparkled with a faraway expression.

Victoria blinked. Goodness. Aunt Phoebe had seen the viscount's stolen kiss? It had been an innocent peck on the cheek, but still . . .

"Have no worry." Aunt Phoebe gently tapped her hand. "The viscount is like one of the duke's own sons. George had a word with him in the library. I won't let anyone harm one strand of that beautiful hair of yours, and neither will His Grace. Now sleep tight, and remember that tomorrow is a new day."

The duke had spoken to Lord Foxcroft? How humiliating.

"Aunt Phoebe?"

"Yes, dearest?"

"What exactly did you mean when you said that the duke mentioned he had plenty of that in his own household?"

"Oh, that." Phoebe clasped her hands together in amusement. "I was referring to his son, you know, the pirate. I had mentioned him before."

Victoria's knees slowly began to buckle, and she leaned against her bedchamber door for support. So, it was true then. "The pirate?"

"Oh, I am not suggesting a real pirate. I thought I made it clear. He only looks like one. Drake, that is George's first born, is the Marquess of Drakefield, you know. They say his hair is to his shoulders, jet-black like James, but even darker and tied back in a silly tail behind his head. They also say his demeanor is anything but docile. But George loves him, and I imagine I will as well. And by the way," she whispered ever so softly as she walked toward her room, "they say he is by far the most handsome man on the face of the earth. Of course, I think his father a rather good-looking specimen myself."

With those profound words, Phoebe let out a girlish giggle and stepped down the hall into her chambers.

Victoria dragged herself into her room, her heart banging against her ribs. But it took only three seconds for her to snap out of her doldrums when she felt a slimy creature slide across her feet.

"WILLIAM!"

Her voice jolted the entire household, especially the snickering blond boy who had quickly retrieved his slimy friend from his cousin's bedchamber, then hid under his own bed, along with his second in command, and a nice soft blanket.

It was just before noon the following day when Victoria awoke. As she dressed for the day, she was informed that Lord Foxcroft was waiting in the drawing room. She drew in an unsteady breath. Tiny footsteps padded in the hall and she guessed it was William with his pile of creatures planning his next move. If that were her only trouble, she could handle the situation.

Phoebe had received the viscount in the drawing room, but as soon as Victoria entered, her aunt suddenly remembered she had something she needed to do.

Alone with Lord Foxcroft, Victoria tried to relax, hoping he was every bit the gentleman her aunt had assured her he was. When he asked her forgiveness concerning his horrid behavior the night before, she was amused.

"I should slap you for the way you behaved," she said

lightly. "As I hear it, perhaps the duke has already done the deed."

He quickly moved to show her one side of his face. "If it makes you feel any better, Lady Victoria, please do. Slap me senseless. His Grace is like a father to me, and I can tell you the man gave me the tongue-lashing of my life." He sent her a mischievous grin. "Yes, I know. I deserved it."

She chuckled. "You are impossible, my lord." She separated herself by walking to the other side of the room, her skirt swishing against her ankles, oblivious to the viscount's bold gaze attached to her backside.

"Lady Victoria?"

She turned, raising a questioning brow.

"Do I dare ask for your company tonight at the opera? I am offered a place in the duke's box."

"And am I safe there?" she asked, mischief dancing in her eyes.

"If you ever have need of a protector, you have one in the duke." Lord Foxcroft grinned and strode across the floor in two long strides. "Of course, the duke is not here now." He took another step toward her, and her eyes widened.

She was saved from scolding the man when her butler Winston interrupted the cozy scene with a stern face directed toward the viscount. "My lady."

"Yes, Winston." Victoria glanced up and fought back a laugh. Sometimes Winston acted as if he were her guard dog.

Her butler spared another stern glance at the viscount, then shifted a firm glare back toward her. The duke was not her only protector.

"Lord Wendover is visiting," Winston added. "Are you receiving, my lady?"

Victoria felt as if Winston had stolen the breath from her lungs. Lord Wendover? What would that man want after all these years? He was the heir to her father's earldom and had literally thrown her out of her home when her parents had died. But how could she deny the man entrance with the viscount standing right beside her?

"Show the gentleman in," she said coolly, missing Foxcroft's frown as he peered back at the butler.

Lady Phoebe entered the drawing room at the exact moment Victoria's second cousin, the Earl of Wendover, entered. The man was clad in a black cloak from head to toe, except for his perfectly folded cravat and crisp white shirt.

The introductions were made, including Lord Foxcroft.

Some would say Lord Wendover was a handsome man with his light blue eyes and fair hair, but to Victoria there was a sneering arrogance hidden in his beady gaze, something the others didn't seem to notice, but something she remembered since she was a child.

Lord Wendover took Phoebe's hand. "Lady Phoebe, my sincere apologies that I have neglected you all these years, but I wish to make it up to you. I admit I have been quite lax in my duties."

Aunt Phoebe's face lit up with pleasure. "Think nothing about it, my lord. We are all busy with our own lives."

Victoria's jaw dropped. How could her aunt be so friendly to the man? But then again, her aunt did not have a malicious bone in her body, not something Victoria could say for herself. Wendover was a horrid man, and she wanted nothing to do with him.

"And Lady Victoria, you have grown into a beautiful woman, dear cousin."

Victoria forced the corners of her lips to curve upward when the man moved to take her gloved hand in his. His clasp was as cold as his heart. "You are too kind, my lord."

Phoebe took Wendover's arm as if they were old friends. "You will join us tonight at the opera, will you not? We must become more acquainted. I fear I have not been on my best behavior since my brother died. It was so good of you to come here and mend the bridge between us."

Victoria almost fainted on the Aubusson rug beneath her.

"I would be delighted, dear lady. It would be a pleasure to venture out with such beautiful women as yourselves."

Victoria felt Lord Foxcroft stiffen beside her.

Minutes later, after the two men left, Victoria climbed the stairs, overwhelmed at the way her life was changing before her eyes. She knew full well that she might see the pirate because she would be sitting in the duke's private box. And then there was Wendover who had appeared like a long lost son. The impudence of the man to show his face after all these years.

There was a knock at the front door, but she didn't think twice as Winston answered it. She began to review what plans she would have to make for the evening. One, how could she avoid Wendover? And two, how could she avoid the pirate?

She stumbled on a step when the familiar voice floated up the stairs. "Good afternoon, I am here to see Lady Phoebe. Please convey to her that Lord Drakefield has come to visit."

Victoria's blood had turned to ice. She barely heard the rest of the words spoken between Winston and the man. Her grip on the banister tightened. She dared not look back. But because she wanted to live, she scampered up the last few steps and flattened herself against the wall. It was the duke's son. But not only that, it was also the pirate from the inn!

Chapter Six

*D*rake stood, patiently waiting inside Lady Phoebe's drawing room, still feeling the brunt of his father's rebuke, and all because he missed being introduced to the new *duchess-to-be*. He had not recalled a tongue-lashing like the one he received that morning from his father since he was fifteen and caught in the stables with the cook's daughter.

The duke did more than boil the morning eggs with his anger. He scorched Drake's ears with words Drake had never heard his father use before. Though the duke's command was never enough to make Drake do anything he did not want to do—at least not at his age—in the end, Drake believed it harder to avoid Lady Phoebe than to meet her, so he chose the latter.

Drake heard the running steps behind him and spun on his heels just as a blond-haired boy rammed into his leg. Stifling his laughter, Drake caught the child's two small shoulders, steadying him and proceeded to lift the wide-eyed boy high into the air, ready to inspect him nose to nose. "Well, what have we here?"

The child wore a black hat that rested sideways on his head making him look like a pirate. To Drake's amazement, two bright blue eyes stared back at him, and it seemed as if the boy were inspecting every crack and crevice in his face. But the color of those eyes looked all too familiar.

Drake's heart picked up a beat. Not just an ordinary blue, but aquamarine. Or was it turquoise?

He tried to keep a straight face, but slowly felt the corners of his eyes crinkle into a smile when the boy began to tug at his queued hair. "Find anything of interest, lad?"

"A pirate," the boy said in awe, squinting at him.

Drake gave the boy a solemn stare, hiding his smile. "Looking for a sword perhaps? Ah, matie, I left that on me ship with me bottle of rum."

The boy smiled. "Oh, I know all about rum."

At the top of the stairs, Victoria felt the panic rise to her throat as she inched from her position against the wall to peer down at the man standing at the edge of the drawing room doors, holding William in his arms. It was the same man from the inn, and he looked even more ominous than he had when she had seen him last.

Yet he seemed different now, too. In fact, he seemed to be enjoying William's preoccupation with his looks, the peacock that he was. Why even that dark brown jacket fitted him to perfection, making him look more powerful than she remembered. And his boots looked as if they were polished only five minutes ago. Of course, he was checking that infernal pocket watch again. The man was preoccupied with order and time, and that was something she could certainly do without. He probably had his entire life timed to the minute. Odious man!

Then as if reading her mind, he showed William the timepiece in question. The boy smiled and put it to his ear.

Victoria frowned, not wanting the man to be agreeable. So, he was kind to children. So what? That did not mean she could trust him. He knew about Nightham, and that was a threat to her and her family, something she'd best remember. He was also the son of the duke Phoebe was to marry. He could easily stop the wedding.

She watched in shock as William ran his hand along the man's clean-shaven face, then jerked his snowy white cravat, almost choking the man to death. Good heavens, William had more nerve than she did. She should have had him with her at the inn.

When William's feet finally hit the floor, Victoria narrowed her brows in dismay as her cousin began to brush his fingers over the man's jacket, touching the row of shiny brass buttons as if they were the most precious jewels in the world. The pair of pokey little fingers moved down past the slick black breeches, all the way to the man's Hessians.

But as William continued his inspection, Victoria caught herself mesmerized by the man herself. For a few seconds she let down her guard and gave the man a chance to glance her way. At least she thought the man had cast a quick gaze up the stairs.

She pulled her head back behind the corner and froze. Had he recognized her?

"So matie, are you a pirate or not?"

The man let out a hearty laugh at William's question. "After your careful inspection, what would you say I am, little man?"

Victoria peeked back and saw the man step halfway into the hall. The skin around his eyes crinkled into a soft, endearing smile that wrapped around her heart. She shook her head. What was she thinking? This man could ruin her.

And he had the audacity to ask her to trust him? She was a fool, but she wasn't that stupid!

"I would say that you are a pirate!" William took his own pirate hat off his head as he started circling the gentlemen. "But a good pirate. Like me."

"A good pirate, eh?"

William slapped his hat back onto his bobbing head. "Yes, a good pirate. One that will protect the treasures in this house."

"Treasures?"

"Yes, and since you are a good pirate, I will tell you something. I am Pirate William and this is Cap'n Whitie."

William pulled out his second in command and grinned. "We protect this house and all the princesses in it."

The man's eyes narrowed as he stared at the white mouse in the boy's hand. "Ah, I see. Espionage at its finest."

"What?" William asked, his nose scrunching. "Oh, yes, es . . . espionage."

Victoria bent over in merriment, her gaze dropping to Aunt Phoebe and Sarah as they came into view. The man was not as stuffy as she had once presumed. Still . . .

"And here are the princesses, are they not?" The pirate peered down the hall.

"Yes, princesses," William went on, "but I saw the villain, too. So did Cap'n Whitie." He tugged on the man's coat.

But the pirate had already straightened from his hunched position, ready to meet the two females coming his way.

"I said," William piped louder, "I saw the villain! And—" but his words were lost in the formal introductions taking place.

"Drat!" William stomped his foot, obviously wanting to talk more about his villain.

Victoria was amazed at the man's gentleness with William. Something in her heart gave a little kick. He was polite, had a sense of humor, and was nice to children. He had been a different man the time she had seen him.

But what would he do if he knew she was the lady at the inn? Did he know already? She shuddered at the memory of those hard gray eyes glaring at her, demanding her cooperation. Would he ruin Phoebe's future?

Phoebe pulled her son aside. "Now, William is that any way to talk to the man who is going to be your brother?"

William jumped with glee. "A pirate for a brother!"

Victoria sighed against the wall and frowned. *Brother.* How wonderfully dreadful. The reality of the situation cut into her heart like a guillotine.

If the duke ever discovered Victoria's past, he would most probably refuse to marry Aunt Phoebe. Her secret would be out, and all would be lost. Frowning, Victoria walked back to her room and plopped on her bed in the throes of defeat. Now she knew how the French felt at Waterloo.

She claimed a headache when she was asked to receive the visitor and could only stare in dread at the ceiling. Had she ruined her family's chance for happiness because of her impulsive actions? Did the pirate know her identity now? Would Aunt Phoebe end up in debtor's prison after all? No, the duke may not marry Phoebe, but he would not let that happen.

"Did you see him, Vicki?" William shouted as he opened her door and slammed it shut.

Victoria lifted her head from her pillow and dropped it again. "Yes, I saw him." *And he is going to ruin us all.*

William hopped onto her mattress, jumping up and down, forcing her to stand. "He's wonderful!"

"Wonderful," she murmured, scooting off the bed.

"And did you see the villain, too?"

Victoria wrung her hands on her skirt and moved toward the window. "The pirate. Yes, I saw him."

"The most magnificent pirate in the whole world!" Bounce. Bounce. "But I asked if you saw the evil villain."

"The villain?" she asked without thinking. But she was more interested in the pirate exiting the townhouse and entering his awaiting carriage. There was something about him that stirred her blood, even though he was her enemy.

She pressed her hand against the window and lowered her gaze in anticipation. He peered up at her. It was so fast that Victoria barely realized what had happened. He had seen her!

Her body went rigid and she stepped back. She could still feel the heat of his gaze burning a path straight to her toes.

"What were you saying, William?"

"I said! Did . . . you . . . see . . . the villain? Are you deaf from a cannonball to your head?" Bounce. Bounce.

"No, I did not see the villain."

"Yes, you did. He was in this very house." William stopped his bouncing. "He was. I saw him."

Victoria narrowed her eyes. Her cousin jumped to the floor and grabbed her hand, pulling her back toward the window. "There. In the carriage. That evil earl! You know, your cousin! Do you see him or not?" By now the boy was shouting in her ear.

Victoria peered out the window and recognized the black carriage that clattered down the street. The coat of arms was her father's. Wendover should have left the house an hour ago.

"The villain's mean, Vicki. Mean as a witch!"

Victoria tried not to show the terror that crawled along her skin. Before today, it had been a long time since she had seen the earl, and for the life of her, she could not figure out what he wanted. But whatever it was, she had a strange feeling he wanted something from her.

Drake relaxed in the carriage, his thoughts centered on the mahogany-haired siren who had eluded him far too long. When he had entered the townhouse, he had smelled roses again, fresh as a spring day. Lady Victoria's scent.

Fox had mentioned Lady Phoebe's niece and her many attributes. Drake, of course, was curious himself, for more reasons than his friend would ever know. And now it seemed very probable that Phoebe's Lady Victoria was the woman from the inn.

The thought of his father being swindled into a heartless marriage based on greed bothered him to no end. Though Lady Phoebe seemed all that was good, the female mind was sly and cunning, as he knew all too well. He felt as if his hands were tied. Should he tell his father his secrets? But could he fulfill his promise to Nightham if he did?

Yet, it was only right that his father knew the truth. Tonight at the opera he would plan his attack well.

Chapter Seven

*L*ater that evening Victoria stood in the duke's box, gazing down at the multitude of people filling the Opera House. A wave of perfume assaulted her senses while the rumble of voices lifted from the pit and the gallery below. She leaned back, feeling a bit dizzy, having eaten nothing since breakfast.

"Lady Victoria," Lord Foxcroft called from beside her, "may I say, you look beautiful tonight, a diamond of the first waters."

Though a bit flustered by all the attention the viscount was lavishing on her, Victoria admitted to herself that she felt somewhat comforted by his presence, especially with Lord Wendover in attendance. "My lord, you are too generous in your flattery."

Then, as if it came naturally, Lord Foxcroft took her gloved hand in his and brought it to his lips as he offered her a seat.

"I cannot tell you how pleased I am that you accepted my invitation. I know you probably would have come as a guest of the duke, but this way, I have you all to myself."

Pleased? She wondered what would he think when he found out about her scandalous past?

She bit her bottom lip in despair, again peering over the crowd as if she were truly interested in what was happening before the performance. She had never been the same after Nightham's death, and at that precise moment, she felt like a wretched fraud.

She exchanged a weak smile with Sarah who sat beside

Lord James. The man had taken Sarah under his wing like an older brother. She wondered if the eldest brother would be as kind.

She turned to look at the duke. His intense gaze never left her aunt. He was a man in love, and the passion in his eyes told her he would marry as quickly as possible if Phoebe wanted it. Now, only to get Phoebe to agree to a special license and a quick marriage. The pirate could try to do his worst, but at least Phoebe would be married to her duke.

She looked over the crowd and shuddered inwardly at her predicament. Time seemed her enemy now.

When Drake's carriage rolled to the front of the theater, he snapped his pocket watch closed, climbed out of the vehicle, and moved purposely toward the stairs near his father's box. As he stood behind the curtain, he smiled, relishing the thought of taking Lady Victoria by surprise. What would she do? She certainly could not climb away from him this time.

He would tell all tonight. His father could not marry into such a family.

"It looks like we have the great Catalani singing for us tonight," Drake announced to everybody as his shiny gilt-buckled shoes plunged past the threshold of his father's box. His steely gaze found Fox sitting next to his prey.

Sarah turned, but Lady Victoria stared dead ahead, her back to him, as if she had not heard him enter. Drake smiled to himself. The little minx. There was no doubt that she was the woman from the inn.

He greeted his father, Lady Phoebe and her neice, James, Wendover, and left Fox and Lady Victoria for last. Even from the back, the lady was quite beautiful, but beauty would not save her now. He reminded himself about his dead wife and the pain that he endured from Honoria's disloyalty, especially her unseemly disregard for his money. His father deserved to know all.

Fox finally turned to him. "Drake, let me introduce you to Lady Victoria, niece to Lady Phoebe."

The duke and Lady Phoebe chattered on, oblivious to the tension in the box.

"Lady Victoria." Drake took her hand and leaned over to peer into a pair of huge turquoise eyes.

She gave a slight curtsy, then lifted her eyes to his. She knew exactly who he was. There was a challenge in her gaze as well as fear. "Good evening, my lord."

"Delighted." He gave her hand a slight squeeze and let it go. "Have we met somewhere before?"

Her lips parted in surprise.

She was more enchanting than he remembered. No wonder Nightham had gone mad. But it was the angry flash in those cerulean eyes that caused him notice. She was daring him to expose her. How very interesting.

"Met before?" Her voice was as sweet as honey.

Drake swallowed a laugh at her pluck and watched in silence as she flicked a glance toward her aunt, then toward Sarah. The instant those big blue eyes softened, Drake felt a slap to his heart. This woman cared deeply for her family, and she was afraid for *them*, not herself. Had he been wrong about her?

No, his mind whispered. She could not be that virtuous. Not a beauty with a heart. But honor would not let him divulge her secret to his father without knowing her ulterior motives.

"Drake, have a care." Fox stepped in and physically jerked Drake away from Victoria, showing the lady back to her seat.

Drake would have thought he imagined the glaring threat from his friend, but the lasting scowl on Fox's face confirmed the man's declaration of war.

Drake flashed a brilliant set of white teeth turning Fox's face a fiery red.

Victoria felt ill. The staring continued between the two men and the uneasiness mounted. It seemed that besides the viscount and the marquess, only she and Sarah, to whom she had confirmed about the duke's eldest son being the intruder at the inn, were aware of the tension escalating in the box. Two silver gray eyes were embedded in her brain. There was no denying that the marquess had planned his attack well.

She knew without a doubt that Lord Drakefield had been

about to unveil her entire escapade with Nightham, but something had stopped him. Had it been the viscount's presence, or something else?

She quickly turned to glance about the crowd. The noise seemed to lower to a murmur now, and all the faces seemed to blur. She felt herself growing warmer by the minute. The marquess was just behind her, staring at the viscount. She fanned her face as tears burned the back of her eyes. She was doomed. He was going to spill her secret and poor Phoebe would be devastated when she lost her duke. All would be lost.

A heavy pressure on her chest made it hard to breathe. But she would rather have it all out now, than wait like a frightened rabbit, burrowing in its hole, waiting for the kill.

Oh, the detestable, hateful man.

Sarah leaned over, her expression worried. "Would you like to walk out for some fresh air, dearest? Lord James would be only too happy to escort you outside."

James rose from his seat and whispered to his brother, "I hold you totally responsible for this evening, Drake. I should have known you had some dealings with Lady Victoria after so many questions this afternoon. You only have to look at the lady's pallor to know she might swoon at any moment. What hold do you have on her?"

Victoria heard the heated exchange and the blood rushed from her face. She cast an uneasy glance over her shoulder at Lord Foxcroft. She was not as brave as she thought. The marquess had won. "My lord," she said, giving the viscount a weak smile, "I fear I am not feeling well. Would you mind taking me home?"

Foxcroft frowned, taking hold of her arm. She swayed slightly in her seat.

"Oh, my." Phoebe grabbed the duke's arm. "Victoria. Why, she never has had a case of the vapors. She must be ill."

Perplexed at the odd turn of events, the suave-looking duke moved to Victoria's side. "My dear, let me help you."

By this time, even Wendover had offered her his arm. "Lady Victoria, lean on me."

Lord Foxcroft argued that it was his duty to take her outside. But Wendover insisted, he was her cousin, distant or not, and he ought to be the one to help her.

"Not likely," was the marquess's retort when he maneuvered his way to take hold of Victoria and spoke in Wendover's ear.

Victoria had no idea what was happening. All she knew was that her head was roaring something horrid, and she felt ill.

In no time, Drake had pushed the hovering gentlemen aside, including his father. He reached out and scooped Victoria into his arms. "I have her now. Make way, gentlemen. Make way." He pressed the woman's body close to his chest, grabbed his hat, and stepped out of the box as Foxcroft reluctantly gave up his spot.

Phoebe swayed. "Goodness gracious."

The duke's arms circled Lady Phoebe's waist, using the situation to his advantage. "Have no worry, my dear, she is in good hands with my son."

Lord Foxcroft took a menacing step forward. "Exactly. Good hands, indeed!"

Victoria sank back against the cold seat of the marquess's carriage and took a deep breath, forcing her gaze on the man entering beside her. The marquess looked at her silently.

She lifted her chin, daring him to do his worst. Though his presence was overwhelming, there was also a strength about him that sent a tingling warmth to the pit of her stomach. But it was the mocking amusement in his silver gaze that sent her rage mounting. How dare he pull her from her family!

A biting silence filled the air, and her teeth began to clatter. She threw her hands around her shivering body, her thoughts scampering dangerously. He may hold power over her and her secrets, but she was furious at his high-handed behavior.

To her surprise, he whipped off his black jacket, placing it about her shoulders. When his fingers brushed her neck, the amusement died in his eyes, and his lips pressed together into a tight line. "You don't need to catch cold on top of everything else. My father would never forgive me if something happened to you. Neither would James or your aunt or your cousin."

He let out an amusing snort. "Or Fox. No, I suppose Fox would not be too pleased with me whatever happened to you."

He handed her the wool carriage blanket beneath the seat and positioned her feet over the hot bricks on the floorboard.

"Warmer?" he asked with a concern that Victoria did not expect.

"Quite," she replied with a shrug, avoiding his steadfast gaze. What was this man's game? Why did he not tell the duke of her flight? Was it because he wanted to keep Lord Nightham's name clear of any gossip? Or was it truly something else?

She wanted to hate him. He was overbearing, dictatorial, and positively the most arrogant man she had ever met. But when she peered up at him, the tenderness in his gaze shocked her.

She tilted her head back toward the window, her heart skipping a beat. "You may take me home now."

He said nothing, and she knew he was studying her. She glanced over her shoulder and faced him. "I wish to go home."

The corners of his lips lifted slightly. "That reddish tint in your hair seems to go well with your temper, my lady."

Her teeth rattled as she lifted her head higher. "You . . . you are insufferable."

His reaction was to frown as he leaned toward her and tucked the blanket tighter around her. "Better?"

His touch was oddly sweet, sending a quivering through her veins. *But better?* Was he trying to suffocate her with his nearness? His overbearing manner, combined with his devilish good looks, sent her heart soaring into uncharted territory.

He glared at her, angling his chin toward her apparel. "If you had worn something a bit warmer, you might not be so chilled."

Her mouth dropped open in shock, just as he tapped the top of the carriage, stood up, and said something to the driver, then sat down, pulling her to his side.

Victoria stiffened as his arm snaked firmly around her waist. "Oh, how dare you."

"I dare anything I want, especially when a lady is wearing my jacket."

"This . . . this is insufferable, my lord."

He laughed, but he would not let her pull away. "I am not ready to tell your secrets just yet. So you may rest easy."

Rest easy? Victoria gritted her teeth, feeling the strength of his fingers pressing into her back. Why, this man could ruin her.

It took her a few tense minutes before she realized the carriage was stopping at her home. She hated to move lest the man believed she was making an advance of some sort. His ego had already eclipsed even her imagination.

However, the stunning thought that she might want him to hold her a bit longer lingered in the back of her mind like a prickly thorn. She let out a distasteful shudder. It was the cold night air making her daft. It had to be.

When he escorted her up the steps and to the door, she handed him his jacket just as Winston appeared. She murmured a hurried goodnight, but was surprised when he stepped in after her.

"Cozy little place your aunt has," he said, walking further into the hall.

"What do you think you're doing?" she hissed.

Smirking, the marquess peered at the butler and gave Winston his hat. "Bring some brandy into the library, my good man, and be quick about it."

Winston stayed put, his questioning brows narrowing into the middle of his forehead. Victoria glanced back at the pirate.

"Oh, good heavens, be reasonable, Lord Drakefield."

The man had the insolence to smile at her, refusing to budge. "Brandy." He paused, raising a brow to the butler. "Winston, is it not?"

Victoria gasped. Of all the unmitigated gall. The wretched man was not going to leave until he had his brandy. She wished she could just give him the entire bottle and shove him out the door. But the way he was staring down her butler and checking that pocket watch of his, it was obvious he was not about to leave until *he* decided to.

She gave a wary glance at Winston. The older man clenched his hands at his sides. Oh, good grief, not him too! She scooted between the two men, dread filling the pit of her stomach. "It's quite all right, Winston. Bring the brandy into the library."

The butler stood for another second, nodded grimly and left, only to return to the library later with a crystal decanter of brandy and one glass. He placed the tray on the mahogany end table and planted his feet on the carpet as though he were rooted to the room like an oak.

A fire crackled in the hearth, sounding more like booming thunder against the silence that swallowed the room. The marquess glared at Winston. Winston glared back at the marquess. No one moved. Victoria grew more uncomfortable by the minute. Surely, Lord Drakefield would not touch the older man.

Smiling, she nodded for Winston to leave. To his credit, the butler took his leave, keeping the doors wide open. But the blood drained from her face when the marquess took three long strides toward the doors, sealing the room closed with a thud. He turned, folded his arms across his chest, and glared at her.

Her heart thumped madly as she fought the anxiety spurting through her veins. No doubt the man would like to skewer her through with the fire poker.

"Well, what is it you want?" Her head, perhaps?

Gray eyes locked with hers. "Now, my little runaway, if I knew the answer to that question, we would not be here, would we?"

Chapter Eight

*V*ictoria watched with misgiving as Lord Drakefield took the brandy decanter off the tray and splashed the amber liquid into the glass. He peered up at her, his steel gray eyes surveying her with a glint of amusement. "To warm you."

He walked toward her and handed her the glass.

Her lips thinned. "No, thank you."

Still shivering from the cold, she spared a glance at the door. She needed a wrap, and she needed him gone.

"Ah," he replied, following her gaze. "Going to be that way, is it?" He put down the drink, and before she knew it, he had her in his arms, depositing her on a soft-tufted chair near the glowing hearth. "Warmer now?"

Victoria gasped in outrage. "You take your liberties too far, Lord Drakefield."

She narrowed her eyes as she followed his long purposeful strides back toward the brandy glass. Then he laughed and started back toward her. "At least we're getting somewhere by calling me by name."

"That is debatable, my lord." She pressed her lips together and glared at him.

But as he closed the distance between them, the devilish gleam in his eye unnerved her so much that she jumped out of the chair and accidentally knocked the brandy all over his cravat. She threw her hands to her face in horror as the liquid dripped down the white fabric and toward his waistcoat.

"Direct hit, my dear." He dabbed at his clothes with a

white handkerchief, stuffing the cloth back into his waist-coat pocket.

Victoria stood, staring in shock at what she had done.

He peered up at her, his gray eyes gleaming with challenge. "Does that mean you are daring to refuse the drink, or is it me you abhor?"

You, of course.

"Very well then," he said with a narrowed gaze, as if hearing her very thoughts. "You are going to freeze to death in that . . . that flimsy gown. Your shoulders are quivering and your teeth are rattling. I will not have you ill. Confound it, woman! You led me on a merry chase after Nightham's death, and now you can hardly stand or speak without shaking!"

She wrapped her arms around her chest. The thought of Lord Nightham and that horrid night brought tears to her eyes. "If you will take your leave, I will take the drink."

"The devil, I will. The drink is nothing more than a medicinal beverage to warm you. I daresay, it is not a ploy to have you foxed. Take it now, so we can have our little talk."

He pushed the brandy beneath her nose, but she refused by twisting her head aside.

"Minx," he chided, wrapping one hand around her waist and pulling her to him. "Warmer?"

Victoria shook her head no. But in fact, she felt much warmer than she ever wanted to be. He smelled of fine soap and brandy, sending her senses soaring.

"Your teeth are still clacking like horses' hooves." His voice whispered along her neck as he rubbed her quivering shoulders. "I assure you it is in your best interest to stay warm."

The mere touch of his fingers sent a smoldering shiver through her veins. "I am feeling much better," she said softly. "Thank you."

He paused, then pulled her closer to the fire. "I'm not going to tell my father about your flight with Nightham, if that's what's worrying you."

Warily, she looked up to find his gaze intent upon her face. At that precise moment, she felt a subtle, but fragile thread begin to grow between them.

"That is, unless you give me pause to do otherwise."

He took hold of her shoulders, and her breath came to a screeching halt. He seemed to recognize her reaction to him, and his lips curved upward into an unconscious smile. "You must trust me on this. Can you do that?"

"Trust you?" she repeated in a suffocating whisper. To put her family's future totally in this man's hands? She shook her head. "No, I can't do that."

He lifted her chin with the tip of his fingers. "Yes, you can," he said in a silky voice and lowered his head, capturing her lips with his. The kiss was oddly gentle, shooting a fiery heat along her skin. He leaned his head back slowly.

"I have wanted to kiss you since the first time I saw you at the inn." His warm breath fanned her cheeks as he gently took her face in his hands. "You must have driven Nightham mad."

The tenderness of his touch began to crack her protective shield. His dark gaze searched her face, and he kissed her again. Her mind said no, but her heart said yes. She did not want to resist him. Like a magical spell, she felt herself sway into him while the room seemed to tilt and spin beneath her.

"What the blazes is going on here?"

"William!" Victoria jumped back and turned toward the open doors. Reality abruptly set in. Shocked at her response to Lord Drakefield's kiss, she groaned out loud.

"Why, ye are the bloomin' pirate!"

William stood at the doors, holding his stick in one hand, flying it in the air like a sword in battle. His white nightshirt flapped about wildly as he circled the marquess.

His black pirate hat hit the ground as if in challenge. "Ye are not supposed to kiss the princess, not unless ye are married!"

The boy pulled his second in command for a look. The furry creature squirmed about William's fingers and emitted a restless squeak.

"Well, well." The marquess's eyes lit up with amusement.

"What do ye think ye are doing?" William stood his ground.

Lord Drakefield's chest began to rumble with laughter.

Victoria looked on in horror, humiliation filling her. The pirate had kissed her, but more mortifying than that, she had kissed him back! And trust him? He must be daft!

William interrupted the tense moment with another slice of his sword. "If you are going to marry her, then I will not have to call you out." The sword fingered back to Drakefield's belly.

"An interesting prospect," the marquess said coolly. "Is it not, Lady Victoria?"

Victoria's eyes widened at the implication. "William, what are you doing up at this time of night?"

"I was watching for that villain, of course!" The boy stomped his foot. "And I saw him! Out there!" His sword flew past the smirking marquess's mouth and toward the tall windows.

Victoria's anger was mounting, toward her cousin and the marquess. She could never trust this man. What in the world had she been thinking?

She patted William's bottom, hurrying him along. "To bed with you, young man."

"Wait just a minute, me brother pirate." Drakefield stepped forward and touched the boy's shoulder. "What villain?"

Victoria glared at Lord Drakefield. Then pushing her cousin along, she said, "I said it is time for bed, William."

But Lord Drakefield gently moved in, brushing her aside. He proceeded to haul William to a nearby chair, then onto his lap, sword and all. "Now, tell me about this villain, me pirate."

"Humph!" William glanced up at Victoria with a winning look in his eyes. "Well." William smiled at the marquess, his expression one of great importance. "The villain always watches us from outside that window."

William pointed across the room. The marquess stood up and held the boy's hand as they took a look.

"He waits on the corner, over there." William stabbed the air with his finger. "He watches and waits, dressed all in black. Sometimes he says bad words. Why, I've heard him say words like—"

"William," Victoria interrupted. "That is quite enough. We have no need to know specific details."

"Go on, William." Lord Drakefield hid his smile. "Continue without the undignified words."

William's eyes grew round, obviously enthralled that someone was finally paying attention to him. "The villain wants one or all of the princesses in the house."

The boy looked back at Victoria, then whispered into the marquess's ear, tugging at his stained cravat. "And I am telling ye, he wants the treasure, too."

"Ah, he does, does he?" The marquess's eyes sparkled. "Depend upon it, William, I will keep an eye out for the villain myself. But I do believe it's time for bed, me pirate friend."

With one fluid motion, the marquess threw the boy on top of his shoulders. William whooped with glee.

Victoria stared, dumbfounded at the man's gentleness with William, and it wasn't the first time he had acted that way either. Drat. She was beginning to like the wretched pirate, and if that didn't go against everything she believed, she didn't know what did. One moment, the man seemed hard and unforgiving, the next moment, he was as soft as pudding.

And the memory of his kisses made her blush. But while her mind was caught in a whirl of emotions, she almost missed the two pirates moving past the library doors and mounting the stairs toward William's bedchambers.

Outraged, she ran after them, not able to believe the impertinence of the man. "Put him down at once!"

"Please, let the pirate put me to bed," William begged, towering above her like some circus act.

"Yes, pleeeeease," the marquess drawled as he continued his flight up the stairs, sending Victoria a surly smile over his shoulder and leaving her at the bottom of the stairs, fuming.

"By the way, me pirate friend," Drake said as he tucked William into bed, picking the mouse from his shirt and placing it in a glass bowl on the bed stand, "do you happen to know who this villain is?"

Drake, now quite amused with William's imagination,

had an uncomfortable feeling in his stomach when he felt the boy tremble.

William's blue eyes widened. He grabbed Drake by the arm. "Lord Wendover. That evil earl. He was here this morning, in this very house."

Wendover? Drake felt a protective surge of anger. He hadn't liked the way the man had leered at Victoria earlier that evening. The earl looked the part of a villain in every way, from that pretty boy face of his to that hideous black cloak and beady blue eyes. And for some uncanny reason Drake knew he had seen Wendover before, but he could not quite place the man.

Descending the stairs, Drake was met by a stern-faced Winston. "My lord, it seems that Lady Victoria has a headache and has asked me to see you out."

The servant shoved his hat into Drake's hands and he, one of the wealthiest men in the *ton*, was out in the streets in a matter of seconds.

A week had passed since Victoria's fateful encounter with Lord Drakefield, and now she found herself entering Percy Hall, the country residence of the Dowager Duchess of Glenshire, the duke's mother and the pirate's grandmother. She shuddered at the thought of her next meeting with Lord Drakefield. The waiting was almost unbearable. She had felt nothing but dread when Aunt Phoebe had accepted the invitation to stay at Percy Hall for an undetermined amount of time.

As soon as they entered the mansion, they met with the duke's mother. The elder lady wore a dark blue muslin gown that hung softly against her slender frame. Her gray hair was piled on her head in a neat chignon, and she was tiny, Victoria thought, such a contrast to her eldest grandchild. But the color of the eyes could not be missed. Gray and calculating.

Since the older lady had been ill at the last gala, and Victoria had missed her appearance, Aunt Phoebe made the introductions. While the dowager conversed with Victoria, Sarah and Aunt Phoebe made their way to their bedchambers to freshen up while William scrambled toward the kitchen.

"Lady Victoria, come sit with me." The dowager duchess tugged on Victoria's hand and led her into a fashionable drawing room painted in soft beige and deep burgundy tones.

Victoria took a seat on the tawny-colored sofa, resting a hand on one of the circular pillows. A maid entered with a large silver tray, setting it on the rosewood table resting beside the marble fireplace.

"I hope my presence will not cause you any inconvenience, Your Grace," Victoria said.

The dowager duchess squeezed her hand. "Not at all, my dear. Not at all. I am so sorry we did not meet sooner. Tea, dear?"

"Yes, please."

"Now," the older lady patted her hand on Victoria's knee, "I want you to be as comfortable as possible. There are horses for you to ride. There will be a ball tomorrow to celebrate your aunt and my son's engagement. Oh, and of course, you will have to view my gardens. They are my pride and joy."

"I would love to see the rest of your estate." Victoria set her teacup down on her saucer, feeling optimistic about her host. "Do you suppose I may take a ride later today?"

"Certainly, my dear." The tiny lady stood and moved closer to the fire. "But if you are in need of anything," she looked at Victoria, "anything at all, please come to me."

Victoria sipped her tea. "I will speak to you if I find the need, Your Grace, but I believe I will have everything I want within my grasp. It is so lovely here."

The dowager smiled at the sound of scampering feet coming from the hall.

"Ith he here?" A little girl with a mane of raven black hair flew past Victoria in a mad rush. "Ith he?"

"Yes, he is." The old lady bent down and scooped the little girl onto her lap as she sat down.

The girl's grin widened. "I will have tho much fun."

The duchess hugged the girl and gave Victoria a wink. Victoria grinned, knowing that the little girl was talking about William.

"Lady Margueretta, I want you to meet Lady Victoria."

"Delighted to meet you, my lady," Victoria said, extending her hand to the girl as she slipped from the duchess's grasp.

Margueretta giggled and shook her hand, but refused to let go, studying Victoria's face with owl-like eyes. "You are a beautiful printheth. Juth like King William told me."

Victoria laughed. "Thank you."

Margueretta raised both her hands to touch the spiral of curls framing Victoria's face.

The duchess gently pulled the girl's hands away. "Gretta, one does not play with other people's hair."

Victoria smiled. "It's quite all right. I imagine she's only curious."

Margueretta studied her. "Do you have any clockth?"

"Clocks?" Victoria asked.

The little girl kept fingering Victoria's hair as if Victoria were a doll in the nursery. "Yeth."

"Her papa collects clocks," the duchess replied. "His life is based on total order."

Victoria smiled. "Well, I suppose he would not like me."

Victoria missed the dowager's raised brows. "I take it you do not keep a schedule then?"

Victoria shook her head, making Margueretta laugh. "Goodness, no. I fear, I'm as impulsive as a child."

"Splendid!" The older lady clapped her hands.

"Pardon me?"

"Oh, nothing." The duchess shrugged and sipped her tea.

Margueretta giggled as she threw Victoria's hair over her face. "Yeth, your hair ith long like a horth tail and my Papa liketh them very much." The girl stretched her hands wide to show the extent of her papa's liking.

The duchess pulled Margueretta away from Victoria. "That means, her papa will adore you, Lady Victoria."

"People call my papa m'lord."

Victoria and the grandmother laughed as Margueretta stepped into the hall to leave.

"But hith friendth call him Drake."

The name came out as *Dwake*, and it took Victoria only a second to make the connection.

"Drake?" Her hands tightened on the pillow beside her. Of course, this was *his* child. What had she been thinking?

She peered up at the grandmother who was now staring back at her with two twinkling gray eyes that seemed to read her mind.

An hour later Victoria approached the stables with thoughts of the marquess swirling in her head. She hated to think of their next meeting. So, he had been kind to William. So what? That didn't mean she could trust the man. Even his kisses were probably a trick of some kind. She had to think of a plan, and riding always seemed to help clear her mind.

Putting on a smile, she picked out a bay gelding in the first stall, hoping that she was probably worrying about nothing. She always thought of a plan, did she not?

"But m'lady, the ground is too wet." The groom shot her a wary frown. "Too many rabbit holes and what not. It takes an experienced horseman to handle this land after a good rain."

"Oh, I have ridden horses since I was three years old. I am quite capable, sir."

The old groom poked his head outside. "Looks like more rain anyway. Ain't ever going to find your way back if you ride into those trees."

Victoria smiled at his concern. "I will not hold you responsible. What was your name again? Mr. Parks, was it not?"

"Yes, m'lady." He frowned.

"Well then, Mr. Parks. I can assure you, my dealings with horses are very knowledgeable." Her hand brushed across the gelding's shining coat.

"Yes, but—"

"Mr. Parks." She interrupted him again with a fluttering of her long dark lashes, and when she touched his hand, a slight grin crossed his grumpy face. She was mounted and out of the stables before he could think of another word to stop her.

Shaking the rain from his hair, Drake hurried into the stables and bit back a smile at the sight of his groom's gloomy expression.

"'Tis a fierce one out there, m'lord." The groom looked away, tending to another horse. "Ain't a day to go riding."

Drake came up beside him. "Ah, you sensed the weather all along. Only a confounded fool would go out in something like that."

The groom hid his wince.

Taking a few long strides about the stable, Drake furrowed his brow. "Parks, where the devil is my bay gelding?"

Parks nervously slipped a hand through his sparse hair. "I told her it was a bad idea to go out there in this weather, your lordship, but she ain't one to listen. No, she ain't one to listen at all. She does what she wants, that one. Impulsive."

"Her? You told her?"

Drake clenched his teeth in frustration. Was the man talking to horses or people? Because the only females Drake could think of were his grandmother, who rode now and then, and Margueretta, who only rode with him.

"My grandmother is out there, you fool?"

The groom shook his head. "No, no, no, m'lord! The lady insisted on riding. She assured me she had experience. I ain't one to argue with the ladies, you know."

Drake was furious. "*She* assured you? Tell me, man, who was mad enough to ride in this? And on *my* horse?"

"I ain't knowing her name, m'lord. But I know she is a lady staying with the duchess for a spell. Niece of Lady Phoebe, I believe. Beautiful mane of hair, m'lord. The color of . . ."

The groom had a glazed look over his eyes that brought Drake's blood to an angry boil.

"Mahogany!" Drake roared.

The horses began to kick and snort.

"Yes. Quite right, m'lord." A silly smile continued to blanket the groom's face as he catered to the animals. "I ain't never thought of it like that. Her eyes seem to cast a spell on me, m'lord. And her small tiny fingers, well, when they touched my hand, I could only—"

"Parks!"

The groom's eyes almost popped out of his head at the booming sound of the Drake's voice. "Yes, m'lord?"

"No one is to ever ride that bay unless I give my permission. Do you understand?"

Parks nodded, shakily.

In minutes, Drake was mounted on the chestnut. He cursed as the rain fell to a steady drizzle. But another storm began as the thunder of horse's hooves pounded the wet grounds of Percy Hall.

Though the rain had stopped, Victoria could not go anywhere unless her horse decided to cooperate. She decided it was part mule. She was cold, drenched to the bone, and sadly regretting taking the horse in the first place. She had found shelter beneath a clump of oak trees, and it was all she could do to hold on to the beast beneath her. She was about to dismount the stubborn animal when she caught a glimpse of a rider coming into view.

She waved her arm high in the air to capture his attention. As the rider neared, Victoria noticed it was the enormous chestnut that she had seen in the stables. Relief washed through her. The groom had come to save her after all. The silly old man.

But her relief was short lived when a crop of black hair met her eyes. Good heavens, it was Lord Drakefield! And he looked every bit the pirate. Well! He had been so agreeable the other day, this was a change indeed.

Instinctively, she pulled the reins of the bay to move in the opposite direction. To her surprise, the animal obeyed.

A chilling wind nipped at her cheeks as she bolted from the trees into the clearing. Without warning, the horse exploded into a fierce gallop, and at that very moment, the clouds burst forth with a heavy rain.

She could hear Lord Drakefield shouting. In fact, she could almost feel the icy glare of his steel gray eyes probing into her back. Hooves thundering beneath her, she stole a quick glance over her shoulder. Rain splattered her face, but she could see him speeding toward her. His black hair whipped in the wind as his chestnut bolted over a large rock.

"Victoria! Pull back! Stop!"

Stop? She cringed as she turned her face back into the stinging rain. It was next to impossible now.

She tightened her grip on the reins, but failed to see the huge boulder in front of her. Instantly, the beast reared back, spilling her into the air. It happened so quickly, she barely

ealized what happened until she slammed into the ground
and felt the pain shoot through her body like an anvil against
her chest.

Drake was only four lengths behind Victoria when he
saw her lifted into the air and thrown to the ground like a rag
doll. Icy fear swept through him. He was oblivious to the
sounds of the rain coming to a slow drizzle or of the thundering hooves hitting the ground.

He heard only the blood-curdling scream he would never
forget. And he would always remember the thud, the eerie
stillness of the wind, and her sprawling form lying motion-
less in a pool of mud.

Chapter Nine

$\mathcal{T}$ he stench of the wet grass drifted past Drake's nose as he knelt beside Victoria's limp body. He pushed back her muddy hair and checked her pulse. She was alive. No broken bones that he could tell. Grimacing, he scooped her body into his arms and whistled to his chestnut. The animal trotted toward the boulder. The gelding would have to wait.

"I am quite fine, my lord."

Pale aqua eyes stared back at him. Her hands pressed against his chest, and his pulse leapt as he tried to suppress his reaction. He wanted to throttle her and kiss her at the same time. But he knew she was hiding her pain well. He lifted a brow and glared back at her instead.

"Fine? You could have been killed."

She raised her chin in indignation, but there was a vulnerability in her expression that tugged at his heart. The little fool! Didn't she know the dangers of riding that horse in this kind of weather?

He drew his cloak over her damp clothes and scowled. She plagued him more than Honoria ever had. But he had instantly sensed her vulnerability and gentleness of spirit that Honoria never had, and those two qualities, more than any other, drew him to her like a child to sweets. Had Nightham seen the goodness in this woman, too? Had he held her close? Had he kissed her?

The questions barely crossed his mind before other ones followed. More intimate ones. More dangerous ones. Drake told himself that he didn't care. But he did. Confound it. He did.

"I daresay, I have survived much worse, my lord."

"Have you now?" His voice was harsher than he intended.

The color rose to her face as she tried to sit up.

Drake pulled her into his arms and instantly felt a surge of anger at Nightham. Had the man taken advantage of her? Or worse, had she loved his friend? Did she still love him?

He peered down at her and touched the soft tendrils of mahogany hair that had fallen across her cheek. She glanced back at him with questioning eyes, and in that instant, Drake wanted to wash any memory of Nightham from her mind. He leaned down and touched his lips to hers. This time the innocence of her reaction was more intimate than anything he had ever felt before. Passion pounded through his body, and he checked himself and pulled back.

Devil take it! The woman had him twisted about her curls like a besotted school boy.

He gave her a twisted smile. "I could not help myself. I do deserve something for coming to your rescue."

Her eyes flashed. "I would not have needed rescuing if you had not followed me."

Fury made him speak the words that had been gnawing at his soul. "You loved Lord Nightham then?"

Her face paled. He might as well have slapped her. "Lord Nightham is dead," she whispered and looked away.

"Is he?" Drake snapped back.

Tears filled her eyes, and Drake fought the jealousy invading his soul. "We'll take the chestnut back to Percy Hall."

Without another word, he swept her onto his horse and mounted behind her. The ride back to the stables became most uncomfortable indeed.

The following evening Victoria changed into her gown with the help of a maid. Her legs were still sore from the day before and so was her heart. But she was determined to face her fears, and she would attend the ball downstairs whether the marquess was there or not. She had felt too safe in his arms and that had vexed her to no end. His hands had held her as if she were going to break in two at the merest touch.

But it was his kiss that she feared had sealed her fate. He was slowly invading her heart, and if she were not careful, the man would live up to his looks as a pirate and steal it, too. And she could never have that. She would have to trust him then, and that was never going to happen.

Besides, what did he want from her? He had said nothing to anyone about her trip to the inn with Nightham. But how long would that last? And did he think her not good enough to love his friend?

"Victoria, did you hear me?"

"Yes, Aunt Phoebe. But truly, I am feeling quite well. Please, do not ask me to stay up here for your engagement ball."

"Please, Victoria." Sarah stepped forward. "You simply cannot go downstairs. You almost died yesterday."

Victoria laughed. "I did not *almost die.*"

"You did!"

"Please. Everyone is treating me as if I were made of fine china. I promise you, I won't break."

Sarah frowned. "You were thrown from that wretched horse. I would think that would be enough to kill anybody."

"I have been thrown off horses before and lived through it."

"Girls, girls. There is no need argue." Phoebe shuffled toward the door. "But Victoria, I implore you, if you do go downstairs, promise me that you will only come down for an hour or two and then return to your room. You need your rest, dearest."

Victoria sighed. "Very well. I promise."

"Good then," Phoebe said, her eyes narrowing. "See that you keep that promise."

As soon as Phoebe left the room, Sarah leaned against the bedpost and drew in a disgusted sigh. "I cannot see why you have to pretend. Your limp is obvious. How are you going to dance?"

"I don't have to dance. I can stand and watch. Is that so dreadful?"

Sarah picked at her gown. "I suppose not."

Victoria decided to change the subject away from herself, anything to keep her mind off that kiss from yesterday.

"I gather Lord James will ask you to dance."

Sarah's eyes lit with excitement. "I do like him. But I am like a younger sister to him. Do you think Drake will ask you?"

"Drake? When did you become so familiar with Lord Drakefield."

"Why?" Sarah's eyes twinkled. "Do you care for him?"

Victoria's lips thinned. Her maid pulled at her turquoise gown, trying to straighten out a small wrinkle.

"Victoria?" Sarah rose to see her cousin's face and laughed. "You *are* interested in him."

Victoria shrugged. Sarah did not know the half of it. "Well, what if I am? He is not the same man I thought he was."

"Yes, but you said you hated him."

"All behind me now. He was only trying to help me yesterday, and it was my fault that I fell, not his. I should never have taken that horse out in the first place." *Or ever have let him kiss me.*

"But will he be dancing with you this evening?"

Victoria frowned. "Why?"

Sarah's eyebrows rose to the middle of her forehead, and she grinned. "Because instead of dancing with you, that pirate might just kidnap you and bring you aboard his ship."

Victoria felt a warm tingle in the center of her body and looked away. "Now, you are being silly."

"Perhaps he can help you out of the predicament you are in."

Victoria sighed and waited for the maid to finish with her hair. After the servant departed from the room, Victoria turned to her cousin. "I have decided to speak to the duke as soon as Aunt Phoebe becomes his wife. I know the longer I wait, the more of a chance I am taking, but I cannot ruin Phoebe's future. I will not seek help, knowing that I may put you all at risk."

"Pshaw! You cannot let this go any longer, Victoria. Something must be done about it. You must find out whether you were truly married. Lord Drakefield was there. He may be able to discover the facts about Nightham and you."

"No. He may seem agreeable now, but I have no idea if

he will tell his family what transpired that day. I cannot trust him." Victoria touched Sarah's arm. "The duke adores Phoebe. If only they would set a date for the wedding."

"But I am not worried about her, Victoria. I am worried about you."

Victoria gave a shaky laugh. "You must not worry about me. Go downstairs, Sarah. I need a few more minutes. Go now. Shoo."

Drake stood in the hall, greeting some of the guests as they entered. He had taken his father's place as the duke had taken a too warm Lady Phoebe for a stroll in the gardens. When the hallway eventually cleared of guests, Fox came up beside him.

"I see you found your lady from the inn," the viscount uttered sarcastically to Drake.

Drake fought to hide his displeasure over his friend's comment. How the devil had Fox discovered his secret? He realized now that it was not only because of a promise to Nightham that he watched over Victoria, he felt a sudden need to protect the lady as well. Her vulnerability had taken him by surprise whether she knew it or not.

"Ah, still upset from the night at the opera, I see," Drake replied.

Fox's eyes blazed with fury as he leaned toward him. "I daresay, are you implying that Lady Victoria prefers you over me?"

"Are you two gentlemen speaking about my niece, per chance?"

Both men started at the sound of Phoebe's voice coming from the seat in the alcove behind them. Phoebe and the duke had obviously returned from the garden, and Phoebe had been resting her feet with the duke seated quietly beside her. A potted palm had hidden them from view. Phoebe's expression was ablaze with disbelief, the duke's red with rage.

Drake stole a quick glance toward Fox, furious that his friend had opened his mouth. It seemed Lady Phoebe had heard at least a part of what they had said.

"Dearest." The duke turned and wrapped his arm around the shaken lady, pulling her from her seat. "I am certain my son and Fox had no such thought in referring to your niece.

This is all a dreadful misunderstanding. Is it not, gentlemen?" His piercing gaze shot through Drake like poison.

Drake nodded in the affirmative. Lord Foxcroft did the same.

Yet Phoebe was not convinced. "Lord Foxcroft," she said shakily, "you had mentioned an inn. Are you suggesting—"

But Phoebe was not able to finish.

"Of course not, Phoebe. Your imagination will get you in trouble some day, dear. Now come along. There's someone I want you to meet." The duke gently pulled his fiancée away from the two men to make the introduction to a visiting baron.

"I am not about to accept your apology for that night at the opera," Fox said beneath his breath, jerking a glass of champagne off a servant's tray as it passed.

Drake sent him a smug smile. "How noble. I was not about to give you one either."

Drake knew this was not the time or the place to confront his friend on the issue. It was enough that he would have to explain the situation to the duke. Before Fox could stop him, Drake strode into the ballroom and asked his grandmother for a dance.

"So you would still dance with your old grandmama." The duchess's gray eyes twinkled with mischief.

Drake grinned. "I always choose the prettiest girls."

"So full of compliments this evening." His grandmother gave his arm a light squeeze. "However, I would guess that if a certain lady from upstairs decided to come down, the dance would have gone to her."

Drake shrugged.

"I thought so." When he did not reply, his grandmother looked up at him. "Jonathan?"

He groaned. She was calling him by his Christian name again. This could only mean trouble. "We are too much alike, Grandmama."

"You were a mischievous little boy, Jonathan. And from what I have heard, you have been a mischievous big boy as well, especially in London."

When the dance ended, Drake avoided her steely gray eyes and glanced across the room as if looking for someone.

Before he could excuse himself, his grandmother took hold of his arm.

"Your heart still aches from Honoria's unfaithfulness, but you must not judge every woman by her."

Drake's brows snapped together. His grandmother was dipping into old wounds he thought healed long ago. He loved the older lady, but she had gone too far this time. No one dared to speak of his late wife in that tone. "You would do best to leave well enough alone."

"That is what I am telling you, Jonathan. Leave well enough alone with your father. He is a big boy, too. And I daresay, if you plan to ruin any of his happiness, I shall come at you with Cook's hatchet!"

Drake's eyes twinkled. He almost believed the woman. "Have no fear, Grandmama. Father's happiness is not in my hands. It is in Lady Phoebe's."

And he knew it was true. No matter what he said to his father about Victoria and Nightham, his father would not cut Phoebe from his life. The lady had wormed her way into the duke's heart, and he would never let her go.

But Drake would never let the same thing happen to him. No, never again would he be subject to a broken heart. Kissing Lady Victoria was one thing, loving her was quite another. Just because he had seen her playing ball with Margueretta this morning and clearly enjoying it, meant nothing at all. The lady enjoyed children. What the devil did that signify?

He realized it meant a hell of a lot more than he wanted it to. Confound it. He would keep his distance from the lady as much as possible. He would keep Nightham's promise by keeping an eye on her and nothing more. No, nothing more at all!

Victoria felt the bruises on her legs as she descended the stairs. It was not terrible, but there was a slight discomfort as her slippers hit the steps.

"Lady Victoria."

Wendover's voice broke into her thoughts, and her stomach churned. She dropped her gaze to the bottom of the stairs. Cold blue eyes regarded her silently.

Yes, William was right, he was a villain.

She instantly recalled the man's words the day he came to her home so many years ago. *Her father was a drunk and a womanizer he had said, her mother a leech on Society and men in general.*

Those wounding statements had stayed buried deep within her heart for the past nine years. Though her father had left her penniless, and both parents were away for much of her childhood, spending time with Society and its pleasures, she had still loved them, and the man had no right to speak like that to a grieving child. He had no heart at all.

"How splendid you look tonight, my dear." All at once Wendover was beside her, his leering blue gaze traveling down the length of her dress. "Beautiful indeed, dear lady. Turquoise becomes you."

His bold assessment baffled her. Whatever he was thinking, it was not agreeable, not agreeable at all. And why had he appeared at her door without a word in the past nine years? Something was definitely askew.

"You must forgive me for being so abrupt, Victoria, but I do need to speak to you about something of great importance." Without another word, he took a possessive hold around her waist.

She stiffened. "I do beg your pardon, but I believe I need to return to my chambers."

"Feeling ill? All the reason to lean on me, my dear."

As his hold on her tightened, an icy chill skittered along her skin. The smell of spirits on his breath made her want to turn her head, but she refused to cower before this man. She was a child when he threw her out of her home, but she was not a child anymore. She would not put up with this kind of behavior. "If you don't release me, I will—"

"My, my, my. Pray, my girl, do not get flighty on me. I am only trying to do the honorable thing for a lady in distress." He slowly slid his hands away, making her feel every one of his fingertips before they left her waist.

His twisted smile made her cringe. "After you, my dear." He bowed, throwing his hand toward the bottom of the stairs, letting her pass.

Chin high, spine rigid, Victoria descended the stairs, feeling his narrowing eyes boring into her back.

"Lady Victoria?" The familiar, welcomed voice rang out, stopping her as her hand tightened on the banister.

Tears of relief clogged her throat as she caught sight of the marquess, clad in his black evening attire. He would never know how glad she was to see him.

"Good evening, Lord Drakefield." She tried to keep her voice steady and calm, but inwardly she was shaking.

His eyes narrowed as he took in the earl. "Wendover."

"Drakefield."

"May I?" Drake said to Victoria, and without waiting for an answer, he whisked his arm through hers and made his way back down the hall.

Drake had seen the paleness on Victoria's face and had instantly come to her rescue. When he detected her trembling lip as she descended those stairs, all thoughts of distancing himself from her vanished. Whatever Wendover had done or said to her had bothered her more than she would admit. As soon as they entered the ballroom he turned toward her. "Did he hurt you?"

For a second, her eyes flashed with something akin to fear, and then it was gone. "No. But you were walking entirely too fast, Lord Drakefield. I fear your horse has made me limp."

"*My horse?* Pray, let me refresh your memory, if you had not insisted on riding the animal, you would not be hurting today."

"You know very well I could not have known about that horse."

When those mystical blue eyes locked with his, he almost lost all train of thought. "My groom told you not to ride, did he not? Therefore, desist your driveling about the horse. I have no wish to hear another thing about it."

He took her gloved hand in his for the next dance.

She jerked her hand from his, her eyes flashing with contempt. "How dare you act so righteous."

"People are starting to stare, my dear. You would not want to ruin your Aunt Phoebe's engagement party now, would you?"

She was furious. "I have no wish to dance with you. And I don't wish you to touch me ever again. Do you understand that?"

"Indeed, I do. However, I believe we never finished our conversation in the library the other evening. It seems we have a mutual friend we need to discuss."

The color drained from her face, and he felt the complete cad. But Nightham's death would haunt them forever until they resolved their differences in the matter. "I mean you no harm. But you must see there are things—"

His words were halted by a loud scream erupting near the entrance of the ballroom. The dancing crowd dispersed. The music stopped. Women began backing up into their partners' arms.

Victoria glanced across the dance floor. "It's Captain Whitie," she hissed. Eyes wide, she backed up and pressed herself against Drake. "Good grief, that wretched creature is heading this way. Do something!"

She turned, her fingers clawing into his chest, and all Drake could think of was how he would have to thank that little cousin of hers for his second in command.

"So you wish me to touch you now?" he whispered down her neck. She smelled deliciously of roses again.

She opened her mouth to reply when Captain Whitie decided he liked the color turquoise and scrambled straight beneath her gown. She jumped. "Oh! I beg you! Dispose . . . of . . . that beast!"

All heads turned their way. More of the ladies gasped in horror, and men raised their brows as they took in the sight of Lady Victoria's ankles. Some mentioned the lively entertainment for the evening.

Drake pressed his lips near her ear and wrapped a hand around her waist. "I daresay, sweetheart, this is not the place for me to put my hands on your legs. Another place and time perhaps . . ." A rumble of laughter erupted from his chest. "Even holding you like this might cause a fury in the *ton*."

Victoria turned her head in agitation. "Pleeeeease." Her grip tightened around his neck. This was heaven. He might never dispose of that mouse. But her eyes pleaded with him. "Please. I abhor the little beast."

Drake swept Victoria into his arms, catching a glimpse of
Fox's hardened gaze, realizing the fun was at an end. "Very
well, my lady."

But he could not very well lift her skirts, so he did the
next best thing. He shook her as though she were a bag of
flour being sifted for a cake. After three hard shakes, out
came Captain Whitie, hurrying toward the place from which
he came.

Clad in his white nightshirt and cap, William stood at the
open doors of the ballroom, his blue eyes twinkling with delight. He shifted his gaze toward Drake as he scooped up his
second in command. "Thank ye my brother pirate," he said
for Drake's ears alone. "I was doing some . . . some *espionage* at its finest."

Drake smiled and slowly disengaged his hold on Victoria.
Her face was cherry red, and she looked enchanting.

"Espionage, indeed." She straightened her gown with a
few swift jerks of her hand.

The hum of voices began to rise while Drake watched her
color darken. "You are very welcome."

The music started, laughter rang out, and the party progressed as if nothing had happened at all. Victoria glared at
him, her eyes narrowing in rage. "Oh, I do believe you enjoyed that little scene."

Drake was about to say that he certainly did enjoy it
when Fox interrupted their little tête-à-tête and whisked her
away for a waltz. Drake snapped out his pocket watch and
scowled. In exactly thirty minutes he would retrieve her,
Foxcroft or not. And then they would have that little talk.

But luck was not with him. For at least a full hour had
past before he could look for Victoria again. By then he realized she had withdrawn to her chambers, orders from Lady
Phoebe.

Frustrated that he had no time to speak with her, he
thought that would be the last he would see of her until
breakfast. However, it seemed William had other plans.

Chapter Ten

At four in the morning Victoria's piercing scream sent Drake, clad in only a pair of tan trousers and an unbuttoned shirt, running to her chambers. He whipped open the door catching sight of her dressed in a thin nightgown and standing on her bed.

"What's wrong?" he asked.

Besides you looking like some angel standing on a cloud of silk, he thought grimly, trying to control his desire.

The chirp of birds seeped into the air, announcing the predawn hour, and Drake realized he had barely slept at all. The duke had ended the ball earlier than the usual hour of *ton* parties, but His Grace had seen Phoebe's weariness for what it was, pure fatigue. No one had questioned the duke's dictate, but all knew he had eyes for only one, Lady Phoebe.

Drake saw his father's ploy for what it was—a move to protect his lady from any discomfort at all. It was that same sense of protectiveness that Drake felt for Victoria. Try as he might, Drake's thoughts had never been far from Victoria or her flight with Nightham.

"Dispose of it," she snapped, jerking her finger toward the bed.

William, he thought, trying to avert his gaze from her lovely silhouette presented against the sliver of moonlight peeking into the room. No doubt the boy had planted something in Victoria's bed. After Victoria had departed the ball, Drake asked Sarah to dance, and she had given him a compact, but decidedly accurate, report about William's mischievous tricks during the sleeping hours.

"D-dispose of what?" he asked, clearing his throat.

Her hand shot toward the end of her bed. "That! There! That thing!"

Drake strode forward. His mouth went dry at the sight of her wondrous hair flowing about her barely dressed shoulders.

There was a large croak, and he snapped his gaze away from her supple form and toward the bed. She jumped to the floor, clutching his arm. The sweet scent of roses reached his nostrils, and he wanted to swing her into his arms and devour her right there. Gritting his teeth, he whipped the coverlet from her bed and released the slippery beast from its tight confines.

"William?" he asked, hiding the laughter in his eyes as he held the gigantic frog in his hands.

"Who else?" she said, still holding his arm.

"Did you call?" Their heads jerked in unison as the small boy emerged from the hall and entered the room. He stood silently, watching their cozy embrace.

"Victoria?" The dowager duchess appeared, her tiny silhouette set inside the door's frame, her nightdress buttoned up to her chin as thick wavy gray hair fell about her shoulders.

"And Jonathan?" Her gray brows lifted as the candle moved toward him. "What in the world are you doing in here?"

Drake groaned and pushed Victoria aside. He could barely see his grandmother's face in the shadows dancing about by the candlelight, but her dictating manner announced her disapproval. He opened his mouth to speak but could not find the words. It was indeed a compromising situation, and blast it, she was using the name Jonathan again.

"I know why," William burst out. "He was protecting Vicki from the villain!"

Drake's mouth twisted. "Hmmm, yes. I was saving her from a frog. She was a damsel in distress, and I came to her rescue."

"This is scandalous." His grandmother's gaze shot to Victoria.

Victoria frowned and clutched one of the linens off the

bed for cover. "It was all so innocent. It croaked, you see . . ."

William shrugged his shoulders. "Botheration, why does everyone make such a fuss about this all the time? It was only a *little* frog." He reached under the bed to collect another croaking possession, and it was all Drake could do to keep from laughing.

"Jonathan," the dowager demanded. "Why are you standing there half naked with that smirk on your face? This is a lady's bedchambers and the middle of the night. If your father ever found out about this, he would demand satisfaction, and you, sir, would be at the altar in no time."

Drake's jaw tightened. "The altar?"

His gaze tilted in Victoria's direction, feeling the treachery of his first wife coming back to haunt him. Had she planned this? "I never thought of that possibility. Did you, Lady Victoria?"

Victoria's eyes grew wide at his insinuation. "Of course not. I am quite certain this little episode will be forgotten by tomorrow." She took a quick step back, away from the light of the dowager's candle.

Drake grimaced. He was not about to be forced. No, indeed!

"Jonathan, did you hear me?" His grandmother took a step toward him. "Out! Now!" Her stiff forefinger pointed the way.

Biting back an oath, he stomped out of the room.

Wordlessly, Victoria slid beneath her covers. William's feet slapped across the wood as he approached the door. "So, it was a big frog! So what!"

"So what indeed," the dowager replied tartly. "Come on, William. Out with you now."

He let out a giggle as the dowager patted his back and followed him, pulling the door closed behind her.

Victoria cringed. If her aunt received news of this, she might insist on a quick marriage.

Victoria recalled the marquess's cool response at the very notion of a union with her. Evidently, it was a detestable thought. Her heart sank. Did he believe that she was replacing Nightham with him?

*   *   *

The following morning at breakfast, Margueretta looked over the table and stuffed some bread into her mouth. "Where ith Papa?"

The duchess pulled some of the food from Margueretta's hand. "Your papa has taken a ride to Grandfather's house."

Victoria felt a blush creep up her neck. She sipped her coffee, peering over her cup at William.

"Why are you looking at me like that for, Vicki?" He wiped his milk mustache with the back of his hand. "It was only a stupid frog and I won't do it again. I won't. Truly." His lips twisted into an amusing grin.

"Won't what?" Phoebe asked.

William exchanged a nervous glance with Victoria. Victoria had enough of his foolish pranks. She turned to the duchess.

"Your Grace, do you think we might try something different for dinner?"

"Something different?"

Thoughtfully, Victoria began to tap her fork gently against her plate. "Yes, well, I believe I would like to try one of Napoleon's favorites."

"And what is that, my dear?"

"Why, frog legs, of course."

William spurted his milk onto the table.

"Yes, I do believe the fattest frogs do best," the dowager said with a sparkle in her eyes.

"Frog legth?" Margueretta snorted in disgust. "Not me!"

Phoebe eyed her son skeptically. "Sounds very interesting, but I believe it would be a tall order. I wonder if Bonaparte had them on the battlefield."

Victoria locked eyes with her little cousin. "We are not on a battlefield, but I believe we have all the necessary ingredients available."

William jumped from his chair. "I will die first!" He bolted from the breakfast room and flew up the stairs. "You will not have him," he cried from the landing. "And neither will Old Boney!"

*   *   *

Later that morning, dressed in a light blue riding habit, Victoria stood in the stables arguing with the groom. Her bruises from her fall had diminished considerably, but it seemed this man was not about to let her ride.

"You jest, sir. I am a guest of Her Grace, and I have it from her that I may ride any time I choose." She may be a bit sore, but she was feeling much better and she needed to clear her mind. Anything to keep her distance from the marquess. Today she had worn her split riding skirt that she had specially made a year ago for riding astride when they had visited their cottage in Yorkshire.

"Sorry, m'lady, but my orders are not to let you ride."

Parks turned his back to her and continued to brush the horse beside him. The mare behind him was already saddled. It seemed the groom was obviously ready to take the animal for a ride when Victoria had stepped into the stables.

"I see. When may I ride then?" she asked.

She met the groom's eyes as he looked over his shoulder. He seemed to shrink back a foot as she continued to glare at him.

Ah, so glaring at him did the trick, did it? "I insist on riding and will not leave here until I do. I may be a bit sore after my fall, but believe me, that was a rare occurrence indeed."

Guilt gnawed at her conscience when she saw the frown on the older man's face. He gulped and wiped the sweat from his forehead. A horse snorted loudly in one of the nearby stalls.

Well, goodness, it's not as if she had bitten the man.

"Please, you have no need to worry about your position with the duchess." Her voice softened. "I won't tell a soul about my little ride, and if by chance, someone finds out," she tapped her riding crop against her skirt, "I will insist that it was all my doing."

She took a step toward him, and the man's eyes widened with something akin to fear. "Oh, please. You take too much upon yourself, sir."

The man flinched as her hand grazed his elbow.

"Parks!"

Victoria turned with a jerk.

"Do not let those turquoise jewels deceive you again," the marquess replied curtly. "You have my orders, Parks."

"Yes, my lord."

Lord Drakefield stood leaning against the stables, his arms folded firmly about his chest, one foot butted up against the hinge of the door. His gray eyes darkened. "You may leave now, Parks."

Within seconds, the groom hopped over one of Drake's boots and dashed outside, leaving Victoria to fight it out alone. The smell of hay suddenly made her cough. She met the marquess's stern gaze and clutched her riding crop tighter. A warm wind whooshed past the doors, blowing a strand of mahogany hair across her cheek. She tucked her hair back into her riding habit and struggled to gain some kind of composure.

The man looked positively dangerous this morning.

He was dressed in a neat brown jacket and buckskin breeches. But he looked more the pirate than ever with his coal black hair tied back in that ridiculous queue and his gray eyes boring into her as if she were some child playing with his treasures.

Jutting her chin forward, she turned her back to him and heard the crunching of footsteps in the straw behind her. Scents of horses and leather mingled in the air as she pulled herself astride the saddled mare with the help of a nearby mounting block.

It was a bold move, and her insides shook like jelly.

Lord Drakefield stood there, hands planted on narrow hips, his face anything but amused. "What the devil do you think you are doing?"

She glanced down at him. "Is it not obvious, my lord?"

He took another step toward her, his lips thinning in displeasure. Her gaze slid to the open doors. She felt a single drop of sweat trickle down one of her temples.

"The mare you are mounted on is tame, but it is not likely to stand still for long with a body on it." His tone sounded calm, but she knew better.

She was barely able to hold back a gasp of surprise when he whipped his hands around her waist, yanked her off the horse, and let her fall against his chest.

"Now, if you would like to go riding"—with a slight quirk of his lips, he lifted her back on the horse and led the animal out of the stables—"you may. But do remember that I am the one who gave you permission to have your morning ride. You have exactly a half hour without a groom, and if you are not back by then, I will send the hounds out after you."

Victoria dropped her jaw in shock as he patted the horse on its way.

Drake slapped his riding gloves against his breeches as he watched Victoria ride over the hill. She was a pauper, and though the similarities to his wife stopped there, he would do best to remember the lady's faults. She was stubborn and impulsive and had placed him in a compromising position. He would not be forced to marry her or any other woman.

It might be best to reconsider his position and wait to marry rich like he had planned in the first place. But plans were much easier to deal with when Lady Victoria was not around.

He gritted his teeth and started back for the house, but not before he instructed one of the grooms that if Lady Victoria did not return within an hour, Drake was to be informed immediately.

By the time Victoria saw the rider approaching, it was too late to start back to the stables. She had already dismounted and was pulling the reins of her horse behind her. The lush field had had looked so inviting, she decided to walk a little.

"Good morning, Lady Victoria. Riding alone, I see. No groom at your side?" Wendover's irritating voice made Victoria ill as the man pulled his horse alongside hers and slid off his saddle.

It was all she could do to be civil and not mount her mare, dig her heels into its side, and make a grand exit. The look on the earl's face had always disturbed her, but now, it was his nearness that caused her stomach to clench.

"Good morning, Lord Wendover. I had no idea you would be riding today." She tightened her hold on the reins, wanting to leave his presence with the utmost haste.

"My dear. No need to be formal. I'm staying as a guest of the duke. The ball was such a festive occasion. I was overwhelmed that your aunt thought to include me in the celebration." He closed the distance between them, and before she knew what was happening, his arm shot out and grabbed her.

Her head whipped back at the sudden jerk. "Let me go!"

"Not yet, my dear. Not until we have a little talk about that shabby little inn that you went to with Nightham."

She gasped in shock. He knew!

Beady blue eyes regarded her with contempt. "No reason to be upset. I know everything. Speechless, are you? Indeed, I know about your little trip with Lord Nightham, our dear, departed friend."

Victoria recoiled. "How do you know?" Her horse snorted, as if sensing her discomfort.

He laughed like a madman. "Oh, come now. Let us come to an understanding."

His grip on her tightened, and she suddenly felt extremely cold. "W-what do you want?"

"Want? There is only one thing I want, and I believe you know the answer to that?"

She stared at him, clearly baffled. "No, I am afraid I don't."

"I want you."

"Me?" He was insane!

"Precisely, my dear. In spite of your horrendous escapade, there will be a marriage between you and me."

She tried to jerk from his embrace, but it was impossible. His fingers dug into her arm like a vise. "Marriage? You must be mad. I would never marry you."

"You will, because if you do not, I will let everyone know about your dear, departed Nightham. That will cause a scandal and cause your poor Aunt Phoebe to be shunned from the *ton*."

His eyes glazed over into a sinister smile. "I daresay, she will not marry her beloved duke then. Or, shall we say old dukie would never marry her. She would be finished. And, my dear, you would not want to spoil her entire life, would you?" He leaned toward her, his sour breath scraping against her face.

Anger swelled inside her. "You would not dare!"

"Dare to kiss you or dare to spoil your aunt's upcoming nuptials? Ha. I dare anything. But if that does not move you, perhaps this pretty piece of information will."

He cupped her chin with a crushing hand. She winced at his hold. Then his hand slid toward her throat. He squeezed her neck until she struggled for breath. "Remember Nightham?"

She nodded mutely, her heart pounding with fear.

"I killed him," he whispered with a slight chuckle.

His horse whinnied beside him as his hand squeezed harder on her throat. "And believe me, I will kill that little cousin of yours as well if you do not do exactly what I say. Do you understand me, Victoria?"

She fought for breath as his hand released her.

"And have a care to keep your mouth shut about this entire encounter. If you say one word to that marquess of yours, I shall slit his throat, too. I will come for you in the middle of the night. Be ready. When the clock strikes two, I will be waiting in the stables. It should be easy to tell the time with all those idiotic clocks of Drakefield's ticking about the place. There will be no excuse for you to be late."

He laughed again. "Remember, the little boy goes the same way Nightham did if you say one word of this encounter to anyone."

Tears burned the back of Victoria's eyes as the sound of hoof-beats roared in her ears. She shook uncontrollably as she watched the black cloak ride off in the direction of the duke's home. Then, she turned toward the grass and retched until there was nothing left in her stomach.

Chapter Eleven

"*I* take it you found Victoria?"

Drake gave a curt glance in the direction of his grandmother, dropped his gaze and threw his riding gloves onto the hall table. "Let us say, she ran into me."

"Come and have tea with me," the lady commanded. "I wish to speak to you."

"And to whom do I owe the honor of this timely meeting?"

"Jonathan, do not use that tone with me."

Drake wanted to roll his eyes. "It is my life, Grandmama. Please, do not interfere. Pray, you will excuse me." He gave her a quick bow and climbed the stairs, surprised that she didn't call him back.

A minute later, the dowager duchess stalked inside the drawing room, her hands waving in the air. "I daresay, I do believe that boy is more stubborn than me. What did I tell you?"

Her son, the duke, rose from the sofa. "What did you tell me, Mother?"

"Jonathan is in love, George. Any nitwit could see that."

The duke's eyes narrowed. "Are we speaking about my eldest?"

"Of course! Who else?"

"James, Sarah, William, Margueretta . . ."

"This is not funny, George. He is simply beside himself. Is it not obvious that he is enamoured with Lady Victoria? Yet that rapscallion cannot see through that thick head of his. All he thinks about is how Honoria deceived him time and time again."

"Come now, Lady Victoria is not at all like Honoria. You are beside yourself, Mother. Please sit down and have your tea."

"I know she is not like Honoria. But if I told you what I knew, you would be beside yourself as well."

The duke lifted a questioning brow as his mother took a seat beside him and took her drink. "Oh, never mind," she said.

"Mother, if you are hiding something, come out with it. I have a right to know."

"Well," she said, frowning, "since it seems you are demanding to know the facts, I cannot very well lie to you now, can I?"

She immediately recounted Drake's story about Nightham and Victoria at the inn, as he had told it to James and Fox. She, of course, told the duke that she could not help but hear every word that was uttered that night.

The duke was surprised, but not overly worried. Money could hush many things these days.

However, when she continued to offer details of his son's infatuation with Victoria, especially and most importantly the part about Drake being in the lady's bedchambers, half-dressed in the middle of the night, the duke's face began to redden considerably.

"The devil you say?" Stunned, George inadvertently tipped his hot tea onto his waistcoat, and he sprung from his seat. "In her bedchambers? In her nightdress and my son clad only in a pair of blasted breeches?"

He wiped his forehead with his hand, then lowered his voice. "Barechested and all?"

The dowager duchess feigned a small frown. "Victoria?"

"Not at all! I mean Drake! Pray, do not jest with me."

The dowager smiled to herself. George was getting upset. A very good sign, indeed. All in all, she thought her son was even more proper and stuffy than her dear departed husband, bless his soul. "Jonathan had his shirt on, but just barely."

George cleared his throat. "And William saw all this?"

The duchess nodded, delighted that her plan was working.

"Confound it, Mother! What will I do? The escapade with Nightham can be hushed. Of course, I will tell Phoebe all about it after we are married. I imagine Victoria discovered the dire straits her aunt was in and was only trying to help. But I don't know why Nightham would want a secret wedding."

"Well, George, I never liked him. The man was a sneaky little twit. And I am sure he had something up his sleeve with Victoria, too."

The duke halted. "You are speaking of a dead man, Mother. Have you no shame?"

"Fudge!" She shrugged, not at all about to apologize.

He began to pace the room, his hand whipping through his hair in agitation. "But then again Phoebe is a delicate woman. Her constitution might not be able to handle a scandal with her niece. Yes, yes, I will tell her after we are married, of course. But this incident with little William as eyewitness . . ."

He shook his head. "I will have to insist on a marriage immediately. Though I believe it was innocent enough, Drake will have to see the right of it."

He turned to her and wiped a hand across his forehead again. "I hate to say it, Mother, but your servants spread gossip like wildfire. This little incident will hit everyone's ears within a week. It cannot possibly be kept quiet like the incident at the inn."

Her gray eyes sparkled with triumph. "I thought you would see it my way, George, and now, it is up to you to see that this marriage is carried out."

"I don't have to tell you that my son is a stubborn mule when it comes to marriage and the like."

"No, but you are a duke, my dear. You can do anything." The dowager lifted the cup to her lips. It was working magnificently! Her heart did a little dance. In no time, she would see a bunch of great grandbabies crawling about the place and filling her life with joy.

"Dash it all, Mother. This is such a disagreeable mess, it will take nothing more than a miracle to fix it."

* * *

Drake's legs ate up the drawing room floor in large angry sweeps as he paced the room. "I cannot believe you are demanding that I marry her. It was an innocent encounter. That is all."

"I am only asking that you think about it," his father replied sternly. "Phoebe knows nothing of this."

The doors opened and then banged closed as the dowager duchess joined the meeting.

"Grandmother." Drake spun around. "So happy you could join us for this momentous occasion."

Her gray eyes locked with his. "Jonathan, I do believe I know what is best for you."

A strangled laugh erupted from his mouth. "Best for me?"

It was not even noon yet and Drake picked up a crystal decanter full of brandy, pouring the amber liquid into a nearby glass. He never drank in the early hours, but it seemed that he had been doing more of everything lately since a certain female came into his life. He had no notion what time it was either. Where was that blasted pocket watch?

The drink did little to settle the bitterness stuck in his throat. He strolled near the fire and threw his glass into the flames, causing tiny glass fragments to spit about the hearth.

He twisted back around, his jaw taut. "I have no wish to have another marriage like I had with Honoria."

"Drake, be reasonable," the duke said, frowning. "Victoria will be ruined. Once the word spreads that you were seen in her bedchambers last night, holding her in a tight embrace, she will never be able to stand in Society again."

The duke glanced at his mother, then shifted his gaze back to Drake. "You can only imagine what people will say. You were half-naked."

"Hell's teeth, Father! I have no care what people will say! And I was clothed."

"Barely," his grandmother whispered as her skirts rustled against the rosewood end table. "You might not care, but Victoria would. No decent man will have her if a scandal broke."

Drake felt the blood rushing to his head. "Can you not see that she planned this entire incident?"

"I am certain that is not true," his grandmother replied.

"But she has nothing. She wants to marry wealth and I will not be her pawn." The words fell from Drake's mouth before he could stop them. He caught sight of the slightly opened door and strode across the room, slamming the door shut.

"Come now, son." The duke patted his shoulder. "Phoebe is without funds, and I am going to marry her. But tell me, do you really believe that nonsense about Victoria making you her pawn? William carries those creatures with him all the time. He is the one who planned this."

"No one heard about last night except William and Grandmother." Drake was determined to stand firm. "I don't recall observing any servants about. Did you?" he asked his grandmother.

The lady's gray eyes widened with indignation. "Indeed not. My servants are most discreet."

"Discreet?" he replied with a snort. Her servants were about as discreet as a howling dog in the middle of a church service. "That does not answer my question." Was no one going to defend him in this? Would he be forced to marry the girl? "I repeat, I saw no servants."

"That is true, Mother," the duke replied, turning toward her. "If no one saw or heard what happened last night, then there may not be a problem. Yes, the more I think about it, the more I realize I should speak to William about this. Discreetly, that is. The boy will have to understand this type of thing sooner or later. And it seemed innocent enough." He cleared his throat. "I cannot have Phoebe upset right now."

The dowager tightened her lips into a grim line. "If no one else knows besides Victoria and William, then you, of course, are correct in the fact that we have nothing to worry about. As long as it does not have a lasting imprint on the boy."

Drake breathed a sigh of relief. Lasting imprint? The only lasting imprint on that boy would be a good whack in the behind.

"But if there is one breath of scandal, it would be your duty to marry her, Jonathan."

Drake stiffened at his grandmother's comment.

"Drake," the duke added, "I fear, if the word is out, then you will have to do the right thing. You must think of everyone that will be affected by such gossip."

Drake stuffed a hand into his pocket. "I truly don't think the word is out. And if it is, then I will have to bow to your will and marry the woman."

"Indeed," the dowager said, "then all is settled." She hurried to the doors to retreat. "If there is any scandal at all, I have your word that you will marry Victoria. Am I correct?"

"You have my word," Drake replied coolly.

However, the more he thought about it, the more he surmised that no one else had seen them. He was certain of it. And he had no desire to be forced into marriage. Choosing was one thing, forcing was quite another. And maybe Victoria's gentleness was indeed a ploy to lure him into her web. He had been wrong before.

"Very well," his grandmother replied and slipped past the threshold. "These doors need oiling, George. Would you see to that for me? I have other business to attend to."

Drake could only stare in awe at the quick way in which his grandmother had left the room, easily changing the subject from marriage to a squeaking door. Frustrated, he flipped his hand through his hair. "Hell's bells!" What a family!

The dowager duchess did a little dance down the hall, heading for the kitchen. There, she would find Cook and any other servants who happened to be around. She would pour out her heart and soul about the sordid details of the events in Victoria's room the previous night. And though it was not considered appropriate for the lady of the house to consort with the servants, she had been doing things out of the ordinary for a lady in her station ever since she had entered into the duke's family.

She would see her eldest grandson happy, even if he hated her for a bit. Oh, maybe a long while. But by tomorrow, every servant would know that Drake had been in Lady

Victoria's bedchambers in the middle of the night. Bare-chested! It wouldn't be terrible, just compromising. By the time it reached London, they would be married, and no one would pay attention to it.

Oh, the blessings of it all!

After her dreadful encounter with Lord Wendover, Victoria tried to compose herself as she slipped inside Percy Hall. She wiped her tear-blotched face with the back of her hand the best she could, all the time wondering if she could make it up the stairs without anyone seeing her. But upon her ascent, she overheard the conversation in the drawing room and stopped when Drake's angry voice reached her ears.

"Can you not see that she planned this entire incident?"

She? Victoria bit her lip. Was he talking about her?

"I am certain that is not true," the duchess replied.

"But she has nothing! She wants to marry wealth and I will not be her pawn."

Victoria's heart plummeted to the floor. With a sob in her throat, she blindly groped for the banister and hurried to her bedchamber.

Three hours later Drake found himself seated in his grandmother's library, wondering if there was a chance that Lady Victoria was as innocent as she seemed. Mayhap Nightham had found a sweet rose within those thorns. But why had they tried to marry by special license in a private ceremony away from home? Was it because her aunt would never have allowed it? Was Victoria taking her family's entire responsibility upon her shoulders and marrying Nightham for their security?

His heart told him yes. The lady loved her family so much that she would have done anything in her power to see them properly cared for. The thought had previously occurred to him, but he had refused to examine it too closely. He wanted to throw her in the same category as Honoria. But Victoria was more than a pretty face. She adored William, the pest that he was. And she loved her aunt and Sarah to overflowing. She even adored his daughter. Honoria had loved no one but herself.

He frowned, tapping his finger on the desk. He wondered if she had loved Nightham with the same devotion. That thought didn't set well at all, because, confound it, he was feeling something for that woman, too.

There was a loud thump in the hall and he looked up. Probably William, he thought with a scowl. He ignored the noise and flicked open his pocket watch that he had finally found on the floor beside his bed. Somehow, it had fallen out of its stand.

Three o'clock. He flicked the timepiece closed and stared at the ink well on the corner of the desk. The letter he had sent to his solicitor might prove helpful. Wilkins always seemed to unearth the most trivial details about any matter, and now it seemed that Drake needed to know a little more about Nightham and Victoria. Perhaps all the pieces of the puzzle would finally fit together, and he would have some answers. It was obvious Victoria was not about to speak to him about it. Whether it was because her heart was broken or she was grieving, he knew not.

"I care not a wit if he wants his peace at the moment, Miles!"

Drake jerked his feet off the desk as Lord Foxcroft flung open the library doors, pushing past the dowager's butler.

"Stand up!" Fox demanded, stalking toward him.

"Something wrong?" Drake's eyes narrowed as he twirled an ivory letter opener in his hand.

"I said, stand up you scoundrel!" Fox drew a fist.

Drake set the opener down, his instincts rising into full alert. "And what brings you to visit at this humble hour?"

"This is not a *visit*." The viscount raised his clenched hand in the air.

"Oh, out with it man." Drake slowly rose. "The suspense is killing me."

Icy contempt filled Fox's gaze. "You know my reason for coming."

"I do?"

Fox rounded the desk. "I am speaking of Lady Victoria."

Drake pursed his lips. Ah, he should have known the very reason when Fox broke into the room. Order was not one of Lady Victoria's fine points, whether she was around or not.

Drake's head suddenly snapped back at the sound of knuckles slicing skin. Though Fox barely cuffed him, the attack was a surprise. "What the devil is the matter with you?"

"With me?" Fox leered at him.

Drake exercised his jaw. "Try that again and you might not be able to stand for a week!"

"We will see about that."

Stunned, Drake could not believe the furor in Fox's eyes. "What the hell is the matter with you?"

"How could you not marry her?"

"Ah," Drake rubbed his face, finally seeing the light. So word traveled fast about his midnight rendezvous. "What did you hear?"

"Enough! Blast it, Drake! I heard enough!"

Drake sat back in his leather chair. "It was totally innocent, but then again, I don't have to explain my actions to you or anybody."

"I don't care if it was innocent or not! You compromised a lady!"

Drake stiffened. "You're daft."

"I warn you, Drake, a man can handle only so much, even if it is from his best friend."

"And what exactly do you mean by that?"

"I mean exactly what I say. I'm willing to marry her as soon as possible. I can obtain a special license at the snap of my fingers. The gossip will die down soon enough."

Drake clenched his hands at his side. How could Fox believe for one minute that *he*, Fox, was going to marry Victoria? "You are willing? Well, my friend, no wish to put you out!"

"I don't see you offering for her hand. And the way I see it, you don't want her. I, in turn, have wanted her from the first time I saw her. She needs a man that will provide for her and protect her. I am a viscount. She will have everything she needs by marrying me."

There was a dangerous edge to Fox's voice that Drake had never heard before. But whether Drake liked it or not, he had wanted Victoria the first time he had seen her, too. But now, the yearning went much deeper than that. He knew the heart that lay within the beautiful lady, and he wanted her more than ever. He would not let Fox or any other man place one possessive finger on her.

"Glad you see things my way. I will go for the special license today." Fox turned.

"The devil you will!"

"Aha!" Fox spun around and sank into a nearby wing chair, folding his arms across his chest in a militant pose. "I was correct in the fact that you wanted her for yourself. Fine then. I suggest that we leave the decision up to the lady."

Drake scowled, knowing that at the moment he was not certain Victoria would want him. "Who else knows about last night?"

"Who?" Fox asked sarcastically.

He shot from the chair, his arms going wide. "Dash it! Everybody knows! And if we don't act swiftly, she will be shunned from the *ton* permanently. No one will call on her or her family. And need I remind you that your father is going to marry her aunt. Do you know the effect a scandal will have on your family? I have no wish to even think about it!"

"Enough," Drake snapped.

"I can see your hesitancy, Drake. Honoria soured your taste for marriage a long time ago. But let me tell you, any man would be lucky to have Victoria as his wife. I, for one, am going to try. I care not if she has a dowry. Not like you. You cannot forget your wife and her poor beginnings. In fact, as I seem to recall, I thought you vowed never to marry a pauper again. To put it in your own words, another poor woman might steal you blind. Besides, it would be best for all if Victoria married me."

"You listen, friend, and listen well." Drake's voice was cold and calculating. "I will make her *my wife*. And I will be obtaining the special license, not you. We will be married as soon as possible. Here, at Percy Hall."

Fox shrugged, stuffing his hands in his coat pockets. "Do as you wish. We will see who wins the prize."

"Prize!" The voice boomed into the room before they knew what happened.

Fox paled.

Drake spun around, his heart stopping. "Victoria?"

Chapter Twelve

*V*ictoria marched into the library, closing the doors behind her as her blue gown swirled angrily about her ankles. She glared at the two men. "I have no wish to have the entire household know everything about my life. But since those doors were open the entire time you two were deciding about my future, there is not much that the servants don't know about me already. Is there?"

"But—"

Both men tried to speak at once, but she cut them off directly, eyeing them both as if they were ants about her feet.

"I cannot believe you two, throwing my name about like a billiard ball." She slapped a finger to her heaving chest. "I will decide whom I will marry. When I will marry. And where I will marry." Her fist hit the desk with a thump. "And, it will not be either of you two fops!"

The marquess edged himself onto the corner of the desk. "I beg to differ."

Victoria seethed with indignation. "What did you say?"

"I said I beg to differ."

Fox cleared his throat. "Drake, I don't believe this is the time to—"

"See here." The marquess unfolded his body off the desk and grabbed Fox by the elbow, directing him toward the doors. "It seems to me there are too many people discussing this delicate matter."

"Too many people! By Jove, Drake, you're mad."

The marquess's eyes gave off a dangerous glint, and Victoria realized she had treaded into unsafe territory. She started inching herself toward the door, two steps behind the viscount.

Lord Drakefield opened the doors to the hall, blocking her passage. "Secure this into your thick head, Fox. Three's a crowd." He pushed the viscount over the threshold, slammed the doors shut, and turned the key in the lock.

"I say!" Fox cried on the other side. "This is not decent of you, Drake. Not decent at all."

"Have you no brains?" Drake's voice boomed past the thick wooden doors. "Two people are all that is needed for a marriage."

"Let me in this minute!"

Stunned, Victoria turned her head to Fox's ceaseless rapping, still not believing what she had heard while descending the stairs. *To put it in your own words*, Fox had said. *Another poor woman might steal you blind. Besides you don't love Victoria.*

In a matter of minutes Fox's voice had disappeared, instantly replaced by the steady ticking of the Madonna and child clock situated on the mantel across the room.

Victoria shifted her gaze to Drakefield, her heart squeezing with pain. He would never love her because she had no money. But never again would she venture into a marriage of convenience.

"Victoria."

She looked up at him, her mind scrambling for some kind of response. She should have checked her impulse to march in here like some queen holding court. Standing here now, she realized it had been the wrong thing to do. Drakefield was not in a mood to listen to anything she had to say. Moreover, Wendover was coming for her tonight. He had threatened William, and now the marquess was going to marry her because honor demanded it.

Nothing was going right at all.

Lord Drakefield studied her thoughtfully. "You must forgive our little conversation, but nevertheless, I can see that you understood my meaning."

Her eyes rounded in outrage. "Little conversation?"

Ignoring her outburst, he snapped out that infernal pocket

watch and pursed his lips. "I will send for a special license, and we will be married promptly."

"Fox was right. You are mad."

His brows snapped into a V. "A special license will stem the gossip. In a few weeks, no one will remember the incident."

Victoria glared at him, feeling every nerve in her body about to explode. "You are calling last night an *incident*?"

"Whatever you want to call it, we *are* getting married."

Her anger had quickly moved past any reasoning at all. Her finger poked into his chest. "I believe not. Have you not heard a word I have said? How could you ever believe I would marry upon your demand? Who do you think you are dictating to me about my life? I would never marry you if you were the last man on earth! I could never marry a man that did not love me. I could never do that again!"

She turned from him, but not before he spun her around and stared at her neck. "What the devil are those marks?"

"Nothing," she replied quickly, realizing he pointed to where Wendover had held her.

The silence thickened as he continued his stare, his mouth tightening into a white line of rage. "Finger marks? Who did this?"

Her heart beat faster. She could never tell him the truth.

"So help me, you best tell me all or I will have every person in this entire household down here until I discover the truth."

She turned away from him, unable to respond.

Suddenly, she felt his fingers tracing her neck and her skin tingled at his touch. His gentleness surprised her again.

"Victoria, let me help you. You cannot shoulder everything by yourself. Can you not trust me with your secrets?"

Her determination began to waver. But trust him? How could she trust any man in her life, let alone a man who would not love her? No, she had to do this alone.

She choked back her tears and spun around, letting out a small laugh. "I was only playing with the children. It's nothing to concern yourself over. We got a bit carried away."

A shadow of annoyance played across his hard features. "I fail to see how children could do this."

Realizing her error in saying anything at all, she began to slowly inch herself toward the door. He must never know about Wendover. She could not put William in danger, or him for that matter. "Please," she said softly, turning from him, her hands fumbling with the lock. "Please, leave me be."

His hand snaked over her shoulder as he unlocked the door. Her heart hammered against her breast. "Why can you not trust me, Victoria? I would never hurt you." There was a strange sound to his voice, and she knew she had hurt him deeply.

"I just can't." Stifling a sob, she jerked open the door and fled to the garden. He could never discover her secrets. Never.

A half hour later in the duke's drawing room, a mile from Percy Hall, Fox lounged on the sofa as he sipped his glass of Madeira. "By Jove, you ought to have seen it, James. I believe I finally did it. After that tiny piece of information I overheard from the footman this afternoon, I did exactly as we planned. Drake was livid when I left."

James grinned. "I daresay, they could use your acting abilities at Drury Lane."

Fox chuckled. "They could not pay me enough."

James rolled back on his heels. "Dash it all. Thought it would never come to pass, Drake settling down. Lady Victoria is an amazing woman."

"Only hope your brother sees it that way as well. Have to admit that in some twisted sort of way, I was hoping he would let me wed the lady. I always had an eye for her, you know."

"Poor Drake. He will never guess the extent to which we conspired to have him married."

Fox laughed. "Certainly hope not. I would like to die an old man."

Victoria walked down the graveled path of the dowager's garden, skirting the small puddles from the rain the previous evening. The anxiety of the last few days was taking a toll on her senses. She had to make a decision about Wendover tonight. The thought of him killing Nightham was too vexing to even think about. But his threats about William made her ill.

"Lady Victoria."

She glanced up sharply at the sound of Lord Drakefield's voice. A flush worked its way up her neck. He had followed her.

She bit her lip, trying to calm her emotions. She loved him. She knew that now.

He treated his grandmother and daughter with such kindness, she could not help but like him. But it was when she saw him with William that she realized the man had a soft heart hidden deep within that granite facade. His late wife must have made him miserable. And that only made Victoria love him more. She ached for him to take her in his arms and wash the worries from her mind. But she told herself time and time again that she could not trust him. She would lose part of herself if she did.

"Victoria, come here." He stepped closer to her, his eyes intent on her face.

She felt her defenses crumbling against his charms. He was going to kiss her, and if he did that, she might tell him about Wendover, thus putting William in danger. Or she might even tell him she loved him. And she could never do that.

She took a hesitant step back. "Stay away from me."

He halted, his hand fisting at his side. "I won't touch you. I only want to talk."

She shook her head and continued backing up. "I simply cannot marry you. You must see how disagreeable we are for one another." She lowered her voice. "You of all people know the scandal attached to my name."

His eyes widened as he watched her movements. "I fancy you may want to stay right where you are."

She stiffened. Anger pushed away any self-pity growing inside her. "You fancy? Let me remind you we are not man and wife."

"I am warning you, you best stop."

"And if I don't stop, what will you do?"

"I won't do a thing. In fact, you will do considerable damage by yourself. It would behoove me to point out that there exists a deep mud puddle directly behind you. Grand-mother was saving that spot for a small pond, but since the storms the past few days, the pit has become a virtual lake."

"Oh, truly?" She choked out a laugh. "As if pigs fly and you have a heart."

"I did warn you." He drew in a calming breath as she took another step back, daring him to fib again.

"Worry not, my lord. You may take your leave and I will—"

Her words were smothered by a gasp of dismay as she plummeted into the pond of mud behind her.

The marquess's laugh rumbled in the air. "I do believe that pigs may actually fly."

Victoria seethed with annoyance as she slopped in the mud, trying to stand. But his next words were said with such conviction, she was caught off guard.

"Though it may seem foreign to you, Lady Victoria, I do have a heart."

She paused and looked up at him. The tenderness in his gaze caused her own heart to turn. She swallowed, ashamed of herself. "Well, perhaps you do after all."

He smiled, putting a booted foot beside her. "Give me your hand then, you little termagant."

She gave him her brightest smile. "Thank you, you are ever so"—the jerk of her arm pulled him in alongside her—"kind," she said with a hearty laugh when he slipped face down in the mud.

He came up spitting for air. He turned and grabbed her by the shoulders. Victoria gasped in surprise.

Gray eyes smoldered as they looked into hers. "Minx," he said softly. He rose, taking her into his arms, crushing his lips to hers in a kiss that staggered her senses.

A warm feeling curled around Victoria's heart as he drew her muddy body against his. Spirals of heat shot through her. She felt warm and safe. For a few moments, she wondered if she could trust this man with her life . . . with her heart. She tightened her hold of him, never ever wanting to let go.

His mouth moved over hers hungrily. "Well, my little minx. Do I have a heart?"

She stared back, dumbfounded at the way he affected her.

But there was a childlike vulnerability in his eyes as he waited for her answer, and her heart became pudding in his hands.

"Hmmm." She plopped her hand over his chest, spattering more mud in his face. His eyes gave off a devilish twinkle, and she smiled. "Why goodness, my lord, it seems you do. And for some odd reason, it seems to be beating quite fast. Quite fast indeed."

With one hand, he pinned both of her hands to his chest. "Will you ever forgive me for my pompous attitude that night Nightham was killed, and then in the library just now?"

"I forgive you."

At that moment, she wanted to tell this man everything. But could she truly trust him? And even if she could, would she be putting his life in danger, too?

"There are questions, Victoria, questions that have plagued my mind ever since I met you."

Victoria knew the time had come. She closed her eyes and rested her head against his chest, knowing she would tell him everything about Nightham, Wendover, and the inn. She loved this man and could do nothing to stop it. She would have to trust him. What else could she do? The torment of keeping everything inside was eating at her soul, making her life miserable. "Ask me anything, and I will tell you all."

He drew her muddy palm to his lips and kissed each finger with such devotion her throat ached. "Ah, sweetheart. I hate to ask this, but I must know if you and Nightham—"

A high-pitched scream ripped through the air. Drake dropped her hands and looked up in horror, a dark shadow of fear falling over his eyes. "Margueretta." No sooner had he said his child's name than he was running toward the stream beyond Percy Hall.

Chapter Thirteen

$\mathcal{A}$s Victoria hurried after the marquess, her gaze clung to a tree leaning precariously alongside the swollen stream. Her stomach lurched at the sight of William and Margueretta perched on a high branch that was swinging out over the water.

Victoria took in the fragile condition of the extending branches, and she could hear the groan of the angry water as it rushed beneath the two children who were clutching each other in fear.

With a pang, she realized the tree could not support much weight, but it looked like the marquess was going to try to climb it anyway. "No!" she screamed.

Her firm command instantly drew his attention. He glanced over his shoulders, his face a mask of worry and fear.

She hurried toward him. "The branches will not hold your weight."

"I cannot stand here and watch them be swept away!" He grabbed for the tree trunk.

"NO!" Victoria tugged on his arm. "Let me go. I'm lighter. I have a better chance of reaching them."

The expression in his gaze told her he understood, but honor would not let her go. "I will not have you lost as well. You are still ailing from your fall from the horse."

"Please, Drake, you know I can climb. I have climbed trees all my life. I have a few bruises from the fall, but nothing else. I'm much better now. Let me go."

"Hurry up, Vicki!" William's cry bit into the wind. "Tl branch is breaking!"

An eerie crack made Victoria shudder. There was n much time. She slammed her hand against Drake's chest ar yanked at his wet shirt. "Do you want to be a dead hero? L you want your child to be an orphan? You might break th branch. Both children would fall. You cannot save the both. You would have to choose. Please! Let me go instead'

Margueretta's wails echoed eerily in the wind. Drake entire body stiffened.

Victoria grabbed him with both hands. "I can do it. climbed down that tree at the inn. I can climb up one just well."

His jaw hardened like steel. The wind picked up agai sending the branches rustling with a ghostly howl.

"For heavens sake, make up your mind! Any minute th branch will break!"

"Get up there then!" Two strong hands circled Victoria waist, giving her muddy skirts a lift. "You best not fall (you will have me to deal with. I am going for that special l cense."

She looked back and smiled. "You are an impulsive ma Lord Drakefield."

Two gray eyes flickered with a caress that felt like a thou sand rays of a summer's sun, warming her, giving he strength to do what she had to do. Her gaze suddenly ros toward the children. "William. Do not move!"

"Botheration! Where do you think I would be going at time like this?" he said, drowning out Margueretta's sob "Me ship's sunk in that roaring sea."

He pointed to the thrashing water beneath them. Log and branches peeked out above the flowing stream. A stron wind whooshed against the branches, teasing their strengtl

Victoria knew there was not much time.

"Take the princess out first," William said, his lips tren bling. "She is afeared."

Victoria's mouth ran dry at the sound of alarm i William's voice. She inched forward, watching her brave li tle cousin slip his arm around Margueretta.

"All right, princess," Victoria said. "Give me your hand.

Margueretta continued to weep as William tried to push her toward Victoria. The branch gave another eerie crack.

By this time, a crowd of servants had gathered and huddled around the tree.

Standing beside the gnarled trunk, Drake cursed, clenching his fists. "Poppet! Take Victoria's hand!"

The little girl sniffed. "I don't want to fall."

"Come on, Poppet. Take Victoria's hand and I will catch you."

Margueretta bit her lip and reached for Victoria.

"Just a little more. Come on, honey."

The branch dipped and swayed over the water. A tense hush fell over the crowd. Finally, one hand clasped into another, and Victoria dragged the girl to her breast.

Drake put out his hands just as a hard wind cut through the trees. "Drop her! Hurry!"

Victoria leaned forward and released Margueretta into her father's hands. The marquess passed her off to one of the servants who headed toward the house.

Victoria felt her breath catch. The branch was ready to break. She could feel it bending beneath her. *Oh, God, help her get to William.*

"All right, me pirate. Just a bit more. Give me your hand."

"No," William cried in anguish. "Too far! The branch is breaking, Vicki! Go back!"

"Don't be a goose, William!" Victoria hoisted herself up further onto the branch. The sound of the rushing water filled her ears. Her bare hands scraped against the bark, and she spared a glance below. The bulging stream raced wildly, throwing sticks, logs, anything in its path. But, she vowed, it would not be her little cousin.

"Vicki, stay back!" She heard his whimpers and couldn't have loved the boy more than at that very moment.

"William, if you don't grab my hand, I will have frog legs for dinner and send your mighty Captain Whitie out into the forest to fend for himself! There are wolves and foxes that love to eat little mice! You hear me, young man!"

William's eyes widened in horror, then he immediately glanced down at the angry stream, his face turning white.

Coming to a monumental decision, he inched toward her. "You will not! I won't allow it!"

Seconds later William's hand slipped into Victoria's, and for an instant, she closed her eyes in prayer. When she opened them, two wide blue eyes peered back at her.

"Aw, Vicki, you would not truly do that, would you? Have frog legs and send Whitie away to be eaten?"

She pulled him close, hot tears slipping down her cheeks. "No, William. I would never do that. Time to go."

She quickly lowered him as far as she could, then dropped him into Drake's waiting hands. The marquess looked up at her and smiled. "Now, come here, madam. We have not finished our business."

Victoria smiled back, and she knew she was powerless to resist this man. She loved him. "Close your eyes and I will be beside you in thirty seconds, my lord."

"Madam, if you believe that now is the time to be attuned to your sensibilities, you are sorely mistaken. Confound it! I will not take my eyes off you. They have been on you every minute anyway!"

Victoria realized that arguing with the man was useless.

As she made her descent, a giant gust of wind whipped through the branches, throwing up her skirts. She tightened her hold on the tree and heard a loud crack. The branch was holding on tenuously at best. She dropped her gaze in horror.

Drake's face drained of all color. He threw his jacket on the ground, and she gasped, realizing that he intended to climb the tree after her. "Don't move, sweetheart! Please, for once in your life, listen to me and do not move one blasted inch!"

Victoria felt the branch breaking and knew if Drake came any nearer, he would fall into the deadly waters with her. She looked out into the rushing stream. The angry flow could wash away an army if they dared to cross it. Her heart pounded wildly as she tried to find her voice. "Stay back, Drake! Stay back!"

He took hold of the trunk and pierced her with a commanding gaze. "Victoria, for the love of—"

But the branch snapped in two before he could finish.

Her scream fell into the wind as she plummeted into the swollen stream below. Cold water sucked her under. Within seconds, a swirling darkness began to overtake her. Crushing her. Stealing her strength. She felt her hands and feet disappearing into the flowing stream of death. And then suddenly, a black rage pulled her deeper and deeper into a numbing abyss until she felt nothing at all.

Fear gripped Drake as he watched slim white hands disappear beneath the stream. Instantly, he kicked off his boots and launched himself into the churning waters.

"Victoria!" His voice was a muffled cry above the roar of violent current. He dove beneath the battering stream, his lungs ready to burst. He came up for breath, his heart constricting with dread. Water bit angrily against his face. Sharp pieces of debris slammed against his body. But then hope stirred within him when he caught sight of a bit of blue floating above the surface.

He swam forward, reached out, and skin met skin. Her face bobbed in the water. He circled his arm around her waist and tugged at her, cupping her chin, trying to keep her mouth and nose above water. Terror crawled along his skin when he saw the blue tint to her lips.

"Hold on, sweetheart. You are not going to die on me. Do you hear me, woman? I will not allow it!"

Two flat blue eyes flickered open for a second or two, then closed. Drake's grip tightened around her waist. Her skirt was snagged on a protruding log. Water filled his mouth as he jerked his head to the side, trying to breathe.

"Open your eyes! Try, Victoria! Come on, sweetheart!" Her lids fluttered open again. "Good girl!"

Pale blue eyes stared into nothingness, then rolled back into her head. Drake's heart shattered. He would not lose her! He would not!

Panic wracked his brain. There was no more time. He said a quick prayer, let her go, and dove below the surface. Feeling for her skirt, he freed the material from the log and hung on for dear life as they were thrust into an endless sea of terror.

He gripped her tighter. Water wrapped around them like

a hangman's noose as he struggled for shore. Then, as if in answer to his prayers, a familiar voice shouted above the raging stream.

"Grab hold of the rope, my lord! Grab on!"

Drake glanced toward shore. Stanby?

His trusty butler stood there, aided by a line of footmen who held on to a rope that had been thrown into the stream. In no time, Drake and Victoria were pulled to safety.

Drake staggered and spit up water as he placed Victoria's limp body gently on the ground. He was barely able to catch his breath as he fell forward, his hands resting on his knees.

"Stanby, where the devil did you come from?"

"My lord." The butler smiled uneasily. "Her Grace sent word to me yesterday. Thought I could be of some assistance to you. Evidently"—a serious crease formed above Stanby's eyes as he glanced toward Victoria's still form,—"your grandmother was correct. She is not breathing, my lord."

Chest heaving, Drake glanced down at Victoria and frowned. "Nooooo," he shouted in grief, gripping her wet body to his chest.

Stanby gently disengaged Victoria's body from his master. "My lord, let me take her." The butler laid her on the ground, turning her onto her stomach. "She may live if we push on her back. The water needs to come out."

But Drake could only stare in horror. Her lips were blue, her body unmoving. He pressed his hand against her cheek. She was as cold as ice.

Then Stanby did the unspeakable. He cuffed his employer on the shoulder. "Get hold of yourself, man! We can still save her!"

Understanding finally dawned on Drake. He knelt over Victoria's lifeless form and raised her arms above her head as Stanby suggested. The large servant then moved her jaw to the side while Drake pushed vigorously on her back.

"Blast it, Stanby. She's not moving!"

"Keep pushing, my lord. I have seen this worked on many sailors that would have drowned."

Drake's hands pressed firmly in a rhythmic motion on her back, his heart twisting in agony with every thump applied to her precious body. "Breathe. Confound it, Victoria. Breathe."

"My lord! The water's coming out."

Drake kept pushing as the liquid came up, spewing past her blue lips.

Stanby frowned. "You will have to blow your breath into her mouth. Now. Pinch her nose, so the air does not go out when you blow."

Drake looked up, horrified. "What?"

"Trust me, my lord." Stanby's voice was firm.

Drake glanced back at Victoria.

"My lord! It cannot wait!" Stanby bent down to take Victoria's mouth in his.

Drake pushed him aside. "Move aside!"

Drake pressed his mouth to Victoria's lips as he blew his breath into her, and prayed Stanby knew what he was about.

"The lady is breathing, my lord!"

Victoria groaned and opened her eyes. Tears dammed in Drake's eyes as he pulled her head close to his chest. "You little fool. I almost lost you."

Her eyes closed again and Drake held her tight. A lonely tear fell from his face and dropped to her cheek. "You sweet, little, adorable fool."

"Drake, my boy, take this. It will help settle your nerves." The duke pushed a glass of claret under Drake's nose.

Drake shook his head. It had been only two hours since the dreaded incident. He sank into the sofa in his grand-mother's drawing room. "It should have been me up there. Not her."

Phoebe put a hand on his shoulder. "I cannot think of anybody who has ever talked my Victoria out of what she wanted to do. And from what I hear, you would have been too heavy to brace your weight upon the branch, my dear."

Drake brushed a hand through his hair that still glistened from his quick bath. He had never felt so helpless in all his life. "It appears her weight was not appropriate either."

He rose from his seat and strode toward the hearth.

"Please, my lord, take this." Sarah's voice whispered be-hind him as she handed him the drink the duke had offered only seconds before. "Victoria would not want you to take the blame. You did the best you could, and now we all have to help her through this."

Drake took the drink and tipped it in one long swallow.

The dowager duchess sat in a corner wing chair, dabbing her eyes. Fox, James, and his younger brother Anthony were whispering in another corner. But Drake's eyes locked on the very tall, familiar figure of the Earl of Wendover.

When Drake caught sight of the man's long, powerful hands twirling a glass of brandy, something snapped inside him. The marks on Victoria's neck suddenly materialized before him. Could this man have had something to do with it?

Drake slammed his glass onto the mantel. He had no proof, but there was something about the man that he had never liked. Clenching his jaw, Drake stalked across the room.

"Wendover, it seems to me—"

"Oh, doctor!" Lady Phoebe's shout turned everyone's attention toward the open doors where the doctor had entered.

The older man glanced about the room. "I gave her some laudanum, but her lungs still have a bit of fluid in them."

"Will she take the fever?" Phoebe asked in fear.

The doctor took his cloak from the butler. "A fever is the least of our worries. I believe her lungs are what we have to fear. Never a good sign when one stops breathing. I'm sorry to leave you so soon, but I have another call to make in the village."

He glanced at Drake. "You did the best you could, my lord. She would not be alive if you had not acted so swiftly. I doubt those marks on her neck will last more than a few days."

Drake grimaced. Marks on her neck! His gaze shifted to Wendover who seemed to be leaving along with the doctor.

"What should we do?" Phoebe asked.

"When she wakes, you must walk her about the room."

Drake moved toward the door, barely hearing what the doctor was saying because when he brushed against Wendover's cloak, the memory of another black cloak suddenly flashed in his mind. The inn? Nightham? Victoria? His mind whirled with unanswered questions. Had the man been at the inn the same time Victoria had been there? Had Wendover been involved in the murder? Or had Nightham plotted with this man? Had Wendover been blackmailing Victoria?

Drake's eyes narrowed. Or was he just going soft in the brain, trying to blame someone else for his foolishness in letting Victoria climb the tree?

"The fluid must not be allowed to build up," the doctor continued as he walked down the hall.

"Can I see her?" Drake finally asked, trying to control his overwhelming urge to flatten Wendover against the wall. Even if the man was innocent, there was still something about him . . .

The doctor shook his head. "She needs her sleep. But when she wakes, keep her drinking hot liquids. Soup or broth is fine. Remember, not too much excitement."

"She will be fine, will she not, Doctor?" Wendover's words floated past Drake's ears as the two men finally took their leave.

Drake glared at the black cloak, deciding to bide his time. Of course, his reasoning was only pure conjecture, but something in his gut told him he was right about William's villain. Wendover was trouble one way or another.

As the days progressed, Drake was pleased to see that Victoria was recovering faster than anticipated. He made a few visits to see her, taking her for walks about the room while her abigail sat beside the bed. How could he ever have thought she was like Honoria?

He decided to hold his tongue about both Nightham and Wendover until after she completely recovered. He was glad when his solicitor finally appeared at Percy Hall to fill in some parts of the puzzle.

Wilkins, a short, stout man dressed in a dark green jacket with pearl-coated buttons, made himself comfortable in the drawing room, sitting on the dowager's favorite chair, the fine art of needlepoint beneath him. A thick stack of papers rested on the rosewood tea table to the man's left.

Drake stood by the fireplace, stuffing his pocket watch

back into place and shifting his gaze back to Wilkins. "You have some information that may interest me, then?"

"My lord, I daresay, I have plenty to interest you."

Apprehension gripped Drake as he dwelled on the possibilities of Victoria's attachment to Nightham. Had she loved him? Did she still love him? "I do want to hear what you have to say, but I also want you to look into the Earl of Wendover's background. What has he been doing the last ten years of his life? Where do his debts leave him? And where has he been spending his money?"

"Very well, my lord. I will see to it as soon as I return to Town." Wilkins cleared his throat. "However, there is much more information than I thought. It is all so fantastic when one gets down to it. Pray, where shall I start?"

Restless, Drake began to pace the length of the drawing room. His expression clouded. "Start with Nightham."

Wilkins grabbed a few papers off his stack and glanced up at Drake over the rim of his spectacles.

Drake's gaze clasped the man in a death hold. "Yes?"

Wilkins visibly swallowed. "I have discovered that Lord Nightham had a penchant for gambling. Months before his death he racked up quite a debt."

"Not unusual. Nightham liked to hit the tables at the clubs now and then. He had his vices."

"Indeed, my lord. It seems he acquired a great deal of debt and owed many people."

"Well, he was no different than a host of gentlemen. The man had plenty of money and never paid on time. Everybody in London knew he was good for it."

Drake stared at the papers in Wilkins's hands and a certain uneasiness swept through him. "How many people did he owe?"

The solicitor pushed the papers toward him. "See for yourself, my lord."

Drake grabbed the papers with one hand and sank into a wing chair. "Lord Finely, seven thousand pounds, Lord Granger, five thousand pounds? Mr. Torrence, eight thousand pounds. Lord Stevens, two thousand!" He peered up at Wilkins, then back to the paper. "Greenbriar, Avelry, Fredders, and the list goes on."

Drake ran a hand through his hair. *Nightham had been in debt? What other secrets had the man been hiding?*

"It seems, your friend was obsessed with the tables," Wilkins said. "The more he lost, the more he gambled. The more he gambled, the more he lost. A rather vicious circle, I would say."

"Nightham gambled at the clubs, but I never stopped to think that it had gone this far. Yet why would he take Lady Victoria to the country to be married? There is no sense in it. She had no money. And I will never believe it was a love match."

Wilkins gave him a dubious look and shifted uncomfortably in his seat. "At that time, my lord, she was penniless."

"You are telling me that Nightham was in debt from gambling? And there is no room for a mistake here?"

Wilkins nodded.

Drake rose. "Then why would Nightham deliberately leave London for a shabby inn to marry a woman with no money? I daresay, she is beautiful . . ."

A hint of doubt began to form in Drake's mind, and he stared at Wilkins. "What else?"

Wilkins frowned and lifted some more papers from his pile. "Here is the true story behind the earl's reason for marrying Lady Victoria."

Drake's lips tightened.

"It seems that she was the daughter of a earl."

"I knew that."

Wilson rustled the papers in his hands and adjusted his spectacles. "Well, from all accounts, it seems that Lady Victoria was placed on the doorstep of her aunt's home when her parents died some nine years ago. Victoria's distant cousin, the new earl, sent her to live with Lady Phoebe. There was nothing in the late earl's will to provide for his daughter."

Drake stiffened. The very thought of Victoria being left penniless by her thoughtless father infuriated him. But knowing that she had been yanked from her home after the tragic death of her parents and sent to live with her aunt, without a penny, enraged him. He wanted to box Wendover's ears so bad, his hands ached. And if that father of hers were still alive . . .

"My lord, there's more."

A maid walked in with a silver tray carrying the tea setting. Drake looked at Wilkins and asked the man if he wanted some refreshment. Wilkins shook his head no just as the maid served a cup to Drake. After the servant left, Drake took his seat.

"There is a decanter of wine on the table, if you wish, Wilkins, but go on. What else?"

"It seems Victoria's Uncle Henry was eventually appointed her guardian. But Lady Victoria had also been left a trust that even she was not aware of."

Drake's teacup stilled on his bottom lip. "A trust?"

"It is from the will of a great aunt who died fifteen years ago. The lady left quite a good sum. No one but Lady Phoebe and her solicitor knew about the money. When Lady Victoria turns twenty-two, she will gain knowledge and access to this trust."

Things were beginning to click into place, causing an icy chill to flow through Drake's veins. "And Nightham?"

"I believe he found out about the trust. He tried to swindle that girl out of her inheritance by marrying her and taking his husbandly rights," Wilkins scowled, "in more ways than one, I can assure you."

Drake slammed his feet to the ground and rose. "I cannot believe Nightham would do such a thing."

"I believe I will have some of that wine you mentioned."

Wilkins stood up, his expression grim as he splashed the red liquid into a glass. The man was the father of three girls himself. Drake could only guess that this act of Nightham's threw the usually sedate Wilkins into a fit of rage.

"Not only that." Wilkins turned. "I have reason to believe his mother knew all about it. The trust. The debts. The special license. Everything."

Drake blinked in surprise. "That sweet woman?"

"She may be sweet, but she is also poor."

The thought of Victoria being swindled by those two people sent his mind reeling with fury. "How much is her fortune?"

"From what I gather, about eighty thousand pounds, my lord."

"WHAT?"

"Eighty thousand pounds."

"Hell's teeth. People would kill for even a pittance of that. She knows nothing about this?"

"No, my lord. But she will. Soon."

"Soon?"

"Yes, in three days . . . on her twenty-second birthday."

Chapter Fourteen

*S*haking, Victoria pulled the covers up to her chin as she watched the furry white mouse scamper across her bed-chamber.

"William, dispose of that creature immediately!"

William looked up from his seat by the window. "*He* is watching us, Vicki."

"You have no need to have Captain Whitie look out for me."

The boy's cheeks puffed out in irritation as he picked up his mouse. "I don't mean Whitie!"

Her fingers tensed, for she knew all too well whom William was talking about.

"The villain is coming here. I can feel it." With a frown, he turned to Victoria and walked to her side. "I am a pirate and us pirates know how to protect our princesses."

Victoria wanted nothing more than to protect this inno-cent boy from Wendover. And she had finally gathered the courage to tell Drake about it. When she was up and about, she would approach him on the matter. "William, I assure you, I am not in need of protection. Now, run along and let me rest."

"Awwww, Vicki." William dropped his shoulders. "Did you know that Drake is speaking to a fat man in the drawing room?"

Victoria swallowed her laugh. "William, that is no way to speak of your elders."

"I don't care." He shrugged and turned to leave. "No one listens to me anyway. Fat! Fat! Fat!"

Victoria frowned as William marched from the room. Wendover's threats echoed in her mind. She had to do something about the situation soon. Drake. She had to tell Drake.

"I say!" Wilkins jumped up with a start and dropped his teacup on the carpet.

Drake spun around. His dark brows rose in surprise when he caught sight of his plump solicitor crouched on top of the sofa. The portly man's arms were flung out to his sides like a baby bird learning to fly. As Drake lowered his gaze to the floor, it was all he could do not to laugh at the pink tail wiggling about the carpet. It seemed Captain Whitie had decided to take cover inside the fallen teacup, which was now upside down and dragging along the floor like a tortoise's shell.

"It's only a mouse, Wilkins."

"Do you mind, my lord?" Wilkins stopped quivering, but his feet stayed on the sofa, waiting for the object to be extricated.

Drake looked up, hiding his grin. "You want me to remove Cap'n Whitie?"

The solicitor gasped in horror. "*It* . . . *it* has a name?"

"*It* does," Drake answered as if it were a common occurrence for every mouse to have its own name.

When the cup started to move again, brushing along the rug in a zigzag fashion, Wilkins almost toppled the entire sofa to the floor. A second later, both men's gazes lifted to the sound of a giggle that emerged from behind one of the wing chairs situated near the door to the hall.

"William, come here this instant!" Drake's stern voice sliced through the air. The maid had come in only minutes ago to serve lemon cakes. Obviously, some other things must have slipped in as well.

A head of tight yellow curls peeked out from behind the chair, followed by a set of laughing blue eyes.

But the moment the small boy's gaze hit Drake's darkened face, all signs of mirth disappeared.

"'Tis only me second in command," William announced with his head held high as he scampered toward his prized possession and scooped it up, cup and all. "Whitie was on the lookout for the villain."

At that moment the little mouse decided to poke its head out of the cup, its nose sniffing and wiggling in fright.

Wilkins groaned. The boy gave a snicker and left the room.

But Drake was no longer smiling. He had not approached Wendover about the marks on Victoria's neck due to the earl's timely retreat from his father's house. And he had avoided approaching the subject with Victoria, but today she was much better. He would seek her out and finally discover her secrets.

"Villain, indeed," the solicitor said coolly.

Now that the gruesome beast was gone, Wilkins scrambled down from his perch. "I say, we did give the tot a good show." He cleared his throat, pulling his jacket taut and straightening his pantaloons. "By Jove, the boy truly believed I was afraid of that pathetic little thing."

Drake tightened his lips, his eyes widening at the ease in which his solicitor had changed his tune so quickly. "Indeed. Quite a show, I daresay. You do have a way with children and animals, Wilkins. The boy seemed to think you were truly scared."

"Humph. Me? Scared? Preposterous!" As if nothing had happened, Wilkins grabbed the papers resting on the table, his hands trembling as he handed the stack to his employer. "I will look into Wendover's background." He nodded shakily, said his farewells, and was out the door in a blink of an eye.

Drake's shoulders shook with laughter. A flash of blue zipped by the doors. Dear, little, mischievous William. That boy would haunt the duke until his dying days.

After placing the papers in the desk in the library, Drake started for Victoria's chambers. She had no idea the true reason Nightham wanted to marry her. Oh, her beauty was unquestionable, but the conversation with Wilkins had shed more light on the matter. Nightham had needed an heiress to emerge from his debts, and Victoria had been his answer.

Fury almost choked Drake as he thought about Charles.

He stopped in front of Victoria's bedchamber door. In

three days time it would be her birthday. A smile crossed his face. He would have a party for her with all the trimmings. Cake. People. Music. Dancing. A waltz or two to hold her close. A walk in the gardens. A kiss. Maybe two—

"Jonathan?"

Drake spun around. His grandmother stood behind him.

"What are you doing here, young man?"

Yes, what was he doing here? He felt as though he were a child, having sneaked a piece of chocolate cake from the cupboards and his grandmother catching him red-handed—again.

He was not a mere pup, he was twenty-seven years old, and yet here he was trying to defend himself. "I came to see if Victoria needed anything."

"Fustian." His grandmother's cool stare hit him smack dab between the eyes. "If she needs anything, she can pull the cord for a servant. Believe it or not, she will be up and around tomorrow. So, stop your fretting. You've seen enough of her the past few days. Let her recuperate."

Her eyes darted toward the door that was slightly ajar, and she lowered her voice. "Besides, she's sleeping. I gave her some laudanum in her lemonade earlier. She won't wake for hours."

She took his arm in a gentle grasp. "I know you have feelings for her, but remember she is not another Honoria. Victoria is different. She's an innocent. I will not have you playing with her feelings. I will not permit it." She looked him sternly in the eye. "But do you love her, Jonathan?"

Drake felt as if the lady had boxed his ears with a sledge hammer. Victoria was not Honoria. But *love* her?

"I don't know," he said coolly.

His grandmother paused. "Why was Wilkins here today? Could the man not wait until you returned to London?"

Drake noted the stubborn set of her chin. She would have her answers or she would have his head. "I needed some information. He is my man of business."

"What kind of information? About Victoria? I am privy to all your secrets about her, you know."

"She told you?"

"No. You did."

"Me? I would have remembered anything like that."

Her gray eyes sharpened like needles. "You, James, and Fox."

Drake thought back to the day James and Fox came to see him at Percy Hall, and his expression stilled. "You heard everything?"

"Everything I needed to know." She crossed her arms over her chest. "Nightham. His death. The entire escapade. Of course, you can count on me to keep everything in the strictest confidence."

He threw up his hands and let out a muttered curse.

"So," his grandmother went on, ignoring his outburst, "you may proceed to tell me the real reason Wilkins was visiting, or should I use other sources available to me to uncover the information?"

"Other sources?" He gave a muffled laugh.

"Do not dare mock me, Jonathan. I do have my ways."

"Grandmama, you are going to send me to an early grave. But just to stifle your curiosity, Wilkins did some detective work for me. I had him investigate Nightham's past, and Victoria's."

She lifted a brow. "And?"

He pushed a hand through his hair. The lady would not give way on this matter. He had heard rumors that many years ago she had even cornered the king on a certain subject at a Christmas ball. Something about the colonies and their freedom. Whatever the discussion, the king had avoided her at all costs after that. Perhaps it was one of the reasons King George had gone mad, he mused.

But knowing it was probably safer keeping his grandmother in his confidence than having her poking her nose where she shouldn't, he took hold of her elbow and escorted her down the hall. "Very well. But this must be held in the strictest confidence. All the papers are downstairs on the library desk . . ."

Victoria sat up in her bed, clutching the coverlet to her breast. She had listened to the entire conversation with rising dismay. To believe that she thought of marrying that wretch! How could he hire someone to investigate her? Who did he think he was? The King of England?

She had almost told him everything. Why on earth did she think she could trust him?

She stared at the lemonade still sitting on her nightstand, then shifted her gaze back to the door. He had told James and Fox about Nightham and her, as if it were nothing at all. And now his grandmother knew everything as well?

His disloyalty burned a path straight to her heart. Trusting the man was out of the question. What if she had told him about Wendover? Would he have disclosed that information to others, placing William in danger?

No, she could never let that happen. She must have been insane to think she could spill her secrets to him.

A wave of pure sadness rippled through her heart. She had thought he loved her and would keep her secrets to himself. What a fool she had been. He had never told her he loved her. *I don't know,* he had said. Her throat ached with a terrible sense of loss. She knew then that she could never be distracted by her foolish emotions again. *He did not love her.*

She wiped her hand across her eyes, determined to do what was needed. She would proceed with her own investigation and see exactly what those papers held. After gathering all the facts, she would decide what to do about Wendover and his threats.

At two in the morning, she did just that and found herself in the library, paging through the papers Wilkins had left for the marquess. Shocked at what she found, she sank back into the wing chair, taking a quick glance at the doors to make certain they were closed.

A lone candle flickered beside her, illuminating the room.

Wave after wave of disbelief slapped her as she flipped through the papers on her lap. What an idiot she had been. Nightham had so many debts she could scarcely tally the total. The man had not a rag to his name. She was stunned. He had deceived her. Used her. Married her! Or had he? She was so confused, she could barely think.

And then there was the thought of his poor mother who probably had nothing at all. The insufferable man!

But it was the fact her great aunt, whom she had seen only once when she was six years old, had set up a trust for her, leaving her eighty thousand pounds to inherit on her twenty-second birthday, that had truly shocked her.

Nightham's deceit clawed at her heart. He had wanted to marry her for her trust. He had needed her money. He had lied to her. Sought her out and wooed her. Though there had been no love between them, she had thought they had been honest about the reasons they had married.

The smiles. The lies. The vows. The extent of his deception made her ill. Not able to look at the papers anymore, she doused the candle on the table beside her and sat alone in the darkness. Tears choked her throat.

She wondered if this was the reason that the marquess had finally proposed marriage? How long had he known about her trust?

She buried her head in her hands. And then there were her problems with Wendover. Wendover!

Her head snapped up, and a sickening heat began to spread through her as the reality of the circumstances started seeping into her brain. Wendover wanted her money, too!

Her birthday was only days away. She would have to distance herself from everything and everyone as soon as possible.

Wendover would seek her out. Drake would seek her out. She couldn't trust him now. Even the scandal with Nightham would haunt her and her family until she could bear no more. She had to find out whether she had been legally married to Nightham.

Overwhelmed, she wiped her eyes with the back of her hands. There was nothing else to do but leave Percy Hall immediately. Most of all, she had to escape Wendover. William would be safe if she were not around. Wendover would not dare to do anything to the boy with that much money at stake and her missing. She knew the one place she needed to go, and that was Nightham Manor.

There were many places to hide in London, but peace would never come to her until she made the truth of that night at the inn known to Nightham's mother.

She needed to make things right. And if the lady were in

need of funds, Victoria would have the means to take care of her. She just hoped the countess would understand and let her stay there until she decided what to do next.

"Pssssst. Pssssst, ye pirate!"

Drake's head lifted off his pillow, and he became instantly awake. His gaze narrowed on the shadow hovering in his bedchamber doorway. "William? What the devil are you doing out of bed at this hour?"

"I came to save the princess." The boy walked into the room, his legs swaggering like a pirate on the high seas.

"Ah," Drake sat up straighter. "The princess." If it had not been the middle of the night, he might have laughed.

William reached for Drake's forearm. "I heard crying."

Drake listened. Outside, a blast of air howled against the windowpane. "It's only the wind."

The little boy dug his heels into the floor, pulling with all his might on Drake's arm. "She's crying. Now, do I have to go there meself or are you coming with me? I know ye love her, so you should be the one taking care of her."

Drake narrowed his eyes. He could not hear his daughter crying. Margueretta slept like a log, and when she cried, everyone in the household knew it. But William seemed beside himself. Perhaps Margueretta was ill. Drake flipped his legs over the side of the bed. "Hand me my breeches over there."

William turned and hurried across the floor, dragging the breeches off the chair.

Drake slipped them on. "How long has she been crying?"

"Hmmm." William pulled his fingers across his chin as if he were a fifty-year-old seaman with a beard. "I would say that she has been crying for almost ten million hours."

Drake met the boy's solemn eyes. Dash it all, what did the boy have cooked up in that head of his? "That long?"

William frowned. "Pirates never lie. Ye should know that. What do ye take me for, a landlubber or something?"

"Now, some pirates do lie. But I believe that you are not that type of pirate."

William threw out his chest with pride.

Smiling, Drake grabbed a candle from his bedside, lit it, and proceeded past the door and into the hall.

William and his second in command padded closely behind.

As soon as Drake stopped by Margueretta's room, William spoke, "Why would ye be going in there?"

Drake opened Margueretta's door a crack. "To see if she's crying like you said. But truth be told William, my little girl is sleeping like a bear. Listen to her snore."

William tugged impatiently on Drake's arm. "If you wake her up, we will never be able to help Vicki."

Drake snapped the door closed. "What do you mean, *Vicki*?"

"Who did ye think we were talking about, the Queen?"

"See here, young man, you will not talk to me in that tone, do you hear me?"

In the dimness of the candlelight, William took a faltering step back. "Yes, your lordship pirate. I hear you loud and clear." He shot Drake a firm salute.

"Blast." It was hard to stay mad at the lad. "Now, what is this nonsense about Vicki crying? I hear nothing."

William cocked an ear toward the stairs. "Yes, me pirate. You are quite right. She has stopped and it is all your fault." He sent Drake a disgusted look. "If you had not taken so long waking up, we could have taken care of her."

"Is she in her bedchamber?"

"Probably." William stomped his foot, as if quite perturbed to have the night end. "You don't move like a pirate."

Drake could not believe he had been pulled out of bed on this wild goose chase. "Go to bed, William. Now!"

William scrunched his blue eyes and hurried to his room. However, Drake was not surprised when the boy stopped in front of his door and glanced back for the last word.

"But I tell ye, me pirate," he said with a lift of his chin that looked all too familiar, "she was crying. I think you had too many cannonballs to the head."

With a candle illuminating the hallway, Drake, half naked, blinked in surprise as William stomped into his bedchamber and closed the door.

After a few seconds, Drake shook his head and decided,

grandmother or no grandmother, he had to see if Victoria was sleeping soundly. He walked to the end of the hall toward Victoria's bedchambers. For some reason, the thought of Victoria weeping sent a surge of protectiveness through him.

He came to an abrupt stop outside her bedchamber and saw that her door was halfway open. Glancing over his shoulder, feeling like some naughty schoolboy ready to be caught by his grandmother, he slipped silently into the room. His gaze turned toward the bed, where a pile of crumpled linens and scattered pillows lay.

"Victoria?" he whispered and came closer.

When he was beside the bed, he froze. She wasn't there.

The hairs on the back of his neck prickled. He looked over his shoulder and strode toward the door. Where was she? Maybe she *had* been crying.

He hastened down the stairs, hoping to find her in the kitchen, sneaking a glass of milk or munching on a slice of bread. But a sixth sense told him something else was wrong. In fact, in the back of his mind he knew something had been plaguing Victoria ever since he had met her at the inn. He should have confronted her when he had the chance.

There was a noise in the library. He stopped on the stairs and listened. A disturbing thought suddenly occurred to him. Had Victoria heard his conversation with his grandmother? He had planned to tell Victoria about Nightham and the trust on her birthday. Moreover, he had been trying to think of a delicate way of telling her about Nightham's wretched scheme.

Another sound. Softer, this time. A whimper? Devil take it. Maybe it was too late for any of that now.

Dreading what he would find, he stalked forward and opened the library door, searching the darkness. He raised the candle up higher, stepping into the room.

"When were you going to tell me, my lord?"

He turned sharply only to see Victoria's shadowed figure huddled in the wing chair beside the desk. She wore a blue satin robe that glimmered against the candlelight. She looked enchanting with the ruffles of her white nightgown peeking over her slippered feet, but it was the glint of anger in her misty turquoise eyes that told him the true story. She knew about Nightham and the trust.

Holding the flame high, he took a step toward her. "Sweetheart, I was going to—"

"Sweetheart?" She choked out a pitiful laugh. "You dare call me sweetheart after you snooped into my life."

Trying to bide for time, he moved to light the candle resting on the table beside her.

She stood. "I cannot believe you would go so low as to investigate your friend, Nightham, as well as me."

He turned toward her. "I thought I was doing you a favor."

"Because you believe yourself above others, you delve into people's lives as if they had no feelings? You were not doing me a favor, my lord. I daresay, you were satisfying your curiosity."

"You're wrong."

He turned his back toward her and lit a fire in the hearth. The rising flames illuminated the room. Before he knew what she was about, she came from behind and tossed the papers into the fire.

She was beside herself. It was understandable. Drake slipped his hands gently on her shoulders. "Victoria—"

She jerked away, the rage still lingering in her eyes. "Don't touch me!"

"I've heard those words before, and it never ceases to amaze me that you change your mind as quick as Beau Brummell changes cravats. But enough of this foolishness."

Her eyes shot daggers at him. "You would not want to be caught in a compromising position, my lord. Or does everything seem all right, now that I am to inherit a good deal of money?"

"You led me to believe you would marry me," he said softly. "This changes nothing."

"I must have been daft."

"No." His eyes found hers, and his heart turned over at the pain that shone in her eyes. "I think not."

She lifted her chin and started for the door.

He stalked toward her. "Victoria, you will marry me."

She spun around. "Why, so you can do the honorable thing for your father and grandmother?"

"No," he said calmly, quickly slipping an arm around her waist. "This is why." Her eyes grew round, but she didn't pull away from him. He leaned forward and lowered his mouth to hers.

"So, I see ye have found her!"

Drake groaned. "William?"

"I told ye she was crying." William sliced his sword through the air, parting the two. "It was the villain again."

Drake glared at Victoria as the image of Wendover came to mind. Her nearness had taken his breath away . . . and his brain. He would confront her now. "Yes, what are you hiding, Victoria?"

The lines around her face tensed. "I should have asked you the same question earlier, my lord."

"I am speaking of the villain," Drake said with an edge to his voice.

"Oh, have you looked in the mirror lately?"

"Are you addressing me, madam?"

"You?" she said sarcastically.

Oblivious to the tension between the two, William began swinging his sword ferociously about the room. "That villain wants the treasure! I know it!"

"Come to think of it," Drake replied, "I believe William may be right. The villain wants something."

William grinned and planted himself next to Drake.

Drake glanced back at Victoria waiting for her explanation. "Could it be your money? Why don't you tell us about Wendover. I saw those marks on your neck the other day."

"Marks?" William let out a cry of outrage. "Marks? What marks, Vicki?"

"It's nothing, William." Victoria glowered at Drake.

The boy stepped back to show her his sword. "Did he hurt you, Vicki? 'Cause if he did, I'll tear him to shreds."

The weapon went flying through the air as William danced about the room. "I'll slice him in two."

Drake hopped back a step as William took a flying leap and jumped on top of the desk. "I'll make mincemeat out of him. Why, the next time I see him, I'll take his neck and—"

"William!" Victoria cried. "Stop it at once!"

The sword came to a halt, clattering to the floor. "Awwww, Vicki."

Drake hid his smile. "Off to bed with you. Tomorrow we will talk more about pirates and villains."

William jumped off the desk. "Truly?"

"Truly." Drake patted his head to move him along.

"Did you hear that, Vicki?"

Victoria smiled. "Yes, and William?"

"Huh?"

"You forgot this." She held up his sword.

"Oh!" He chuckled and retrieved his weapon. "One cannot be without a sword when Wendover is about. He scares the bloomin'—"

"William!" Victoria took a menacing step toward him.

The boy glanced mischievously up at Drake before he started for the library doors. "Never mind."

Her lips grimly set, Victoria slipped her hand into the boy's and started for the doors. "I'll see that you make it to bed, young man."

William looked over his shoulder at Drake. "The princess is leaving with me because she likes kissing me better than you."

Drake lifted a concerned brow. "I daresay, I'll have to remedy that situation very soon then."

But to Drake's astonishment it was not William who snorted with disgust, but Victoria.

Chapter Fifteen

"Lady Victoria's birthday party will be a wonderful surprise for her tonight," Stanby said, turning toward Mrs. Dorling in the hall outside the Percy Hall drawing room.

The older lady had arrived the previous day to care for William, as the boy seemed to be a handful to all involved.

"Is everything underway?" she asked the hovering giant.

Stanby smiled. "His lordship is going to ask for a waltz."

"A waltz!" Mrs. Dorling clasped her hands together in delight. "My, Lord Drakefield is a rather sly one, is he not?" Her eyes twinkled with mirth.

"I would say he is more like his father than any of the other sons," Stanby replied with pride.

Mrs. Dorling raised an inquisitive brow and Stanby winked.

"When they see what they want, they don't give up," he said suggestively.

"Oh, my." Mrs. Dorling's cheeks turned pink with giddiness as she brought her hands to her face. "Truly?"

"Indeed." Stanby took a step closer. "And it seems that same quality has rubbed off a bit on me." He hovered over the small woman and set his hands on her shoulders.

Mrs. Dorling giggled. She had been a widow for twenty years. "Oh, my, Stanby. You are incorrigible."

The giant man took her hand and slowly led her away into the drawing room. Standing behind the doors, he picked her off her feet and fastened his lips to hers. "Ah, my love, where have you been all my life?"

"Oh, Stanby. You are so very strong." He kissed her again.

William popped out from behind the sofa. "Oh, Stanby,"

he mimicked in a high-pitched voice. "You are so very strong."

"Zeus!" Stanby cried.

"What is all this?" the boy said in disgust. "I tell you, a pirate's life is a life without peace! Does everybody have the kissing bug?"

Stanby lowered the woman in his hands, his gaze penetrating William's face like an English cannonball directed at Napoleon's nose. The little boy gulped. Mrs. Dorling turned beet red and flew out of the room, flapping a hand to her large bosom as if she could not breathe. "Oh, my, my, my."

Stanby took in a deep breath, gritting his teeth as he spoke. "Pirate's life, indeed!"

"Worry not, old boy," William replied coolly, his hand flicking in the air as if he were twenty instead of six. "I won't say a thing. No one believes what I say anyway. Villains and treasures. They all think I make it all up."

He walked out of the room with a mute Margueretta trailing behind him, her owl-like eyes growing wider.

Stanby clenched his teeth in frustration. "Indeed!"

"Did you say something, Stanby?" Drake appeared in the hall, his expression blank as he looked at his butler, whose face seemed rather flushed. "Are you ill?"

"Not ill, my lord. I am ready to drown a discourteous imp."

"A what?"

"I said, I am steady, but frown at my discourteous limp."

Drake watched Stanby sweep out of the room and down the hall. Why, the man was not limping at all!

Later that day, Drake rode his horse back to the stables and turned to his groom. "Parks, did I see my grandmother's carriage heading over the road?"

"I believe so, my lord."

As he dismounted, Drake shook his head, thinking that perhaps one of the guests for the party needed to return to London. Yet he was surprised that they had not used their own carriage or his father's coach for the drive. The birthday party was a surprise for Victoria, and the guests were staying in either the village or the duke's home. It was probably one of his grandmother's friends.

"William, what are you doing?" Drake noticed the boy's frown as he stood outside the stable, throwing sticks at the ground.

The boy looked up. "Nothing."

"Nothing? Somehow, I believe you are only telling me a half-truth."

William kicked a pebble. "Botheration! At least you listen sometimes. I will tell you because you are a brother pirate."

It took every bit of effort for Drake to keep a straight face. "And we pirates stick together?"

William nodded and took a confident step forward. "Well then, you can see how things be, matie. Tonight is Vicki's birthday party, but if you're still planning to have it, you might want to know about her surprise, too."

"Drake, a word with you!" James came striding toward them.

Drake patted William's head. "Go on and play, lad."

"But I have important information about the princess."

"Tell me later."

"Never," William said as he stomped ahead of them. "Never. Never. Never."

Drake turned to James. "What's so important?"

"The subject concerns Wendover and it's not pretty."

"What?"

"Fox has discovered the man owes a great sum from White's betting books. The handsome earl may make the ladies swoon, but the man is not allowed inside the club until he pays up."

Drake watched William hurry away. What the devil was the boy so fired up about? "I know about his debts."

"You do?"

"Yes. But I don't know where he is. At least he won't be at the party tonight." *The wretch.* "I was hoping to corner him in the library." *And pummel his brains.*

James frowned. "There's something you are not telling me."

Drake looked off in the distance. "Wilkins was here."

"And?"

"He had surprising information about Victoria that I believe Wendover may have had an interest in." Drake gave his brother the details of the findings and James looked back, stunned.

"So you're telling me that Lady Victoria is eighty thousand pounds richer as of today and our dear departed Nightham was a crook. And now Wendover wants her money, too?"

Drake's jaw went rigid with rage as he thought about the information Wilkins sent him yesterday. "I believe so. In addition, Wilkins informed me by letter that the man had two previous heiresses for wives who died under mysterious circumstances."

"And the man just popped up in Victoria's life," James said grimly. "Devious man."

"Not only does he have debts at White's, but he's been spending time in Brighton and Bath trying to swindle many a wealthy gentleman. Seems his luck keeps running out. My guess is while in a drunken stupor he might have said something to Nightham about Victoria or the other way around. Somehow they both discovered her trust before she did." He recalled the pain in Victoria's eyes and felt a stab of guilt. "Confound it, James. I'd like to strangle them both if I could."

"By Jove, Fox was right after all. You love her!"

Drake stiffened. "Love has nothing to do with it."

"But of course you love her. She is nothing like Honoria."

"Now, you're beginning to sound like our grandmother."

James grinned. "The lady has you coiled and twisted like one of those curls hanging from her head."

"If you wish to live out the day, James, make your way back to the house. Now!"

James scooted back a step, his eyes sparkling. "Ah, I shall depart and leave you to your daydreams then. Adieu, Romeo."

After his talk with James, Drake walked into Percy Hall, knowing his feeling for Victoria was more than the boyish crush that he had felt for Honoria. But love her? She was different from most of the beauties he knew in the *ton*. Victoria cared for others more than herself. She was devoted to her family. It was a quality hard to find in London Society where appearance and money were the world. Moreover, Drake knew Victoria was not immune to his touch. The birthday party this evening would be just the thing to prepare her for his announcement of their engagement. Though she had avoided him the past two days, he hoped her temper had cooled enough to at least have a dance with him. He had a few last minute details to work out with his grandmother.

"Drake!" William called from the floor below. "I have to talk to you. Pirate to pirate."

"Not now, William."

"But—"

"William, I distinctly said, not now."

"Humph!" The small boy sat on the bottom step and took out his second in command. "They never listen to me, Whitie. Never. At the party tonight, I'll show them all."

Sparkling chandeliers shimmered upon the dance floor. The orchestra played a sweet concerto as Drake strolled into the ballroom holding a glass of wine in his hands. It would be at least an hour before the guests appeared.

"Drake," Sarah said, stopping him. "Have you seen Victoria?"

"No, I was rather hoping she would be with you."

Sarah lifted her shoulders and laughed. "Oh, I imagine she's still getting dressed. All Aunt Phoebe told her yesterday was that we were having a little party tonight with a few close friends. I have tried to avoid her for the past few days in fear that I might tell her of our little surprise. There is not much we don't confide in each other."

"Nothing?" Drake lifted his brow. How interesting? He wondered if Victoria had mentioned anything about the inn.

Sarah's eyes twinkled. "Almost nothing."

They suddenly directed their gazes toward William, dressed in a dark blue jacket and pants, standing behind the damask curtains at the end of the room.

"The boy looks rather uncomfortable in his outfit," Drake said, a smile on his lips.

"William wished Victoria a happy birthday," Sarah said with a chuckle. "But he almost told her everything else before I had to wrap my hand around his mouth and drag him from her bedchamber. She has been sleeping all afternoon and she gave the maid the evening off to celebrate her birthday. I suspect she's having to use your grandmother's abigail this evening."

"Do I dare ask you to excuse yourself and deliver her as soon as possible? I believe we should inform her who the guest of honor is before the guests arrive."

Sarah's blue eyes twinkled. "Of course, I was meaning to leave and check on her. I should be but a minute."

Five minutes later, Drake noted Sarah's return to the ballroom. She seemed distraught as she made a direct line to her aunt. He could not help but feel a faint twinge of foreboding.

"Gone! Mercy me, I cannot believe it," Phoebe replied, swaying precariously toward Sarah.

The duke immediately grabbed the older lady's elbow and escorted her to the nearest chair.

"Is something amiss?" Drake demanded, making his way across the room.

The duke turned, a frown settling across his face. "It seems Lady Victoria had business in London. She has left the premises."

"Left the premises?" His voice rose above the music.

Sarah dabbed a handkerchief to her wet face. "She left us this letter."

"It is inconceivable that Victoria left by herself," Phoebe wailed. "Oh, to leave without a maid. What is to become of her? George, the danger that one comes across with highwaymen and such. A lady alone out there. Why on earth would she leave us?" The lady looked up at Drake as if he were the reason Victoria flew from the bosom of her family.

The duke's raised brow suggested the same.

Drake clenched his teeth and snatched the letter from Sarah's shaking hands. Danger, indeed. It was more likely danger from him than anyone else.

Dear Aunt Phoebe,
  Please forgive me for my hasty departure, but I must leave for London. I cannot tell you my reasons, but by now you must know that I have a trust worth

*80,000 pounds, so you need not worry about my
situation. I hope that I will return to you as soon as
possible. Please do not seek me out. I am staying
with a friend. I love you all, and tell Sarah and
William not to worry.*

    Your loving niece, Victoria.

"Not to worry," Drake mumbled sarcastically.

He crumpled the paper in his hands. Why the blazes did
she leave? Was she afraid of him? Had he been so callous
that she could not stay near him? Or had it something to do
with Wendover? Bewilderment yielded quickly to a white-
hot fury.

"I tried to tell you!" William's voice blasted through the
orchestra's melody. "But noooooo, you would not listen to
me." The boy held his chin high and began to walk out of
the ballroom.

Drake grabbed the back of William's coat, dragging the
boy backward. "What do you mean *you* tried to tell us?"

"I tried to tell you that she was in trouble, but you ignored
me. Remember?" His eyes welled with tears.

Drake recalled the boy's constant interruptions earlier
that day. Guilt sank into his belly like a cold, hard ball. What
kind of man was he that he couldn't listen to a six-year-old
boy? Or that a woman would flee his side because she was
afraid of him? What terrible thing was she hiding that she
couldn't trust him?

The women in London adored him. He was a prize on the
marriage mart. Mamas of eligible misses scurried his way
like dogs to a bone for just a word with him. But one lady
was not impressed. Was it his pride that was hurt? Or did he
hurt because he loved her? Or blast it all, was it the combination of the two?

Chapter Sixteen

*W*hen Victoria arrived in the West End of London at Nightham Manor, she was led to the drawing room by a tall, skinny butler named Cutler. Taking a seat on the worn sofa beneath her, she gazed nervously about the room. The few lit candles solidified her thoughts. Nightham and his family had been in desperate straits. Charles must have used everything he had, leaving his mother with nothing. Victoria's heart turned as she thought about the destitute lady being pushed out onto the streets by Nightham's heir. She knew very well what that felt like.

Anger began to build inside her at Nightham's treatment of his mother. But she intended to remedy that. She would use her inheritance to help the lady. Though she knew her marriage to Nightham was still not clear, she desperately hoped the countess would let her stay at Nightham Manor until the situations were resolved with her possible marriage and with Wendover.

She dare not return to the family townhouse. The danger of Lord Wendover returning was too great. She knew her family was probably devastated at her quick departure, and the thought of how the marquess would receive the news pressed heavily upon her conscience. Pride would force him to look for her, for it certainly wouldn't be love.

She sighed and wiped a gloved hand across the dusty end table, wondering how the countess had taken her son's death.

"My dear, my dear."

Victoria stood as Lady Nightham walked into the room.

She was a slender, reedlike woman, with a dainty nose and a creamy complexion. Victoria, expecting a much older, more portly woman, realized that the countess had probably been the toast of the *ton* in her day. It was that blond hair, much like her son's, that made the countess appear almost angelic, even dressed in a black mourning gown.

The lady took Victoria's hands in hers, and there were tears in her eyes. "I received your letter, my dear, and am so sorry you were embroiled in one of my son's harebrained plots. He was a good boy, you know, but sometimes Charles would get himself in the worst scrapes. Always such a secretive boy."

Victoria had sent the lady a missive as soon as she had discovered the facts about Nightham and her inheritance. She had conveyed the entire episode to the countess, including her possible marriage with Charles, hoping the lady could forgive her. It was a risky undertaking, but she had felt at a complete loss after Drake had deceived her. She needed a place to hide.

"I insist you stay with me until we have everything sorted out, my dear. I am certain if Charles had a special license that you were indeed married to him. However, I will have my own solicitor look into the matter, inconspicuously of course."

Victoria fell into easy conversation with the lady and discovered that no provisions other than a small amount of money had been made for the frail lady after her son's death.

After a few minutes, tea and lemon squares were brought for refreshments. Victoria sat on the sofa, still apprehensive about staying, but she knew it was her only course of action.

"I do appreciate your generous offer, letting me stay with you while my aunt is still in the country," Victoria went on. "And though there still is the question of my marriage, I beg your forgiveness for the entire episode. If it were not for me—"

"My dear, my dear," the lady interrupted, trying to set her mind at ease. "It was not your fault. Not at all. Though Charles was a selfish boy, I always loved him. And if you were truly married to him, then we will get along famously. I admit his death came as quite a shock to me. But the arrival of your letter picked up my spirits, because you see," she sniffed, "I find that I may no longer be alone in this world."

Victoria felt the beginning of tears pricking her lids. "I'm overwhelmed with your kindness. But I must ask you not to say a word of my visit to anyone. At least for a few days."

The lady raised a curious brow. "You are in hiding then?"

Victoria placed her teacup down. "Until I know whether I was married to your son, I find my life at a standstill. I need to ponder my situation alone, without the influences of people I love telling me what to do. I know this may sound silly to you, but I beg you to allow me this time. I have told no one but my cousin of my, um, situation with Charles."

"Well, naturally, you can stay here, my dear. I can promise you my strictest confidence. There certainly is no need for you to leave. Though, I was thinking of having a few guests in honor of my daughter-in-law, it is a little too soon after my son's death. A year, you know." She sniffed and patted Victoria's hand. "I am so alone, but am terribly grateful you have come into my life."

A heaviness centered in Victoria's chest. She had made a terrible mistake going away with Nightham to be married. If it were not for her, the man would be alive today, and this poor woman would still have her son, though a gambler he may be. She could only hope the countess would keep her word and not mention that she was staying here.

She could not have her family know where she was, because she had no idea what the future would bring, especially in the form of Lord Wendover. But she knew it was only a matter of time before the marquess would find her. By then she hoped to discover whether or not she had been married. She felt somewhat relieved to know the countess would be discreetly looking into the matter with her solicitors. And Wendover could not blackmail her while she was gone. He would not dare do anything to William because she was his only hope.

She had already decided that after she figured out if she were married to Nightham, she would make her dealings with Wendover known to her aunt. Perhaps the duke could help her then. For it seemed the man was in love with

Phoebe and nothing would deter him from breaking off their
engagement, not even her scandalous past.

She certainly could not tell Drake. There was no telling
what he would do behind her back. She ached for his help,
but she also knew she could not completely trust him. She
did love him. She knew that now. But trust was another matter entirely.

"I will help you anyway I can, my dear," the countess
said, dabbing her eyes. "I will send word to my solicitor
posthaste. Now, I'm certain you are tired. Cutler will show
you to your chambers."

Her gaze shifted away from Victoria to encompass the
entire drawing room. "As you can see by my humble sur-
roundings, my servants are few and far between. I do not
even have a maid to serve you. There is my housekeeper and
my cook, and of course, Cutler, but that is all. Nevertheless,
if you need anything, anything at all, they would be only too
happy to help."

The lady crumpled the handkerchief in her hand. "I can
see that we are going to get along famously, my dear. Thank
you so much for telling me the truth. You cannot believe
what a comfort you have been already."

Tears tightened Victoria's throat. She knew she had done
the right thing in coming. "And I thank you for your understanding, Lady Nightham. Your generosity is overwhelming."

"Think nothing of it, my dear." She gave Victoria a
tremulous smile. "Or should I say daughter?"

Drake slammed his hand on top of his solicitor's desk. "I
cannot believe she disappeared just like that. Where the
devil could she have gone?"

No doubt Wilkins had seen his employer angry before,
but this, well, this was far past angry.

Wilkins adjusted his cravat and cleared his throat. "She
did have a good sum to spend, my lord."

"The lady has eighty thousand pounds at her disposal,"
James said with exasperation. "She could have gone anywhere."

Anywhere, Drake thought. She was a little magician in that department.

James and Fox had followed him to London. All three men had been there one week with no clue as to where Victoria had gone. Back at Percy Hall, Drake had almost killed the groom when the story came out that Parks had known of Victoria's departure in the dowager's carriage. He would have shaken the poor man to death if not for his brother and Fox who came to the man's rescue, pulling him from Parks in the nick of time.

"She could have gone anywhere," Fox piped in. "By Jove, even to the Continent."

Drake shot his friend an icy glare. "I will find her, and when I do, heaven help her or anyone else who helped her hide."

"I do have another suggestion, my lord," Wilkins offered. The three gentlemen turned with a jerk. "Lady Victoria's solicitor may be of some help. I have recently discovered who is in charge of her trust."

"Her solicitor?" Drake said, trying desperately to hold his temper.

"The name is Washington," Wilkins replied. "Washington and Sons, to be precise. Located a block from Hyde Park."

Drake repeated the name, snapping out his watch and replacing it with an irritated thrust.

Wilkins sank back into his chair. "As to the other matter, I have not been able to locate Wendover. The man has disappeared as well. He's in quite more debt than even you expected. I believe he wanted Lady Victoria's inheritance to cover his losses."

Drake's lips thinned as his mind raced with thoughts of Wendover intercepting Victoria. If the man had taken Victoria, he would kill him.

After leaving Wilkins, Drake directed his coachman to drive to the office of Washington and Sons. James and Fox had returned to the duke's London townhouse to inform Drake's father of the new information. Even Phoebe had removed to London, too horrified at Victoria's disappearance to even think of marriage to the duke—a situation that did not please the duke at all.

Drake pinched the bridge of his nose with his fingertips. He now had some concrete reasons for why Victoria had left. But the threat of Wendover alone should not have made her flee. Why could she not trust him? Because he had gone behind her back, that's why. Even Nightham's treachery had affected her. Her father had failed her. Her uncle had failed her. Why should she trust any man at all?

The carriage finally pulled in front of a small, red brick building housing the office of Washington and Sons. Drake strode past the front door, his expression grim.

"May I help you?" A stylish man in a dark brown waist-coat spoke from behind a grand mahogany desk.

"Mr. Washington?"

The man stood up, extending his hand. "At your service."

Drake made his introductions and squeezed the man's hand hard enough that he received all the information he needed. Drake now knew where Victoria was residing. Relief coursed through him. He felt as if a steel weight had been lifted from his chest as he hopped into his waiting carriage.

It was lucky he'd made the trip to Washington's office. He had swiftly put a stop to any of her money departing from the credit she had with the bank. Once he told Washington that he was Victoria's fiancé and would give the final word on where the money went, the solicitor warily agreed.

Drake assured himself that he really had not threatened the man, he had just exercised his voice of authority. A very loud voice of authority.

It seemed that Nightham's mother, working through her own solicitor, had been taking large sums of money from Victoria's account. Victoria, the little fool, had given the lady full access to her trust fund via Washington and Sons. Ten thousand pounds were already deducted from her credit.

Drake checked his timepiece, then stuffed it back into his pocket. Of all the places, he never once thought to look for her at Nightham Manor. What a fool he had been. Nevertheless, he would have Victoria in his hands by sunup tomorrow.

Chapter Seventeen

*T*he warm rays of the morning sunrise poured through Victoria's window waking her from a deep slumber. The sun seemed unduly bright as she pulled the pillow over her head. She didn't want to rise this early in the day. There was no need. Life in the countess's house had proved to be quite dull.

But despite the monotonous existence, there was no other way she could think of to avoid Wendover, at least not until she was sure of her marriage one way or another. She was still awaiting the news from Lady Nightham's solicitor regarding her situation with Charles. When Victoria learned the facts, she could then make a decision on what to do.

But the horrid thought of William dying like Nightham made her sick to her stomach. And there was also Drake's life, too. She assured herself she had done the right thing. Staying here had bought her some time.

"Victoria?"

She shook her head and squeezed the pillow tighter around her ears. She must be dreaming. It sounded like Lord Drakefield speaking to her.

"Victoria."

Her name was voiced with such authority, she turned sharply and her eyes flew open in dread. Good heavens, it was him.

"W-what are you doing here?"

He hovered over her as if it were the inn all over again. He wore a neat blue jacket with buckskin breeches hugging his powerful legs. His ebony hair gleamed in the sunlight while eyes the color of dark rain clouds glared into hers. The strange thing was, she was glad to see him.

His reaction was swift as he wrapped a powerful hand about her bare ankle and pulled her toward the edge of the bed. "It seems to me that I ought be the one asking the questions, madam."

She was shocked by the heat of his touch, and she swallowed past the lump in her throat as she tried to devise an acceptable explanation. For once in her life, her mind went blank. Her cheeks warmed under the fiery heat of his gaze.

He let go of her ankle and leaned over her. He smelled of coffee and bayberry soap. "I am waiting for an explanation."

Her answer was the fleeting thud of her heart against her breast. She wanted to tell him she loved him, that she wanted to trust him. But something inside her rebelled when he spoke to her as if she were a five-year-old child.

"If you do not start explaining yourself, madam, I believe I will take you over my knee right here."

She gasped in outrage, pulling the covers over herself. "You would not dare?"

A surly smile tilted the corners of his mouth, and she felt herself color.

"You have vexed me to no end, madam. If you are not willing to speak to me, then I will explain a few things to you."

She flinched when his hand sliced through the air. There was an edge to his voice that she had never heard before. But it was that odious pocket watch that vexed her to no end. Why was he snapping it out now?

"First of all, fill your mind with this little fact. Your little pirate did not stop weeping for hours after we found that note of yours. He thought he failed to protect you."

Her stomach churned with remorse. "I can explain—"

"Second of all," he continued with a harsh set to his lips. "Sarah refused to eat until you returned. It was Mrs. Dorling who finally forced her."

Heat singed Victoria's face.

"And on top of that, your Aunt Phoebe swooned every time she reread your letter. She refuses to marry my father until you are found. Needless to say, the duke has an army out searching for you. Trying to keep the gossip down has cost him a fortune."

"I had no idea." Guilt stabbed her heart. She hadn't meant to cause such misery. *Just tell me you love me. Please.*

"You had no idea?" he growled. "Confound it, woman. Do you always do what you want, when you want?"

"Please stop shouting. Everyone will hear you. This is most improper, you being in my bedchambers."

His gray eyes darkened to black, and she realized she had gone too far. "You have the insolence to tell me that I ought not be here? You being here is improper!" His hand waved about the room. "Did you ever stop to think how *I* would feel? Or how people would look at me after you fled Percy Hall?"

She blinked and felt a piece of her heart die. He was worried how he would look? How obvious could it be? He did not love her. It was his pride that was hurt.

What had she been thinking?

She looked away, a suffocating sensation tightening about her chest. His kisses meant nothing at all. Oh, she realized now that she had hurt her family, but William's life had been at stake. She stiffened as he continued to glare at her.

She glared back at him with a decided coolness. "How did you gain entrance into my chambers?"

His face suddenly turned into a mask of contempt. "I climbed the tree outside your window."

"You climbed in here?"

"I do know how to climb trees, too."

"Why don't you climb right back down then?" she said, boldly lifting her chin.

There was a tense pause, then suddenly he grabbed her shoulders and whipped her out of bed. "If you act like a child, madam, you will be treated like one."

"How dare you?"

"I dare that and more." He pulled out that infernal pocket watch again and looked up at her. "I will allow you all of fifteen minutes to make yourself presentable and give your farewells to your host. You may send for your things later."

He snapped the watch closed and stuffed it back into his pocket. "Starting now."

Victoria's mind reeled. "I cannot leave. You don't understand."

"I understand completely. You can and you will."

She pressed her lips together, knowing that he would make good on his threat. She had no choice but to comply. "Very well."

"I will be waiting for you outside in the carriage. Remember fifteen minutes or else."

His dark gaze bore into her with calculated precision. She swallowed tightly. The next moment, she watched, dumbfounded, as he made a swift retreat out the window.

Drake took a seat in his carriage and whipped out his pocket watch. "Ten more seconds," he repeated to himself. "Then so help me, I will plow past that door and—"

His head jerked up as Victoria came bounding out of the townhouse, one hand clasping her bonnet, the other hand holding her shawl about her breasts.

A wide-eyed countess stared from the window as the carriage door opened and Drake jerked Victoria inside.

The vehicle clamored down the otherwise quiet street for a few taut seconds before Victoria spoke. "I simply cannot believe you treated me like that. A gentleman would—"

Drake gritted his teeth. "At this point, if you are wise, you would not call me a gentleman or anything else."

The thinly veiled warning in his voice caused a blush to sweep across her cheeks. But she was not about to be bullied. Besides, he was only doing this for his pride. "If you could have only seen that lady's face when I departed. She is devastated that I am leaving. I am her only hope."

"Lady?" Drake's chest began to rumble with mocking laughter. "I take it you had knowledge that that so-called lady was using your inheritance to her heart's desire?"

"Of course." Victoria smoothed her skirt with her hand. "After all, what happened to her son was partly my fault." Her hands trembled at the thought of Wendover killing Nightham. She wanted to tell the marquess all about it, but the odious man was being so pompous right now. "I thought it only right—"

Drake broke in. "That lady snatched close to ten thousand pounds from your precious little account! She bought a pretty little cottage in the country. Not a castle mind you, but a pleasant little place to do her business. If I had left you there another week, she would have robbed your pockets blind. You would have no credit in your account at all. May I remind you, the trust is not settled as of yet. The bank is only lending you the money until everything comes through."

Victoria clutched her shawl tightly. "Lord Nightham left his mother virtually nothing at all. Since he was killed, she has no one to look after her."

"She is not your responsibility," he snapped, hitting the side of the carriage with his fist.

She watched his anger mounting and realized with absolute conviction that this was not the time to tell him about the possibility of the lady being her mother-in-law or of Wendover's threats. "What is the lady to do then?"

"Lady? That lonely widow is not a lady at all."

"I don't understand."

He turned and glared at her. "Sweetheart, you have been aiding a lady of the night."

Victoria gasped. "No?"

"Yes. To put it bluntly, the Countess of Nightham services the gentlemen of the haught *ton* with females of . . . hmmm, let's just say, ladies of ill repute. You have been shoveling money into the oldest business in the world, my dear philanthropist."

Victoria felt her cheeks flame with embarrassment. She opened her mouth, but found she could not speak.

Drake's jaw hardened as he stared out the window. "Believe me, the countess will be able to live without you and your little inheritance for a very long time."

The hooves of the horses drummed against Victoria's brain. She was deeply ashamed of being taken advantage of in such a manner. Not once, but twice. She could not believe that Lord Nightham's mother had fooled her just like her son had done. What a peagoose she had been.

"You are not to take a shilling without my permission."

Victoria barely caught the last of his words. "What?"

"I said, I put a halt on your account."

His words finally dawned upon her. "That is my coin to do with as I wish."

"Not for long."

Victoria clenched her teeth, almost too angry to speak. "And what do you mean by that?"

"After we are married, you and your money will belong to me."

"You are fooling yourself, my lord. I have already told you I will not marry you." *He would never love her.*

"Ah, yes, I do seem to remember something to that effect. Nevertheless, you *will* marry me. You seemed to have changed your mind when rescuing Margueretta from that stream."

"Yes, well, I believe I already told you I was delirious at the time. And I do not believe I ever said yes."

To her surprise, he turned slowly, taking her hand in a warm clasp. His eyes softened. "You little fool. For days I thought Wendover had kidnapped you. A silly thought. But I was beside myself with worry. I would have killed the man if he had laid one finger on you."

Her lips trembled and she looked away. Her emotions were swirling out of control. *Wendover killed Nightham,* she wanted to say. *And he might kill you and William. And I love you so much it hurts inside. I don't want you hurt.*

"Victoria, look at me." He pulled her gently toward him.

She tried to fight the staggering desire to be near him. To love him. To trust him. But it was impossible to resist him. He moved her hand to his lips. The touch was warm and sweet, sending a quiver of delight through her. He pressed his mouth against hers, and she never dreamed a kiss could be so passionate and gentle at the same time. She tried to ignore the nagging voice in the back of her mind that she would be putting him in danger and William as well. But she couldn't. She loved this man too much.

"No." She pushed her hands against his chest.

Stunned, Drake pulled back. "I didn't force you to kiss

me, you know." The stark pain in his eyes squeezed her heart.

She looked away, feeling him stiffen beside her. She wanted to tell him everything, but she didn't want him killed. And how could he treat her so tenderly and not love her? "Where are you taking me?"

"Home."

"What should I tell Aunt Phoebe?"

There was a slight pause, and she felt him stiffen beside her. "Mayhap you ought to have thought about that before you left Percy Hall so quickly."

The condemnation in his words drained the blood from her face.

"Do you have any idea what grief you have caused everybody? I will never forgive you for this, Victoria. Never!"

Standing in her aunt's drawing room, Sarah turned her back on Victoria and fled from the room. By that time Phoebe and William had entered, and Victoria made her feeble apologies all over again, but even her aunt seemed disheartened at her flimsy excuse of visiting a friend who needed her.

But Victoria could never tell them the entire truth. It was too dangerous for them. She had decided to hire a Bow Street Runner to follow up on Wendover's claim of killing Nightham. In the meantime, she would apply to her own solicitor about discovering the truth concerning her marriage. It was obvious Lady Nightham's man had done nothing with the investigation since it would not have served the countess to dispute her son's marriage.

"My dear," Phoebe said sadly. "You made us sick with worry."

Victoria's feet shifted uneasily and her eyes welled with tears. The pain she detected in her aunt's face was so acute that it shattered her heart. Aunt Phoebe, William, and Sarah meant everything to her. "I . . . I never meant to hurt anybody." Her hand flew to her mouth and she rushed out of the room.

Drake frowned as he turned to Phoebe. "I will return tomorrow."

Phoebe sniffed back tears and gave him a kiss on his cheek. "Thank you. I won't even ask her where she's been. I'm just glad she's home. You must forgive me for giving you the impression that I thought Victoria left because of you. She is an impulsive child, always thinking she has to take care of things herself. I let her have her way since she came to me. I may have been wrong in her upbringing, but I loved her as if she were one of my own."

She let out a small sob, then climbed the stairs, leaving only William and Drake alone to stare at each other.

William whipped his sword about, slicing it through the air. "Why are you looking at me that way, me pirate? I'm the one who has three crying princesses." He pointed his weapon toward the stairs. "This is unsufferable. Simply unsufferable."

"Insufferable, William." Drake's lips thinned as he listened to the three wailing women. "Downright insufferable."

Chapter Eighteen

*V*ictoria sat back on her chair and drew in a weary sigh as she stared at her reflection in the looking glass. Dark circles surrounded her eyes. Her hair was a messy nest of curls, and she desperately needed a bath. A copper tub full of warm water waited beside her bed.

The pain of the past few days overwhelmed her. Lord Wendover continued to plague her thoughts as well as the marquess who had visited her every day since she had returned. Knowing he would want some answers, she refused to see him. She had to have some kind of plan. Her every move was watched by her family, and it was impossible to get a letter out to Bow Street without someone being suspicious. But sooner or later she had to do something.

A knock at the door pulled her from her thoughts.

"Come in."

"My lady," Mrs. Dorling replied. "A caller to see you. Lord Wendover."

Victoria froze. Wendover was here? The nerve of the man. Fury soon replaced any fear she had of the earl. The impudence of him to show his face at her aunt's home after what he had done. She had been a victim long enough.

"Says you would be wanting to see him as soon as possible," Mrs. Dorling continued with a face of disapproval. "Something about some unfinished business. Should I send him away? I know the marquess isn't fond of him."

Victoria dug her fingers into her rosewood vanity. She would see him. But he would have to wait. "Tell him if he wishes, he will have to wait until I finish my bath."

Mrs. Dorling's face grew grim. "But your aunt has left for the day. Sarah and William have gone with her. You have no chaperone. It isn't proper."

"I have Winston, Mrs. Dorling." But Victoria knew that the old butler would not stand a chance against Wendover. Yet she knew the earl had been too secretive by far to chance anything at her home. She looked at her water and doubted that even a hot bath would ever wash the dirt from his black heart.

Drake gazed out the window at White's, then turned his stony countenance on Fox and James who sat beside him. "The woman is as stubborn as a child. She speaks to no one but Mrs. Dorling."

James peered over his wineglass. "Drake, you are letting her make a cake of you. I daresay, if you would only take a firm stand here, you could get on with your life."

Drake eyes flashed a subtle warning. "And you are an expert on women?"

James frowned and poured himself another glass of wine from the decanter. "I am merely pointing out the fact—"

"That you are a useless man in matters such as these, little brother. So shut up."

James narrowed his eyes and downed another drink. Drake did the same, as well as Fox. After about an hour of constant spirits, the two younger gentlemen stumbled to a standing position.

"I s-say," Fox said, staggering against Drake's shoulder. "If I were you, and of course, if you were me, that is to say, if I . . ." He swayed slightly toward James. "The way of it is this. I would demand that Victoria come out of that room at once."

"Easier said than done," Drake replied grimly, as James and Fox swayed from side to side. They were stone drunk and yet he felt nothing.

James fell against Drake's chair, slurring his speech. "Yes, Drake. If you showed her—" Without warning, he fell face down onto the floor with a smack.

"Ouch!" Fox replied, casting his gaze downward. "Do believe your brother has taken a fall."

Drake cast a wincing glance in James's direction and jerked him upright. "Devil take it! I don't know how you two imbeciles go anywhere without me. Help me drag this sot out into some fresh air."

As soon as Drake and Fox pulled James past the doors of the club, Drake shifted his gaze to where a young footman had jumped down from a hackney and was running toward him.

"My lord," the boy puffed. "I have an urgent message for you from Winston, Lady Phoebe's butler."

Drake threw his limp brother into Fox's arms and took the letter from the boy.

"What is it?" Fox demanded.

Drake crumpled the paper in his hands. "It seems Wendover has taken it upon himself to visit Lady Phoebe's home."

"Wendover?" Fox asked, wide-eyed.

"The devil himself. It's beyond me that the man had the gall to appear in London at all." Drake gestured for his carriage and glanced back at Fox. "Take James home. He's of no use to me in that state."

"Dash it all, Drake," Fox protested, seeming to have regained some sobriety. "You may need us."

But Drake had already hopped into his vehicle, shouting commands to his coachman, leaving Fox and James to catch a ride with an inebriated viscount departing at the same time.

"My lady," Winston whispered bluntly, his wary gaze glued to Victoria as she descended the stairs. "You do not have to meet with this man. I can and *will* show him out if you only say the word."

Victoria rested her hand on the old man's arm. "Thank you, Winston. But you must not worry. I know what I am about."

By the feel of Winston's stiff shoulders, Victoria knew there was no hope in coaxing her butler to leave. Her heart turned over when his jaw jutted forward in disapproval. He was as steadfast as a soldier in battle. "Very well, my lady. But remember, if you need me, I will be but one step away."

"Thank you, Winston. I will remember."

She took a step toward the drawing room, and a surge of dread filled her as she opened the doors. But she would not cower to this man or any man ever again. She would tell him that Bow Street would be following his every move. Blackmail would do him no good. He would never lay a hand on William.

"Lady Victoria."

She glared at the earl from across the room. He stood relaxed, his hand resting on the marble mantel, one boot crossing the other at the ankle. His fair looks might strike most women as handsome, but to her, he was as ugly as Medusa.

"Lord Wendover, I must say I am surprised to see you in London. Forgive me for missing our last appointment. It was such a bother, you know."

She felt her spirits lift at the sight of his frown. If he thought to bully her, he had better think again. Evading her problem had evidently been the wrong thing to do. She would see this man hanged for murder.

Without a word he stalked across the room, his dark blue gaze piercing the distance between them. His mouth stretched into a thin-lipped smile as he took her hand and kissed it.

Shocked, Victoria shrank back.

He continued to hold her, then glanced over her shoulder at a narrow-eyed Winston standing guard beyond the door.

"How clever, my dear. But since we have business matters to discuss, I feel it ever so important to keep this conversation just between the two of us." In two quick strides the man strode toward the doors, jerking them closed with a thud.

Victoria felt a frisson of alarm, but dismissed it immediately. She was in her aunt's home, for heaven's sake.

The knock on the door was Winston, of course. "Are you well, my lady?" he asked from the other side.

Victoria went to open the doors, but was stopped by the hand on her wrist. "It would be in your best interest to hear me out, my dear. Alone. I meant what I said the other day."

A brief shiver of uncertainty shot through her. She opened the doors a crack and looked her butler in the eye. "I am fine, Winston. I will be but a minute."

Winston opened his mouth to speak, but Wendover closed the door in his face. "Very nicely put, my dear."

Victoria took an abrupt step toward the sofa and turned. "What do you want?"

"Want?" He closed the distance between them. "You mentioned our last appointment, did you not?"

Victoria commanded herself not to panic. But when he drew his face closer to hers, she backed up a step. "We have nothing to discuss. You are insufferable to suggest anything else."

His horrid chuckle sent her heart racing.

"A little spitfire? I like that." He moved toward the decanter of brandy resting on the sideboard, then stopped to let his gaze rake over her. "I never proclaimed to be anything but insufferable. In fact, sometimes I think I'm barely human."

Victoria swallowed the bile in her throat. She glanced at the door and knew that Winston was standing there, ready to defend her virtue if she so as much squeaked his name.

Wendover cradled the drink in his hands and stared at her.

Victoria suddenly had a bit of empathy for Captain Whitie when he had been cornered by the neighborhood cat.

"You see, my dear, I need you. As you have probably guessed by now, I need your money. And I cannot have one without the other." He took a seat on the wing chair, crossing one leg over the other as if it were a visit between friends. "I only found out about your little trust by mere chance. A letter came to my home addressed to you. Of course, I opened it, and to my surprise, discovered your little secret. I imagine Nightham found out by mere chance, too. Probably knew someone related to your generous benefactor. So, my dear Victoria, you will marry me, and in return, I will not hurt your precious William."

Her fists tightened against her skirts. "You're mad."

"No, I will do whatever I have to do in order to have that money." He rose and drew nearer. "You will never be rid of me."

"I would never marry you. My family would never allow it."

"As if they would have allowed your marriage to Nightham?"

Victoria shuddered and took a few steps toward the closed doors. But before she knew it, he cornered her against the wall.

"It would be best not to scream, my dear."

Her heart thumped against her ribs when he pulled out a knife. She thought of Nightham and her stomach somersaulted.

"I have used this before, as you well know. And no screaming, if you please. You would not wish old Winston hurt now, would you?" A chuckle erupted from his thin lips as he slipped the knife back into his inside pocket.

Victoria squeezed her eyes shut as burning tears silently spilled down her cheeks. "Please, don't hurt him."

"Hurt him? This is only a warning, Victoria. I will come for you when you least expect it, and you'd best be ready. And if you dare say one word of this to anybody, and that includes Bow Street, you will find your little cousin dead. Oh, and maybe that old butler, too." With those last words Wendover spun around, downed the last of his drink and departed from the room.

Victoria felt the trembling build inside her. Pressing a hand over her mouth, she slid down against the wall and stifled a sob.

Chapter Nineteen

Drake picked Victoria off the floor and carried her to the sofa, muttering a curse. He glanced over his shoulder at a shocked-faced Winston. "How long has she been like this?"

"Two minutes at most, my lord. I only wish I were twenty years younger."

"Drake?" The duke stood at the drawing room doors with Phoebe by his side. "What the devil happened?"

Phoebe gasped, seeing her niece lying on the sofa. "Goodness, what happened to Victoria?"

Drake barely looked up. "Wendover was here, is what happened." The anger he felt was beyond boiling.

Bewildered, Sarah followed behind her aunt. But it was William who slipped between his mother and the duke, pushing his way toward Victoria and putting a hand to her head.

The boy frowned at her disheveled appearance. "It was the villain! He did it! I know it!"

William wiped his hand gently across Victoria's forehead and gave her a loving kiss on the cheek. "I would have left Whitie in charge of the ship if I had only known, me princess."

Victoria's lips turned upward in a shaky smile.

"Victoria, is it true?" Phoebe asked with a frown. "Did Lord Wendover threaten you?"

Drake's lips thinned. "The man was here. Make no doubt about that."

Phoebe's face paled. "I should never have left her alone."

Drake cast a knowing glance toward his father, as if he would to speak to him later. The duke acknowledged his son with a nod.

"I felt lightheaded," Victoria said, closing her eyes. "Nothing happened."

"Nothing happened?" Drake snapped, pacing the room. "You will not go anywhere near that man again! Do I make myself clear?"

"I heard you, my lord," she said calmly, holding her reeling emotions in check. "It is very hard not to hear you these days."

Phoebe, Sarah, Winston, Mrs. Dorling, and William seemed to be observing the couple with great interest while Victoria felt an embarrassing flush blanket her face.

In the meantime, the duke poured her a brandy and handed it to her. "I must agree with my son, Victoria, you must not put yourself in that man's path ever again."

"If I can help it, I will keep myself far away from the man."

"If you can help it?" Drake asked sarcastically. "The man is without morals. You will never go near him again. Do I make myself perfectly clear, madam?"

She lifted her chin up a notch as she stared back at him. "Oh, yes, you have made yourself perfectly clear, my lord."

"Confound it," he muttered as he departed from the room. "Confound it all!"

The following day when Drake returned to Phoebe's townhouse to visit Victoria, William swung his sword, stopping him in the hallway. "You take a swing at his belly, me pirate! That will take care of the villain!"

Drake grimaced, his mind trying to concentrate on finding the man in question. He had searched the clubs and gaming hells for Wendover, but the man had eluded him. He guessed the earl was hiding in a remote part of the city, or being bold as brass and biding his time in some elegant hotel in Town under an assumed name. The chances of finding the man were slim.

Drake dodged William's jousts as Winston escorted him into the drawing room. Scampering feet followed behind.

Victoria had taken a morning ride with Phoebe and Sarah to visit an old governess. Winston insisted that they would be home within the hour. Furious that Victoria had left the premises with Wendover still at large, Drake decided to wait until the entourage returned.

"Then you head for the neck!" William whirled past the fireplace. "Like this! See!" The boy dropped his sword to his side and scowled. "Are you listening to me? If you want to fight off the villain, you will have to learn some of my secrets."

Drake cocked his head toward the boy when the sudden realization came to him that Wendover had said something to scare Victoria. A threat of some kind. He was sure of it. He would stay with her twenty-four hours a day if he had to.

"Did you hear me?" William tugged on his arm, pressing his nose into Drake's face.

"I have other things on my mind today, William." Drake glanced at the boy and smiled when he saw a trace of red gel on a pair of dimpled cheeks. "But I daresay, me pirate, is that some type of fruit I detect on your lips?"

William squirmed out of his arms. "Well, um, yes. But I did not steal Cook's raspberry preserves. I only borrowed them."

"I see."

"Now, as I was saying," William replied, taking a seat beside Drake on the sofa. "We have to protect the princesses and all the treasures in this house."

Drake thought to humor the boy. He was not about to leave the house anyway. "Hmmm, I know all about the princesses, but what about the treasures?"

William snorted in disgust. "The treasures? What kind of pirate are ye if ye don't know about the treasures?"

"I don't have to look for treasures, William. I have enough of my own."

"Margueretta told me about your clocks. But all pirates seek treasures. And the treasure in this house is most val . . . lable."

Drake leaned forward, his interest piqued. "You have a valuable treasure for me to see?"

William planted his hands on his hips. "Of course."

"And where do you keep this treasure?"

"I don't have it with me," William said, chewing on his bottom lip. "I'm guarding it for Vicki. The treasure is in her bedchamber."

Drake's eyes lit up with interest. "Her bedchamber?"

"Top drawer."

"What is it?"

The boy's face spread into a mischievous smile. "Now you are speaking like a pirate. The treasure is a ring with a big red jewel that shines when I put it by the candlelight."

Drake shoulders tensed and a sinking feeling started growing in the pit of his stomach. "A ring?"

"Yes, me pirate, a ring." William puffed out his chest, quite pleased with himself for the knowledge he had just bestowed upon his fellow conspirator. "But the villain might want that ring. So I must guard it with my sword and Cap'n Whitie."

Drake rose from his seat. What was Victoria doing with a red ring? He hoped against all odds that it was not Nightham's. Had she been lying to him all this time? Had she stolen Nightham's ring? Had she been involved in his death? No, he told himself, she was not like Honoria. She was not.

"Does she have the ring up there now?" he asked with deadly calm.

William visibly gulped. "Well, the princess does not allow me to hold it. 'Tis a pirate's job to be sneaky. Right?"

"Sneaky, indeed. The top drawer you say?"

William grinned, grabbing his sword. "Shall I fetch it?"

"Why don't you do that?" Drake replied flatly. "Be a good pirate and gather that treasure. But be careful not to be seen."

"Aye matie." And William was off and running.

After visiting Mrs. Weber, Phoebe's old governess, the women decided to stop at the milliner's, but Victoria feigned a headache and asked to be dropped off at home.

Gray clouds hung overhead as she stepped out of the carriage and gazed down the street. A brisk breeze whipped the dark brown hat off Mrs. Mellows, the housekeeper next door. The stout lady hastened after it, looking like a toddler running after her runaway puppy.

Victoria drew in a heavy sigh as she stepped into the townhouse. The past few months had been like that hat, flying out of control wherever the wind decided to blow. Her planned marriage to Nightham had been a mistake, and now, she had no idea what she was going to do. She had penned a letter to Washington and Sons, hoping they could settle the matter one way or another.

She climbed the stairs to her bedchambers, knowing that it was time to tell Drake everything. Whether the marquess loved her or not, Wendover was a threat she could no longer ignore. She had no options left. Bow Street would have to be informed.

"Victoria."

The sound of Drake's voice sent her heart thumping. She turned toward the drawing room. "Drake?"

Two icy gray eyes pinned her to the floor. Was he worried about her?

"I was out with my aunt and Sarah. There's no reason you should have been worried. But as long as you're here, I would like a word with you." She would confess everything. She had to trust somebody.

"A word with me? By all means."

She stepped into the drawing room and he closed the doors. "I was thinking about the past few months and—"

"Take a seat. Now." His stern words sent her grappling for the nearby wing chair.

"I know you are upset."

"Upset?" His eyebrows raised in challenge. "That, madam, is too mild a word. Enraged is more like it."

The cold contempt that flashed in his eyes surprised her.

"Are you finally going to tell me the truth?"

"W-what do you mean? If you are speaking of Wendover, I was going to tell you, but—"

He threw his hands to his hips, forcing his jacket aside. "Do not think me an imbecile. I am not speaking of Wendover."

Victoria watched in alarm as his long legs pounded across the room. A cold knot formed in her stomach, and a little voice told her she ought not be alone with this man, not now. He truly looked like an enraged pirate.

When his back was turned, she rose to leave. "Perhaps I should speak to you another time."

He spun around. "Stay exactly where you are. I don't believe you want anyone to hear what I have to say."

A sliver of uneasiness snaked down her spine as she sank back into her seat. Had he discovered that she had been married to Nightham after all? But she had planned to tell him. She had.

He thrust his hand into his pocket and pulled out a ring. "Have you ever seen this before?"

Her cheeks bloomed with color, and she rose, barely able to control her gasp of shock. "Where did you get that?"

"Where? I think you know the answer to that." He looked at her accusingly, the bitterness in his voice puncturing her heart.

"You took that from my room! Have you no decency? To ruffle through my things! I have never felt so violated in my life. How could I ever thought of trusting you!"

"Trusting me? I believe you have things backward. Your little cousin did some detective work on the treasures of this house. So do not blame me because William brought this little gem to my attention."

"How . . . how dare you send a child to do your dirty work."

He dangled the ring in the air. She raised her arms to grab it. With lightning speed, he caught her arm and jerked her toward him, his warm breath against her face. "When were you going to tell me about Nightham's ring, Victoria? When?"

He opened his palm and shoved the ring beneath her nose, then uttering an oath, he released her and slapped the ring onto the end table. She opened her mouth to defend herself, then shut it as she stared at the ring. The ruby glittered beneath the rays of the sun like a piece of her shattered heart.

She peered up at the marquess and shuddered, trying to think of the right words to explain herself. But it was the glint of suspicion flashing in his slate-gray eyes that cut the last spark of hope between them. It mattered not. She still had to tell him everything. She had already made the decision before she had entered the room. Other people depended on her. "I can explain."

"You stole it?"

The vile accusation snapped her senses into full alert. "Stole it? How could you believe such a wicked thing?"

"What would you call it? Borrowing, just as William borrows the raspberry preserves?"

"Oh, do not bring William into this."

His short bark of laughter infuriated her. "That boy is an innocent. You, madam, are not."

She walked toward the window and stared off in the distance. "You are a fool, Drake. A blind fool. I heard about your wife and her infidelities. This has nothing to do with the ring and you know it."

Tears stung the back of her eyes as she turned to meet his sneering gaze. She was surprised how calm and controlled her voice sounded. "You will allow a dead woman to dictate your life? You believe all women the same as your cheating wife? You even have the audacity to think that I stole from Nightham? *She* was only one woman, Drake. Not all women put together."

Then with her chin held high, she marched forward and snatched the ring from the table. Why had she ever thought she could trust this man at all?

"In fact, I almost feel sorry for you, *Lord Drakefield*. You have no notion of what is important in life."

"I want an answer from you, Victoria. Explain yourself."

Her laugh came out in a sad rumble. "How very sorry I feel for you."

"Victoria, I will not leave this house until I have an answer."

"An answer?" she laughed, hardening both her heart and her resolve under his withering glare. "No."

His brows snapped together. "No, you will not answer?"

She strolled slowly toward the door. "No, I will *never* marry you." Her voice cracked as she opened the doors and left him standing by himself.

"This is not the last of our conversation, madam!"

Drake's only answer was the slap of slippers up the stairs.

He took an abrupt step toward the hall and stopped with a curse upon his lips. Had he lost his heart to this woman, only to have it thrown back in his face with lies and deceit like Honoria?

No. It was more than that. He was jealous of the possibility of Victoria loving Nightham. It was ludicrous to believe she had stolen the ring. There had to be a plausible explanation. What the devil had he been thinking?

"Is it worth anything? The treasure, I mean?" William stood beside him in the hall, his blue eyes looking up expectantly.

"Worth anything?" Drake let out a hollow laugh. "Dear boy, I believe it cost me more than a thousand treasures."

"What?"

"Nothing, William. Nothing at all."

Later that evening, when James and the duke visited Phoebe's townhouse, they decided that one of them would stay on watch during the day until they determined the best course of action to take concerning Wendover and his bizarre behavior.

Phoebe took her fiancé by the arm and led him to the library, leaving James and Sarah alone with Winston standing in the hall as guard dog.

"Winston," Sarah turned to her butler, "I was wondering if you would check on William. I fear he has been spying on our neighbor Mrs. Shelby, certain that she is working for Napoleon."

"I believe Napoleon is no longer a threat," Winston said, pursing his lips, obviously not taking the hint to move.

"But William is a threat," Sarah replied, smiling. "He has taken it into his head that the lady is a foreign agent. Mother caught him using his spyglass the other day."

"That should not pose a ready problem, Miss Sarah. I daresay, a harmless venture."

Sarah frowned. "Not a harmless venture when our neighbor is in the process of taking a bath, Winston."

Winston's face turned red. "I will see to the boy right away."

Standing near the hearth in the drawing room, James gave Sarah a brotherly wink. "Smart thinking. Winston has felt quite useless the past few days."

"Lord James," Sarah said, her expression serious, "I need to speak with you."

James's expression suddenly became somber. "What is it?"

"I want to speak to you about your brother."

James's eyebrow arched in question. "What does Drake have to do with you?"

"Everything."

He frowned. "Everything?"

Sarah sighed and gave him the details of Victoria's adventure with Lord Nightham and the special license.

James smiled and gave Sarah a brotherly tap on her hand. "I already know about that. You must not worry about it."

"But you don't know that Victoria married Nightham, do you?"

"By Jove, you jest?"

Sarah, having extracted more details out of Victoria, gave James the remainder of the story, including the part about Drake finding the ruby ring and accusing Victoria of stealing it.

James shook his head. "My brother is a fool when it comes to women. Ever since he married Honoria, he has hardened his heart to any female at all."

"Then you will have to tell him the truth."

James pulled nervously at his neckcloth. "Me?"

"Yes, you. There is no other gentleman that I trust. Why, you are like a brother to me. I beg you. Please."

"Hell's bells." He flushed at the sound of Sarah's gasp. "Beg your pardon, but that is simply out of the question. No one tells Drake something like that and lives to tell about it."

Drake sat at the card table at White's, betting outrageous amounts of money, but much to his regret, it did nothing to drown his sorrows or his memories of the turquoise-eyed siren who had claimed his heart.

"Drake," James whispered over his shoulders, "I need a word with you."

Drake picked up his cards for another round. "No."

"A word, if you please."

"As I recall, you are hypothetically to be stationed at the townhouse at this very moment. I believe father has set up an around the clock schedule to guard the place."

"Father is there."

"So then," Drake glanced up, "why not join us for a game of vingt-et-un after this?" He leaned back and dragged another chair across the floor. The other players were paying attention to their drinks and cards, ignoring the two brothers.

James frowned. "I need to talk to you, not play games."

"If you don't want to play, go away."

Scowling, James removed himself from the card table and waited in another room. But Drake sensed his brother's impatience. Could he not drink and gamble in peace without his entire family interfering?

After a half-hour of cards, Drake gathered his earnings and headed for James who was nursing his second glass of brandy. Drake leaned against the wall with arms crossed. "Well, what the hell do you want?"

Voices lifted from the adjacent room.

James pointed to the chair beside him. "Sit down. I would like to speak to you about Victoria."

The only other gentleman in the room had his ear to a corner table due to too many spirits.

Drake's answer was to push away from the wall and stalk across the room to another table, grabbing a glass of Madeira.

James shot from his seat and before Drake could take a sip, his brother slapped the drink out of his hands. "By Jove, Drake, you will listen to me."

Drake's hand shot out as he grabbed his brother by the cravat. "Another act like that and you will find yourself on the floor like the last time you were here, except this time I will help you to it."

James gave his brother a belligerent stare. "I have no wish to fight, but for your sake, I will. Besides, I promised Sarah."

Drake released him. "Sarah? What has she to do with this?"

James took a seat and lowered his voice. "I am like a brother to her now. She has confided to me that she's afraid for her cousin and only wants her happiness. She told me about what you found in Victoria's room."

Drake's expression stilled.

"I know how you feel, but hear me out. Victoria did not steal that ring. Nightham was her husband."

Drake stared at James thoughtfully, then sank into a nearby chair. "Go on."

"Sarah told me the vows between Nightham and Victoria were said by special license minutes before our friend was murdered."

"I thought it a slight possibility"—the shock was apparent in Drake's voice—"but she never said a thing to me."

"Perhaps she was afraid to tell you. You do have a way of frightening people."

Drake felt about as small as Captain Whitie. Had his anger at Honoria caused Victoria not to trust him? He gazed into James's pitying eyes and said the words before he could take them back. "I was a fool."

"Yes, you were," James said curtly. "A blind fool at that."

You are a fool, Drake. A blind fool. Drake recoiled in his chair as Victoria's words came back to haunt him.

After a moment he stared at the sickening smile on his brother's lips. "And why is that so funny, pray tell?"

"Funny? It's hilarious." James slapped the table with an open hand. "Heaven help us all when you two have children."

Drake smiled, warming to the idea of having children with Victoria. Was this what love was? To want to live the rest of your life with someone and keep her safe? To give her children? To worry over her every need? Yes, his heart answered back. Yes.

A commotion near the front door drew their attention.

"I say," James said, frowning as he made his way toward the crowd. "I believe there's been a fire at one of the hotels."

Drake stood behind him.

The crowd was so loud James had to scream. "Lord Hamilton's family was staying there! His two children are dead!"

Drake grimaced. He barely knew the baron, but the thought of two small children dying in the fire made him ill.

Suddenly, James turned and grabbed his brother's shoulders. "Wendover was staying at the same hotel. Fire's out now, but it seems the earl was one of the victims."

Drake questioned one of the gentlemen who was at the hotel. The man told him the earl's signet ring was found on his burnt body. Drake hated to admit it, but a part of him reveled at the man's death. Now that Wendover was gone, Drake would travel back to the Boxing Boar Inn and find out exactly what had transpired between Nightham and Victoria.

Had they truly been married? No vows had been recorded at the church. Something was definitely askew. There had been no witnesses, and the local vicar had denied servicing any such ceremony.

Drake wanted to marry Victoria as soon as possible, but he wanted to clear the slate first, and if that meant going back to the Boxing Boar Inn, he would do so without Victoria the wiser.

He felt a grin stretching across his face. Heaven help him. He loved her.

Chapter Twenty

"Vicki! Do you want to go with Mrs. Dorling and me?"

Victoria felt every bounce of William's feet as he jumped on her bed. It was early morning and she was barely awake.

It had been three days since she had seen the marquess, and he was still avoiding her, even though she had received a dozen roses and a written apology about his behavior with the ring.

But the misery of that last meeting still plagued her mind. By apologizing, she knew he was dissolving any ties to their relationship in a gentlemanly manner. Yet in the letter, he begged her to trust him.

Her heart ached, but it mattered not, because this morning she was going to take a ride to see her solicitor. Whatever information he had gathered, she would take the news back to Aunt Phoebe and tell her the whole of it, from the flight with Nightham to Wendover's threats. Wendover was dead and a scandal seemed far less dangerous now than the thought of Wendover killing William.

"So, my little pirate, where are you going?" she finally asked her cousin when he stopped jumping.

"A drive in Hyde Park. Old Georgie's going to let us use his fancy phaeton when he comes for breakfast. We can all take turns."

With a roar of triumph, William leapt off her bed, his sword whipping excitedly about his head. "One of his drivers will be at the reins, and I might be able to have a go at the horses. Four white horses, Vicki!"

His voice was so ecstatic that Victoria could not hold back her chuckle of delight. "William, you should not call His Grace, Old Georgie. He will be your stepfather in a few weeks, you know."

William looked away, then put one hand on his hip and let out a weary sigh. "Listen, we are leaving in a few minutes. There will not be anyone at the park this early. We can have it all to ourselves. Do you want to go with us? It will be a tight squeeze, but I am rather small, and you can ride beside us and then Mrs. Dorling can switch places with you."

Victoria felt a grin tug at her lips at the thought of Mrs. Dorling riding her horse. "Not today, William."

"Awwww, Vicki."

Victoria sighed as he jumped on her bed again and continued his bouncing. She quickly moved to her sitting table, pulling a brush through her hair. Her mind ran over the past few days, including the facts about Wendover's death. She felt sinful, but she was glad that he was dead. It was only Lord Drakefield and Nightham who haunted her dreams now.

William jumped off the bed. "Vicki! Look at how your hair flies in the air and crackles like those bugs I step on every summer." He took the brush from her hands and pulled it through her mane of mahogany curls and squealed in delight. "It makes snapping noises like guts squishing on the rocks in the hot sun."

Victoria grinned at her reflection in the looking glass. William had her hair standing on end like some madwoman. She frowned suddenly. Was she mad for loving someone who would never love her back?

"You best get going, William. Save a ride for me another day."

"Oh, very well, me princess. But I will not always have four white horses to take along." He slapped her brush on the table and made a sinister face in the looking glass. "I will look for tiny, tiny creatures. An entire hat full." He ran to the door and laughed. "So beware!"

"William!"

He glanced over his shoulders and quirked a blond brow. "Don't worry. This time they are for Sarah."

She heard him giggle as he closed the door, and she thought she heard the word *guts.* She would have to warn Sarah about checking her bed before she turned in for the night.

A half-hour later, the duke and James showed for breakfast. Stanby personally delivered another bouquet of roses for Victoria from the marquess. Of course, the giant was deflated when he heard that Mrs. Dorling was out riding with William.

The duke glanced up from the breakfast table and chuckled at Stanby's frown. "Mrs. Dorling went along to watch over the boy. By now William is gallivanting about Hyde Park with my new phaeton. Hopefully, they will have the place all to themselves. If you wish, Stanby, stay here and wait for them."

Stanby gave a stiff upper lip and nodded. "Thank you, Your Grace. I believe I will."

Phoebe smiled at the giant. "Mrs. Dorling would enjoy seeing you when she returns. Why do you not wait for her in the blue salon?"

"Thank you, my lady." Stanby hovered by the door.

Phoebe noted his tight expression and frowned. "What is it, Stanby?"

"If you will forgive my rudeness, my lady. I feel quite ill at ease about Mrs. Dorling and William going out by themselves."

"Ah," Phoebe sighed. "McGraw is driving. So you see they are not alone."

James let out an amused snort and turned toward his father. "Are you saying it is only McGraw and Mrs. Dorling with that boy? You truly believe they can handle the situation?"

The duke cast his son a stern glare. James adjusted his neckcloth. Sarah giggled and Victoria pretended not to hear.

"My dear," Phoebe grinned at the duke. "William is a handful. I can see James was only concerned about the boy." She inclined her head toward James. "But depend upon it, Mrs. Dorling can handle him."

Stanby cleared his throat, and all heads turned in his direction.

The duke looked on, his brow furrowed. "What is it, Stanby?"

Stanby looked over the table. "I do beg your pardon, but Mrs. Dorling can usually handle the boy, however, I cannot put it out of my mind that Lord Wendover is still in the area. The man seemed quite unstable."

Phoebe's face paled.

"The man is dead," Victoria said with a frown. "The paper said so."

"If you pardon my bluntness, Lady Victoria," Stanby said, "the earl's body was not recognizable. They only assumed it was him because of his ring."

Victoria visibly paled.

"What Stanby says is quite true," James said as he cut into his kippers. "The thing is, the body was assumed to be Wendover's, but it could be someone else. However, the investigators were almost positive it was the earl's remains. Since the man has not shown his face at all the last few days, and his death has been in all the papers, I fail to see how it could be otherwise."

"Nevertheless," Stanby said with a grimace. "Something don't seem right."

Victoria felt herself grow warm as Stanby excused himself and moved to the hall toward the blue salon, his face showing every wary emotion he felt.

After a stunned silence, the duke tried to change the subject. Nothing from the weather to Prinny's latest escapade seemed to help the icy feeling that flowed through Victoria's veins.

After breakfast, Phoebe, the duke, James, Sarah, and Victoria gathered in the drawing room.

Sick about the possibility of Wendover being alive, Victoria put on a calm face as she prepared to leave for her solicitor's. She glanced out the window when a stylish phaeton whipped into view. She almost laughed when she saw the harried driver conduct the four magnificent white horses to a halt in front of the townhouse. William must have driven the poor man daft. The amusement died on her lips the second she realized that the crazy driver was not McGraw, but her very own Mrs. Dorling with the driver slouched over the lady's lap.

Panic burned a path straight to her heart. "William!"

All heads snapped in her direction when she shouted the boy's name. She picked up her skirts and hurried toward the door.

"William?" Phoebe sent an alarmed look the duke's way. "Is he hurt? Oh, my baby!"

The duke pushed his chair back. James followed.

"McGraw's hurt!" Victoria cried to the two men behind her.

A sobbing Mrs. Dorling helped lower the man to James and the duke. The lady slipped Victoria a sealed letter, her entire body shaking. "Oh, my lady! It was someone with a mask. I was to give this only to you. That ogre took William. McGraw tried to defend us, but—" The housekeeper let out a deep sob. "The blood. Oh, the blood."

"He'll make it," the duke said grimly, looking over McGraw's wounds.

"Alice!" Stanby came bounding out the door and ran toward Mrs. Dorling, his face almost as white as hers. The large man cursed as he gently brought the older woman up the stairs and into the townhouse.

Victoria felt ill as she clutched the letter to her pounding chest. Wendover was alive! The man had taken William. Her throat tightened with dread. Dear, precious William. All that mattered was William. She had to concentrate on William.

The doctor was called to attend the driver, and by that time Phoebe had taken ill on the sofa in the drawing room. Sarah hovered over her aunt, tapping her face with a cool cloth. The duke sat at his fiancée's side.

"Everything will be quite all right Phoebe, dearest. William will be returned." The duke's voice was calm, but Victoria knew he was anything but tranquil. His face was hard. His gaze the same. She recognized the lethal glint harboring in those dark eyes. They were a different color from Drake's, but they gave off the same surge of power and determination that no one would want to cross.

However, it seemed in all the confusion, no one had seen

Mrs. Dorling hand Victoria the letter. Victoria moved to the hearth and broke open the seal, her heart beating madly.

James quickly moved beside her. "It would be best if I saw that first, Victoria," he said in a firm voice. "I saw Mrs. Dorling slip it to you. The others may not have seen, but I did."

"The letter is for me, not you."

"That does not mean a thing. Give it to me." He shoved out his hand. "This is William's life that hangs in the balance. Do not keep your secrets from us any longer."

The fire flickered beside her and her mouth went dry. *William. Think of William.*

"After I have read it, you may have it." She said the lie as smooth as silk. At this point she did not care. No one else would be hurt because of that horrid man. No one.

"Very well." James waited impatiently, his gaze hardening with every passing second.

Victoria turned her back to him. Her shoulders slumped forward as she read the letter. Wendover wanted her to meet him one block from the townhouse at precisely twelve o'clock noon. He had William and would kill the boy if she were but a minute late. No one was to come in her place and she was not to share the contents of the letter with anyone. He would be watching closely.

Dear merciful heaven! What was she to do? She glanced at James. She could not let him read it. Her stomach turned with indecision. He would hate her for what she was about to do, but she had to do it and do it quick.

He took a threatening step toward her. "Victoria, I will have that letter now."

"Goodness, has Sarah fainted, too?" As James abruptly turned his head toward the doors, Victoria took the moment to crumple the letter into a ball and send it flying into the fire.

"Why, there's nothing wrong—"

As James turned back, his face filled with rage the moment he realized what she had done. He pushed her aside and grabbed the poker to fish the remains of the paper out of the fire. There was nothing left but black cinders. If looks could kill, Victoria thought she was about to die. She held her breath.

"Lord Wendover has William," she replied softly. "We are to wait until he sends another note."

She lied to him, of course, but she had told some of the truth. By the time they guessed the whole of it, William would be back home and she would be long gone. But she could not dwell on the horrid notion of being with Wendover. She had to focus her thoughts on her sweet little William. She would welcome any little creature he put in her bed, if only he would be returned.

Less than a half-hour later, Drake blew into the house like a storm wreaking havoc with anything in its path. "Where is she?" His loud voice bounced off the crimson wallpaper in the front hall. Winston had sent a message, telling him about the sordid happenings and the marquess was fit to be tied.

"You may find her in the dining room," James replied coolly, suddenly appearing in the hall. "We made a call to Bow Street."

Drake fisted his hands at his sides. "Victoria!"

A shudder shot through Victoria's body. Her teacup rattled, and she spilled the hot liquid on her skirt. Sarah peeked up, her eyes puffy from crying. Phoebe rested her head on George's shoulder.

Victoria blinked. The pirate appeared in the doorway. Two long, muscular legs were planted firmly on the floor as if they were holding up the entire room with his hovering stance. His neckcloth was askew and his hands were clenched at his sides. Inky black hair hung loosely around his shoulders and over one eye. His fitted brown jacket made his shoulders look wide and powerful. But it was those piercing gray eyes that froze Victoria to her seat.

"Yes?" She made an extreme effort to hold her chin steady.

He strode toward to her and lifted her firmly from her seat. "I wish to speak to you. Now."

She did not fight him, but followed him to the library where he settled her in a wing chair and hovered over her like some dangerous pirate.

"What the devil is going on in that little mind of yours?"

"Nothing," she said, her guilty gaze sweeping the floor.

He leaned over and straddled her with his arms. "Do not lie to me. You received a letter from Wendover. What did it say?"

"H-he has W-William." She could not keep the shakiness from her voice.

His voice instantly softened. "What else, sweetheart? What did Wendover say?"

Sweetheart. She peered up at him and saw the lines of strain across his face. She did love him so.

"What else, Victoria? What else was in the letter?"

She bit her bottom lip. "I cannot tell you."

"This is no game, Victoria." His nostrils flared. "You will tell me the contents of the letter or else."

Her gaze narrowed. "Or else what?"

"Can you not trust me for once?" He glared back.

But she did trust him now. She just didn't want him hurt.

A numbing silence blanketed the room. The standoff continued until Drake threatened to have her watched day and night until she told him what he wanted. To Victoria's surprise, she ended up in her bedchambers, treated like a prisoner at Newgate, with one of the duke's barrel-chested footmen guarding her door.

Frustrated, Drake slapped the wing chair with such force, it went careening on its back. He checked his timepiece, then snapped it back into his pocket. His mind raced with fear, because as sure as the ocean was blue, he knew that Victoria had some little scheme that she was not sharing with anybody but herself. No doubt, she would act on it if given half the chance.

Chapter Twenty-One

*D*rat! Victoria paced the floor of her bedchamber. The nerve of that man posting a guard. She had bested him once, and she could do it again. She glanced over her shoulder at the window and pursed her lips thoughtfully. With a quick jerk, she started pulling the sheets off her bed.

It was twelve o'clock when she stood on the street corner, the hood of her dark blue cloak hiding her face. Her heart picked up speed as the clip-clopping sound of a carriage rolled slowly toward her. She glanced up at the glossy black door that stopped in front of her. The steps were let down by an ugly-looking footman. She took one last glance over her shoulder before she hitched up her skirts and climbed inside.

"Good afternoon, Lady Victoria. So nice you could make our little rendezvous."

"What do you mean she has left the premises?" Drake bellowed. "Gone is more like it!"

He grabbed the sizeable footman who stood guard outside Victoria's bedchambers and shoved him aside. James came bounding up the stairs just as Drake plowed past the door.

Drake's eyes widened in alarm as he took in the sight of her naked mattress. He spun toward the open window where a light breeze whispered against the curtains. He stood there gaping.

She had done it to him again. He looked at the sky as light ribbons of pink fell against the sinking sun. When he found that woman he would shackle her to his leg and never let her go. They would be married before she knew what happened to her.

Back at the Boxing Boar Inn, he had discovered that Victoria and Nightham had never been married. Some drunk pretended to be a vicar, only wanting Nightham's coin, but Drake suspected someone else was involved because the man's wife had found him dead the very next day. The imposter had two witnesses to go along with the jest, as he called it, for a very old friend. But it had not been a jest at all, it was a hoax, and stupid Nightham had never caught on.

The possibility that Wendover had something to do with the imposter and the man's death was not far from Drake's thoughts. However, it mattered not. All that mattered was retrieving Victoria and William safe and sound.

James peered out the window, an incredulous look blanketing his face. "Hell's bells! She tied the sheets together."

Drake slapped his hand against the frame of the bed. He cursed a blue streak as he stalked from the room and hurried downstairs.

News of Victoria's disappearance spread through the house in no time. Drake turned to leave.

James stood beside him. "Let me go with you. Father has no need of me here. You do."

"Get your things and let's go."

Victoria trained her gaze on William's slumped shoulders. Dark golden lashes swept across the boys pale cheeks as he slept. How she hated Wendover. Her eyes slowly lifted across the leather seat to meet the man's sinister smile.

"Enjoying yourself, my dear?" He swiftly placed his hand on her knee. Angrily, she flicked it away. His eyes narrowed, and he gave her a swift slap across her cheek. It felt like a crack of a whip, and Victoria's head snapped back to the side.

Her hand instinctively came up to rub the sting away. Tears began to well in her eyes. But she would not cry. She would not give the scoundrel the satisfaction of knowing he had hurt her.

"Go ahead and weep, my dear. The sniveling boy will not hear you. I gave him enough laudanum to last an entire day, if not more. Not enough until we arrive in Gretna Green, but then I do have more."

Gretna Green? Did he believe he could marry her in Scotland? It would take days to drive there. The man was mad.

"I suppose you are wondering who that dead man was at the hotel." He raised a brow and chuckled. "The stupid servant did not fetch my dinner fast enough. Ah, but it was fortunate that he also decided to steal my signet ring at the same time, do you not think so, my dear?"

Victoria felt her stomach roll. Had he killed the servant at the hotel to make it look like his own death? She was a fool to have believed that once she showed her face Wendover would honor his word and release William. She did not want to hear anything from this vile man.

"Lord Drakefield will follow, you know."

"If he does, he's a dead man."

But Victoria would not give in to defeat. Drake would find them. She knew that now. She did trust him. It was only a matter of time.

Ignoring the earl's glare, she placed her hand protectively on William's forehead. She knew Wendover wanted her inheritance. But the stipulations of her aunt's will stated that she must be married for a minimum of six months for her husband to have access to her sizable trust.

But she guessed that Wendover would probably kill her first, pretending she was alive somewhere, saying he sent her off for a little trip to the Continent or something of that sort.

She fought to clear her mind of the horrid thoughts. For William's sake, she had to find a way out of this. If only she had left a letter, telling Drake of her plans. But he would find her. Time would be of the essence, and if Victoria knew anything about the Marquess of Drakefield, time was his specialty.

It took Drake and James all night to find anyone who had seen Victoria or the boy. The witness, a drunken Lord Hazelby, had seen Victoria's descent from the window and other attributes of the lady as well. The baron happened to be passing through the neighborhood and had seen the lady in question jumping down from the last knotted sheet.

"Quite a good show," he had said with a hiccup, grinning. "Handsome ankles. And those shiny locks of hers . . ." Hiccup. "But it was those legs that got my attention. Long and slim and, well, you know, old boy, they—"

He stopped his informative speech as soon as he caught sight of the marquess's hardened gaze. "I only meant to say that she was rather fetching—"

"You say one word of this to anyone, Hazelby, and I will meet you at dawn. Do you understand?"

The baron gulped at Drake's command. "You can depend upon my utmost discreetness, Drakefield. No need to recall a thing. Saw nothing at all. Not at all."

Less than an hour later, Drake paced the drawing room of his London townhouse, having ascertained that Victoria had stupidly hopped into a carriage only a block from her home. Bow Street had discovered that Wendover had hired a carriage from a stable near Cavendish Square early that morning.

James picked up his drink. "Doubt if Wendover's still in London, if that's the case."

Drake strolled about the room, his jaw tightening. "Gretna Green is always a possibility. If my guess is correct, he wants to marry Victoria to make certain he retains the rights to her inheritance." He paused. "Not only that, I believe Wendover killed Nightham."

"Are you certain?" James asked.

"Nightham was in the way. It all makes perfect sense."

James paled a little. "Cold-blooded murder?"

"Yes," Drake said, making a fist. "They have almost a day's ride on us. But if I'm wrong, I need you here, James. Do you understand?"

James put down his drink. "I understand, but that does not mean I like it."

A bundle of yellow curls brushed against Victoria's cheek as she swayed in her seat. "Laudanum," she said, her head tingling like tiny pins.

"Yes, my dear," Wendover drawled. "I slipped it into your tea at the last posting inn. It was the only way I could get you here without speaking to anyone."

"Here?" she said, frowning. Had it been days or merely hours since she had been away from home? Somehow, she vaguely recalled a dirty inn where she'd slept, or was it two or three inns? The laudanum was clouding her mind.

"Yes, laudanum does seem to make time go by faster, does it not?" Wendover was so close to her, his sour breath blew across her face. His hand slipped to her knee. "Soon you will be my wife. Then I care not who you tell about what. For once you are my wife, I will own you." His hideous laughter resounded off the walls of the carriage.

Victoria felt stripped as his gaze traveled over her person. Dear heaven, what had he done to her while she was sleeping?

He seemed to read her mind. He smiled like a lion ready to devour his prey. "I am not such an ogre as that, my dear. I would not force you before we are married. I do have my scruples."

Victoria felt the bile rise to her throat. What kind of madman was he?

William began to wake beside her. "Vicki, where are we? I had a terrible dream about old Wendover. He was so mean. He was an evil villain."

"Thank you for the compliment, boy." Wendover chuckled as he sipped from his bottle of whiskey.

William huddled close to his cousin, his eyes wide with fear. "I'm . . . hungry, Vicki."

"You should be hungry," Wendover said sarcastically. "Tea and laudanum are not quite the diet for a growing boy. Are they, Victoria?"

Victoria cradled William in her arms. She could feel his body trembling uncontrollably. Anger lit a fire inside her. "How could you terrify a child like this, much less letting him starve?"

"Starve?" he said calmly. "That is the least of your worries, my dear." His hand touched her leg again and he laughed. "Starving comes in many forms, Victoria. Many forms indeed."

Drake pulled into the yard of the coaching inn and jumped down from his horse. He hoped his information was correct. Wendover would make his stop here. While taking a short cut across the fields, Drake had seen a black coach along the road, most probably Wendover's.

He had questioned the owner of an inn about twelve hours back. Money and threats helped the owner remember a man of Wendover's description and a woman with a sleeping boy. They had ordered two rooms, the lady and boy having been guarded by an ugly-looking brute harboring a pistol in his coat pocket. Information was also supplied that this inn was to be their next stop.

Drake knew it would be better to surprise Wendover at the inn, rather than stopping the carriage along the way and chancing a shoot-out, putting Victoria and William in danger. It would be more than an hour before they showed. He would wait.

Taking a seat inside the inn, he ordered food and drink. He was tired. Hungry. And mad as hell.

Chapter Twenty-Two

*T*he moment the carriage rolled to a stop, Wendover turned and grabbed hold of Victoria's arm. "Do not even think of leaving, my dear. The door will be locked, and if you dare make a sound"—he pulled a pistol out of his coat pocket and pointed it at William—"the boy will suffer."

A sudden chill hung on the ends of his words as he left the carriage, but instead of fear flooding her senses, Victoria was fuming with rage. The insolence of the man. She would not be his next victim and neither would William.

There would be no help coming from the driver. In fact, the big lummox was guarding them now. And William was still sleeping off the laudanum.

She gazed frantically about the carriage. The curtains were drawn closed, and she dare not open them in fear Wendover might see her. She eyed the small black case that he had stashed beneath the red wool blanket resting on the floorboard. The case held laudanum and heavens knew what else. She found the bottle of whiskey stuffed in the corner of the leather seat and jerked it beneath her skirts. If nothing else, she would be ready when he came for her.

"Vicki," William asked, his eyes blinking against his drowsiness. "Is he going to kill us?"

"No." She turned and patted William's head, her throat growing thick with emotion.

"He said he would kill me if I caused him any trouble." William's voice trembled with fear.

Victoria held him close. "I will not let him hurt you. Now,

sit up and take some very large breaths. That's it. Feeling better?"

A shot rang out. Victoria jumped.

"Do you think he shooted someone?" William asked, his eyes widening.

"I wish someone shot him, but I highly doubt it. If luck is with us, it was a highwayman." Victoria shook the carriage door, trying desperately to open it. Drat! It was locked!

"Vicki," the boy whispered with a shaking voice. "I hear footsteps."

"Shhhh." She crouched on the seat cushion and pushed William to the far corner of the coach. "He's coming."

William whimpered. Victoria took a few deep breaths, trying to control her pounding heart. "When I hit him on the head, William, you run out of this carriage. You may feel drowsy now, but once the air hits you, you'll wake up soon enough. And scream like a real pirate. Someone will come to our aid."

For the first time in days, William's eyes lit with excitement. "I can scream quite well, you know. I have been practicing. Can I curse like a pirate, too? Like Drake?"

"I don't care what you say, just jump out when I tell you. Here he comes. Now act like you're asleep, and when I say go, you run like the devil."

"The devil?" William asked incredulously. "How does he run? Mama said I'm not supposed to be like him."

"William, run when the time comes. Now, hush."

Victoria pushed William back and huddled against her seat, her hands shaking. For not the first time, she wished she had told Drake the truth and that she loved him, whether he loved her or not. Now, she might never get the chance.

She stilled when the door began to rattle. She could hear Wendover cursing with words she had never heard before. His sinister face appeared in her mind's eye and a wave of nausea rolled through her.

"Vicki." William peeked up. "That is not—"

"Quiet."

"But—"

"Hush."

William covered his head with his hands.

A second later, the door flew open. With a powerful

swing, Victoria slammed the black case toward the man's face. Then came the bottle of whiskey barreling down onto his head. The man groaned in protest. Glass sprayed all over the carriage. Her feet slammed his neck to the floor. "William! GO!"

"But Vicki—"

"Leave! Now!" She gripped the boy's arm, yanked him across the seat, then over the man's head and threw him outside.

"But Vicki!" William was almost sobbing now.

She could not believe him. "I will be all right William. Run!"

She was just about to step over the body and out of the carriage when a strong hand gripped her ankle and pulled her down. Her bottom hit the floor with a thud. Oh, merciful heavens! He was going to kill her!

"HELP!" she screamed.

"Confound it, woman! Do you always have to fight me?"

Victoria stared back into the most heavenly pair of gray eyes that she had ever seen. "Drake." With a groan of relief, she threw her arms around his beautiful head of black hair, now dripping with whiskey and bits of glass.

He whipped his head back and pulled a few of the glass fragments out of his hair. "Devil take it. Gentleman Jackson's is nothing compared to you." He raised his hand to rub his head and winced.

"But Wendover?" she asked shakily.

"Dead. I shot him in self-defense."

"You shot him?" William's awed voice came from behind the carriage.

Victoria shuddered with relief. "He was a horrid man." She would have cried if it were not for Drake's awkward position. She giggled instead and held her hands to her mouth. "You should have told me it was you at the door. I could have killed you."

"Hey, are you listening to me?" William stomped his foot as a crowd began to form in front of the inn.

"Listening is not one of your cousin's good points, William," Drake said, glaring in Victoria's direction.

"Drake, I had no idea it was you at the door." She scooted back, her hand trying to push him away.

He scooted forward, pulled her out of the carriage, and scooped her into his arms. "You, madam, are going with me."

"Truly, I did not think . . ." she said, cautiously.

"You never think. You act on impulse, and I for one am going to stop that once and for all."

Victoria did not want to ask how he would do that. But her pulse quickened at the speculation. For once, she kept her mouth closed.

His lips pressed tightly together, Drake carried her toward the inn with an excited William by her side. The boy looked radiantly happy as if he was not affected by Lord Wendover's death at all . . . or the laudanum.

"I did try to tell you, Vicki, but you refused to listen." William's little chest heaved up and down while he panted.

She glared over Drake's arm that was wrapped around her shoulder. "Tell me what, William?"

"I knew it was me pirate at the door all the time. I could tell by the way he spoke."

Victoria glanced up at Drake, recalling the string of curses spewing forth from his mouth. He shrugged as if to show her he had no idea what they were speaking about.

"And pray tell, how did he speak, William?"

"He talked like a pirate," William said with pride. "I told you he would take care of the villain for us."

Victoria's heart swelled as she looked into Drake's smiling eyes. "I knew you would come. I should have trusted you before. Will you ever forgive me?"

"I will only forgive you if you will only trust me."

She peered up at him, her heart in her eyes. "I do trust you. I did trust you. I just didn't want you hurt."

"Good." Drake gently set her down just outside the door of the inn, and made no attempt to hide the fact he was studying her. By now a crowd had gathered around them.

"Drake?" she asked hesitantly. "Will they hold you for questioning? What about the magistrate?"

The crowd began to murmur. Drake locked eyes with hers and she longed for him to hold her. Her throat filled with emotion, and she knew she needed to tell him now. "I love you, Drake."

"I know, sweetheart." A muscle flickered in his jaw and he bent down on one knee, taking hold of her hand. "And I love you, Victoria."

Her face blushed. "Please, Drake. For goodness sake, stand up. I know you love me. But everyone is watching us."

"Confound it, woman. Would you please close that beautiful mouth of yours for one minute and let me have my say?"

Her lips snapped shut.

"Better." He pulled her naked hand to his lips. "I am asking you to be my wife. Please do me the honor of accepting."

The crowd hushed, waiting for her answer.

Tears spilled over her lids. "I would be pleased to marry you."

"Don't ye know? Pirates don't speak of love!" William frowned and threw up his hands, disgusted. "You just shot a man!"

Drake rose and gave William a stern glare. "I shot the earl in self-defense, not because I wanted to. And love is very important for pirates."

"Oh, yuck!"

Though William was disgusted, the crowd applauded as Drake carried Victoria to another carriage owned by the proprietor of the inn.

"We will be married today, my love." His voice was soft and gentle, caressing her heart.

Victoria frowned. He did not know about her marriage to Nightham. She had to tell him. "But I cannot marry you. At least not—"

Her mouth was smothered by his kiss. "Sweetheart, I have a special license and the vicar is waiting in the next village. Do not ask me how I managed. Suffice to say, the deed will be accomplished and we will be married tonight."

Before she could answer, Drake captured her mouth again. She felt in heaven as she succumbed to the hunger of his kiss. All thoughts of Nightham and Wendover dissolved.

"Hey," William interrupted. "What about me?"

Drake let Victoria slip from his hold as he turned, lifting the boy into the carriage. "Inside, me pirate."

"But what about Wendover?" Victoria whispered as she entered the carriage.

Drake hopped in after them and closed the door. "The magistrate happened to be in the inn when Wendover drew his pistol. There will be no investigation. We can leave free and clear."

The wedding took only a few minutes. Victoria had tried to tell Drake of her former marriage, or at least the question of its finality, but he refused to listen about Nightham at all. It mattered not. He would not hear another word about the man. He asked her to trust him, and she finally agreed. What had she been thinking?

When Drake bent down to kiss her, William protested uproariously. The witnesses took their leave and the vicar moved from the room to grab some papers to be signed.

"You don't understand, Drake. I do trust you. But you must listen to me."

His gray eyes devoured her. "Everything is fine. We are married. William will not come between us with his sword. The boy has seen us kiss before this." He turned to the small boy and winked. "Am I not correct, William?"

"Aye me pirate," William said, frowning as he stomped his foot. "I have seen it all before, and I don't like it."

Drake turned back to his wife. "I believe it is time you call me Jonathan?"

"No, I—"

Drake set her away from him. "What do you mean, no?"

"I mean no, Jonathan. I cannot marry you."

Drake laughed. "Too late."

"But what about Nightham? I married him at that inn. I tried to tell you before but you would not listen."

"No, you did not."

"Maybe you did not hear me the first time since your kisses stopped whatever explanation I was going to say. But please, you must believe me that I married Nightham, or at least I believe I did, but I have no papers to prove it."

"I heard you the first time, sweetheart. And I said, no, you did not."

"I did."

"Did not."

She was simply beside herself. "Oh, why do you tease me?"

"I have information that you were never married to Nightham. The man who was supposed to have performed the ceremony was not a vicar at all, but an imposter, and he was found dead the very next day by his wife. I don't have proof, but I believe Wendover may have had something to do with the man's death. The imposter threw in a few words that sounded like a wedding ceremony, and it seems Nightham was duped as well. You have no certificate stating you were married. Nothing was found on Nightham to contradict my findings. The old man, a painter by trade, had done this before when in his cups. Whether Wendover had something to do with the fraudulent ceremony or the man's death, we will never know. The two witnesses are missing, too. But in essence, you see, my sweet, you were never married. Ever. Until now."

"I was never married?" Her eyes grew wide.

Suddenly his jaw went taut. "You were not with Nightham later, were you? I mean, as man and wife?"

She felt the blood surge through her veins at the implications of his words. "I most certainly was not." She lifted her chin. "As you said before, I was not married."

He let out a light-hearted chuckle. "Sweetheart, then I am your one and only husband." He grabbed her by the waist and pulled her gently toward him. "And you are my wife." His hungry kiss was a command with promises of things to come.

"Drake, please. William is but only a few feet away."

"Almost ten feet," William cried out. "But this pirate can hear everything loud and clear, matie!"

Drake's chest rumbled with mirth. "Hop in the carriage, William. We will be with you momentarily."

"Very well, me pirate." But William stayed where he was, watching the two of them with wide, curious eyes.

Drake turned his most fearsome glare upon the boy. "Now!"

"Very well!" William groaned and scurried out the door.

Drake pressed a light kiss on Victoria's open wrist. "I love you, *wife*. Margueretta loves you, too. She told me so."

"And I love you and your daughter, *me pirate*."

"And I will always love you," his gray eyes twinkled, "even though you are a pauper."

She pushed him away. "What do you mean, a pauper?"

"Your trust was not a trust at all. Your great aunt's money was invested in a shipping company that went under. I retrieved that information only recently. The trust seemed solid enough at the time it was made, but evidently there was nothing to it as of two months ago. The credit at the bank is worth nothing. They were as gulled as you were."

"What about the countess?"

He laughed. "Nightham's mother will have to hand over everything she bought, including that wee little cottage."

"The poor lady."

"Oh, she is not as poor as you believe, sweetheart."

Victoria smiled, trying to ignore the foreign aching in her limbs. "But I thought you married me for my inheritance."

"Inheritance be gone. I love you."

His lips slowly descended to meet hers. His hands moved slowly down her back. She never dreamed it would feel like this.

"What kind of pirate are you?" William bellowed, peeking through the church doors. "The carriage is waiting to take us to that inn up the road. Are you coming or not? I heard someone say there is only one room left. Hurry up or that will be gone, too."

After speaking to the vicar and signing some papers, Victoria hurried toward the carriage. Drake followed behind her, his eyes widening in horror as William's comment finally registered in his brain. "One bedchamber? Confound it, Victoria! There must be some mistake. I cannot bear to be with that . . . boy . . . on my wedding night!" He flipped open his pocket watch and scowled.

"Oh, Jonathan," Victoria said with a twinkle in her eye as she glanced over her shoulder. "It's only one night."

"One night too many if you ask me."

"Who was asking?" William screamed from the carriage.

Victoria bit back a laugh, and before there would be another shooting, she had to kiss her husband long and hard before he would enter the carriage.

Chapter Twenty-Three

$\mathcal{V}$ictoria and Drake followed behind William as the boy burst through the door of Phoebe's townhouse, his feet thumping on the floor sounding like a stampede of wild elephants.

"Anybody home?" he yelled, climbing the stairs.

George, James, Phoebe, and Sarah appeared at the drawing room doors.

Phoebe grabbed her little boy, crushing him in her arms. "William. Oh, William!"

The boy hugged her just as hard. Then he looked up and twisted his lips into a frown, embarrassed by her show of affection. "Mama, I feel like a lemon you squeezed for tea."

"Victoria." Phoebe sobbed again, hugging her niece. "Are you all right, my dear?" She pulled Victoria back and held her by the shoulders. "Did that madman hurt you?"

"I'm fine. Truly."

Drake threw his arm around Victoria's waist. "She will be fine as soon as we have her home." He swallowed his words when Victoria's elbow caught him in the ribs. Blast. It was the same place William had been jabbing him all night. The boy had refused to sleep in the extra bed.

"Home?" the duke asked, narrowing his brow.

But before the duke could ask any more questions, Phoebe grabbed Drake by the neck and kissed him on the cheek. "I don't know how to thank you for all you have done for me."

Drake squeezed Victoria's waist a little tighter. "I take it you received the missive that we were quite fine. But I hate to tell you, I had some rather selfish reasons for finding these two rapscallions myself."

"But Drake," James broke in, "the story is that you shot Wendover."

"Wait!" William's hands waved wildly in the air. "I want to tell the story. Me, me, me!"

All eyes turned his way.

Victoria laughed. "You may tell everyone the story as soon as we all take a seat. I feel as if I have not slept for days."

"This way, maties," William said, marching into the drawing room, staring back at Drake and Victoria. "I am waiting for you two to sit down. Or do you want to leave and start kissing again?"

All heads snapped back to Drake and Victoria.

"Indeed, now that you mention it," Drake drawled, but stopped abruptly when he felt another sharp poke to his back this time—his wife's finger to be precise. "Now that you mention it, I think that maybe I should be the one to begin."

"No!" William began jumping up and down. "I will! First, I was kidnapped!"

Victoria tugged Drake toward the sofa.

The boy drew in a heavy breath as his arm shot out toward Victoria. "Then, Vicki was kidnapped! Then the villain gave me a sleeping potion!"

"Oh, my poor boy," Phoebe wailed.

George patted her hand. "Go on, William."

"Then, the villain brought us to a wicked old castle."

"You mean the coaching inn, William," Victoria said.

"A castle!" William's jaw jutted forward in defense as he pointed to Drake. "Then our pirate saved us."

"How did he do that?" James asked, grinning.

William lifted his finger to his forehead and pulled the trigger. "He shot the villain right between the eyes."

"William," Victoria admonished. "It was not that way at all."

But it was too late. Phoebe was out cold, lying on George's lap. Despite the predicament, the duke seemed to be enjoying his hold on Phoebe. He lifted his gaze to the boy. "Go on, William."

With Drake's help, the story of Wendover's demise continued with the added note of Lord Nightham's murder at the inn.

William plopped himself on the Aubusson rug and blurted out, "The next thing that happened was the wedding."

"Wedding?" everyone asked in unison. Phoebe woke up.

"Yes, the wedding!" William ran to the sofa and threw his arms around Victoria and Drake. "We were married!"

The newlyweds left Phoebe's townhouse two hours later with Victoria's trunks in tow. When the carriage door closed, Drake drew in a deep breath. He was finally alone with his new bride.

However, before the vehicle moved on its way, Drake turned in surprise when he heard William's voice, bellowing like a foghorn at the bottom steps of the townhouse. "Wait, me pirate!"

Drake gazed out the window in disgust. The boy's feet were slapping hard against the walk.

"Wait!" William shouted, waving his hands.

Without hesitation, Drake grabbed the attention of the driver. "Move, Henry! Now! Double your wages this week if you lose him!" The horses moved faster.

Victoria's dark lashes swept off her cheeks in surprise. "But Jonathan, could we not—"

"No, we certainly cannot!" In one swift jerk he pulled his wife onto his lap.

"But what about William?" She laughed and turned her ear toward the curtained window. "What is he yelling about?"

"Who cares?"

She frowned.

Drake blew out a tired sigh. "Very well. I believe he said something about a wedding gift."

"A gift?"

He lifted her chin with his finger. "Forget about the gift. I love you."

"Oh, Jonathan. I love you, too."

He slipped a hand to her hip and could hear the thumping of her heart as his mouth swooped down to capture hers.

And then she screamed.

He screamed back, and she flew off his lap, ending up in the corner of the carriage. It happened so suddenly, Drake thought it was a dream. But he watched in horror as his wife crumpled into a tight little ball of shivering fear.

Despite the horrid fact that the exact moment he touched her, she had blasted his eardrums straight to hell, it took him five wretched seconds to deduce the exact cause of her scream was not because of him.

"Confound it all," he snapped. "I cannot believe this."

Victoria's arms flew wildly in the air as she scooted further into the corner. "Remove it at once! Jonathan! Pleeeease!"

"It's only Whitie." Drake stated in stupefied amazement as he grabbed the mouse off his wife's quivering legs and dangled the little beast by its tail.

"Are you laughing at me?" she asked. "Because, if you are, so help me . . ."

She left the threat unsaid, and Drake grimaced, swallowing his chuckle as thoughts of that little pirate invaded his mind. He stared at the shivering creature hanging mercilessly in the air, its pink feet running nowhere fast.

"Do you understand, sweetheart?"

Victoria's brows slammed into a large V. "No, I do not!"

Drake smiled, watching a pair of dainty ankles tilt his way. "*This,*" he wiggled the mouse, "is William's wedding gift. He must have put the beast inside the carriage before we were packed."

"Oh," was all she said when Drake plopped the poor little creature inside one of her hat boxes, replacing the lid.

"Come here, sweetheart." Drake grinned and gently eased her back on his lap. Her hold on his heart tightened. Precision and order in his life had flown out the window the minute he had laid eyes on this woman. But who cared about order in his life? Not him. Not anymore.

"And Whitie will not chew through that box?" she asked, clutching him tightly.

"Trust me, sweetheart."

"Oh, Jonathan, I do trust you. Always." She put a soft hand to his cheek.

When his wife's shaking hands circled his neck, he groaned. Yes, indeed, he would have to thank that little pirate many times over for the little wedding gift. And to think he only had to ask for a few of those furry gifts whenever his wife was angry with him. He would have her in his arms in no time. Yes, marriage would be wonderful.

"Jonathan?"

"Hmmm?" He glanced over her shoulder and took a quick peek at his pocket watch. Time was of the essence here. He snapped the watch closed and placed it on the seat. If everything went as planned, he would be at his townhouse in seven and a half minutes. Up the stairs. In his chambers—

"Jonathan, I said I loved you."

"I love you, too. For all time. Now trust me and don't worry. Not even about Captain Whitie. He's safe and secure. There is no way out." He watched a smile play across her lips and kissed her with all the passion he had held in for months.

He had no notion that only two feet away, a small white mouse peered through a freshly bitten hole in one red-striped hat box, and was chewing as fast as its little teeth could to rejoin the party.

This time Victoria's scream slammed clear down to Drake's toes. He jerked back, biting back an oath.

"Depend upon it! I am going strangle that cousin of yours!"

To Drake's horror, Captain Whitie scampered off Victoria's skirt and moved beneath the seat, dragging Drake's beloved timepiece behind him like some prized medal won in battle.

"Devil take it! Look at that!"

Victoria giggled. "It looks as if your time is gone forever, my lord."

Pausing, he shifted his gaze back to her. "Well, what the devil are we going to do about that hideous beast?"

"Confound it all," she said. "Forget about it."

His jaw dropped. "What did you say?"

She smiled. "Forget about the time, Jonathan. Trust me." With a saucy smile, she snaked her hands around his neck and brought her lips to his ear. "We can make our own time now."

After those endearing words, she kissed him, ending all discussion about the mouse that had by now found a hole in the floorboard, and was dropping a certain gold pocket watch onto the cobblestone streets below.

The ceremonious clank turned Victoria's head. But to Jonathan Gorick Kingston, the Marquess of Drakefield, he heard nothing but the whispers of silk and lace.

He had lost all track of time, all track of order, all track of anything and everything but love.